METAMORPHOSIS
ADVANCED READER COPY

ROSS JEFFERY

Copyright © 2024 by Ross Jeffery

All rights reserved.

No part of this book may be reproduced in any form or by any electronic or mechanical means, including information storage and retrieval systems, without written permission from the author, except for the use of brief quotations in a book review.

Please note that any shifts in tense or style within this work are intentional and a reflection of the author's artistic choices. These changes are not errors and have been carefully considered by both the author and editor to enhance the narrative experience.

INTRODUCTION

*TO BE ADDED

*TITLE DESIGN

'Nothing ever really goes away – it just changes into something else. Something beautiful.'

Metamorphosis – Franz Kafka

'Well, I've been afraid of changin'
    'Cause I've built my life around you
    But time makes you bolder
    Even children get older
    And I'm getting older too...'

Landslide – Fleetwood Mac

PART ONE
EGG

CHAPTER 1

Two years ago, Cynthia had had her eggs frozen, for use at a later date, if she decided motherhood suited her. Little did she know, the later date she'd imagined would never come. Due to the minor inconvenience of no longer having any eggs, and the fact of her being human, she knew that laying one was impossible.

What she decided to do instead was to lay something altogether different; a trap. A honey-trap, to be precise. And her OnlyFans© site had brought her everything she'd ever needed – *motherhood aside.*

It had provided her a boyfriend, money, a nine to five job which she didn't mind clocking in for. She was her own boss after all, as well as her own accountant, and being the only staff member on the payroll meant that if she wanted a pay rise, then she'd damn well give herself one.

Her nine to five started at nine PM and ended at five AM, but because it was all done on her laptop – *remote working people started calling it after Covid* – she never had to leave the comfort of her house, her room, or, most of the time, even her bed.

She'd achieved a luxurious, extravagant, and envious lifestyle, all by the ripe old age of forty-one.

Now she was forty-three, yet with the right lighting, the correct make-up and the proper accompaniments, Cynthia could pass for mid-twenties at her best, and early thirties at her worst. And she had all the accompaniments, because she had the financial security and the time to manicure her lifestyle any fucking way she wanted.

Through all the preening and all the skin regimes, the little bees who swarmed to her honey(pot) trap didn't actually care what age she was. Decorum, it seemed, was just a word to the avatars which appeared on her screen. They weren't choosy or picky in the least, and all they seemed to care about was that she remained obedient and submissive to their flagrant wants and desires – they were paying for this shit after all.

It didn't matter how she dressed herself up, her fans were only ever interested in her nakedness.

Her flesh.

Mouth.

Legs.

Breasts.

Arse.

Eyes.

Were eyes flesh?

Whatever piece of her they could see, they wanted. Yet, Cynthia was in control. *Always in control.* She was the boss, the dominatrix, and in a way, she was also her own pimp. She alone decided what to show, for how long, and, most importantly, how much she'd charge them for the pleasure of their voyeurism.

She was good at her job – *damned good* – and many, if not all of her subscribers told her so.

Cynthia was in control, of *this*, and of *that*, always. She knew it, and her fans knew it too, however much they tried to deny it and presume *they* were in control.

There was an unwavering confidence about her in how she could hold captive her audience, and she knew – *unwaveringly* – whatever piece of her *she* chose to show them, and whatever price *she* demanded for the pleasure, they'd pay for it and devour it like jackals, like maggots.

Her fans, it would seem, were anything but fussy. And when the bell chimed on her laptop, denoting another payment received, she'd smile, flirt, become the object of their affections, and, more importantly, their desires. It made her feel alive and powerful.

It made her feel like a goddess.

Men and women sought her out. Married or single. Sexual deviants or sexual predators. None of it fazed her. She'd just open her arms wide and sometimes her legs – *if the price was right* – and she would welcome them into the fold. They had their needs and *desires*. Itches that needed to be scratched.

And, well, Cynthia had *hers*.

One part of the job never came easy to her, however. Even though, on reflection, it was the most important thing she *needed* to remember – *even more important than paying the tax on her considerable earnings* – and that was to remain subservient.

It pained her gravely having to be the doe-eyed, '*come save me daddy*' or '*mommy*' – *whatever floated their boat* – damsel in distress for all the twisted people out there. Yet it was all part of the act. The role she was called to play. She'd even taken some amateur dramatic lessons to help her get into character, although her showmanship seemed to come pretty easily to her, and she'd quit after the three-week taster session.

She just couldn't afford to let her subscribers see the deep sadness in her eyes, or the loneliness of her soul.

She'd had everything she'd ever wanted, yet last year, she lost it all.

She'd masked her pain the only way she knew how; through a collection of close-fitting dresses which made her feel *all* woman and *less* widow.

Could you be a widow if you'd never been married?

It was a thought which plagued her. A ponderance which disabled her most days and made her feel *less*, when all she longingly craved was to feel *more*, than she was. She wore brassieres which accentuated her curves, instead of showing the world the hollowed out husk she'd become. Negligees were another favourite and left little to the imagination, leaving her fans – *her OnlyFans©* – hot under the collar, and her '*hotness*' helped to mask the cold blood coursing through her frozen veins.

PING.
A notification.

PIMP_RASCAL <Can U Count down 4rom 10 4 me>

Inclining her head, she pouts before blowing a little kiss at the screen.

They love it when she does that, sends them wild in the digital aisles.

Instantly her speaker on her monitor chimes.

Once.

Twice.

Thrice.

Three money bags appear on the toolbar briefly, before a slick animation has them disappearing into her bank account as if they've been suck down a drain, accompanied by the sound of coins being jangled in a bag.

Like taking candy from a baby.

A smile wrinkles her heavily glossed lips before she flutters her long – *fake, and ridiculously expensive* – eyelashes at the screen. Rolling a French-manicured hand in front of her, she bows slightly to those in attendance, the picture of a courtroom jester, ready to appease her master or mistress.

"Your wish…is my command." A soothing voice which is not her natural voice. There's a throaty warble to this character she plays, more Marilyn Monroe than Cynthia Wright.

"Ten."

Eyelids flutter.

"Nine."

Tongue licking at her top teeth.

"Eight."

Plays with her hair. A wig. Black. She'll never show them the real her. That's how you get caught, or develop a stalker, and there's no way Cynthia's planning on getting caught. Not when she's so close.

"Seven."

Her breathing speeds up, not because she's out of breath, but more because she knows this panting is what drives the viewers wild.

"Six."

Did I get the rabbit out?

The sudden thought throws her, and she's forgotten the count momentarily, however, she's the consummate professional and sticks the landing just in time, albeit a little flustered.

"F-F-F-Five."

The stutter, not planned, more of a happy accident – *as Bob Ross would have said* – seems to have struck some sick-chord with her fans, and another chime rings out from the speakers, announcing a deposit.

"Four."

Winks at the screen, knowing whoever made that last deposit thinks that wink was for *them*. They always think what she does is for *them*, gullible fools.

"Three."

Drawing close to the camera, she crosses her arms out of shot, giving her once pert breasts – *which sag slightly due to her age* – the added boost they need. She's all natural, and folks seem to really dig that about her. But she knows she must keep up appearances, and as she leans forward, she makes a mental note to pick up a new push-up bra tomorrow.

"Two."

Whispered, slow and breathy.

"One."

Staring into the camera lens for a moment, she places her thumb to her mouth where she begins to chew on her nail demurely.

Heart emojis begin to fill her screen, flowing up the side in a steady torrent of red, as if each were filled with helium. Once they reach the top, they pop. The whole thing is bittersweet, observing all those hearts dying on her screen, because every time she witnesses it, they remind her of how her heart burst, exploded, shattered into infinitesimal pieces almost two years ago; and how she doesn't have a heart left.

Only hurt, sorrow, rage and a thirst for wholeness.

CHAPTER 2

The clock above Cynthia's desk reads 5:30am and she's long since clocked off from her OnlyFans©.

Now, instead of a busy commute home, fighting her way through the hordes of zombies on the bus and train, she reclines in her chair and smiles at how simple her life is.

With the computer on standby, and plaster stuck over the webcam – *because you can never be too careful who's watching* – she finally closes it.

The one thing Cynthia prides herself on – *now more than ever* – is being careful. Remaining hyper-vigilant is how she's been able to get away with her terrible, mistempered deed for so long.

As her speakers play Fleetwood Mac's majestic album, *'Rumours,'* she wonders what rumours are flying about in the real world. About her. About him. She ponders if her family are concerned about how she's coping and why she's become so withdrawn over the past two years. The ponderance dies quickly though, as she remembers that no one will come looking for her. She's warned them off; given polite excuses at first, but when those hadn't worked – *with her nosey family mainly* – harsh rebukes had worked a charm.

Slipping off her wig, she drapes it over the mannequin's head next to her laptop, the porcelain-faced observer of all she does on and off screen.

But does it observe? When it has no eyes, only the impressions of eyes?

She peels her fake, expensive lashes free from her eyes as Christine McVie sings about *'making loving fun,'* and Cynthia recalls a time when it was, indeed, fun; instead of the onerous chore seduction had become over the past year, as she continues to cling to the lifestyle that she's become accustomed to, even as other, pressing, matters contend for her time and effort.

Sticking the lashes on the smooth eyelids of the eyeless head, she smiles. She actually enjoys this time. Finds comfort in the crafting of a face where there is none, a friend where there are only strangers, and a significant other where there is no other and when life seems, well, insignificant. This strange ritual makes her feel less lonely, because since *he* left – *left makes it sound as he popped out to the shops and never came home.*

Severed. That was a more apt descriptor for what happened.

And so, since Daniel had been crudely and cruelly *severed* from her life, amputated as if he was a limb, or a leg which had supported her. She now walked with a metaphoric limp, comforting herself with only half an embrace.

Severed, and even *amputated*, are better words than *lost* for what happened. Both sum up the sheer trauma of Daniel's passing and how it devastated Cynthia, ruined her completely, as the removal of something which was once integral would do, to anyone. If you removed the foundations someone had built their house on – *and we can replace house with life with the same outcomes* – the bricks, the walls, the roof would come tumbling down.

And sometimes, there was a person in that wreckage.

"You make loving fun, Daniel."

She whispered it, before shaking her head, no. "Well, you *made* loving fun. For a while... at least...we'll always have that..." her gaze finds the porcelain face, made up with her wig and fake lashes and her thoughts grow maudlin and bitter with resentment.

Since *that* day, the day Daniel was hacked and removed from her life – *like a melanoma* – Cynthia's been alone, surrounded by people, yet utterly, totally alone.

Well.

Almost alone.

The sudden trilling of an alarm pulls her out of her stupor. Reaching a hand to her phone, she taps the screen with the pad of an immaculately-manicured finger, silencing the alarm.

Leaning closer to a small mirror above her computer, she pulls the ever-growing bag under her eye down with the pad of her middle finger before using her thumb and forefinger to remove a contact lens.

The turquoise blue of her *'stage-eyes'* gives way to the murky, greenish-brown of the ones she was born with. Holding it between her fingers she opens the lens case with her other hand before depositing it within, repeating the process with her other eye. Two squirts of contact lens solution are added to the box, to bathe, clean and keep them supple. Closing the box, she shakes it like a maraca along with the music from her speakers before placing it down next to her computer.

Cynthia takes each part of her ritual de-masking seriously. She's got a reputation to upkeep: *cleanliness is next to goddess'ness*, her mother had often tittered.

The alarm sounds again and she silences it with another tap, she won't be rushed.

This lady is not for turning.

She shakes her head at the interruption.

Each layer of her stage makeup that gets wiped away are pieces of the *her* she is to many, revealing piecemeal by piecemeal the *her* she hides so well. The *her* she was for Daniel. Reaching forward, she reclaims the contact lens box, opens it, and adds two more squirts of solution for good measure before returning the box to its place. She doesn't want to get an infection. The last thing her adoring fans want is a pouting woman with a seriously bad case of pinkeye staring back at them. They want her pristine, they want the goddess who they worship, and Cynthia would provide.

Taking a cucumber scented wipe, she begins removing her makeup.

First, she tackles the thick eyeliner and mascara. Another three wipes are required to remove her contouring and foundation, and even then, she needs more – *seven in total* – as she always underestimates how she applies her second skin – *with a trowel* – because she's no longer the spring chicken she once was. By the time she's done, her face is as smooth as the porcelain head on her desk, and her skin can finally breathe. Numerous wipes later, the task of removal, of her personal devolution, is complete and she deposits the sandy, rusty, mud-coloured wipes in the bin.

Another alarm trills from her phone and she lets out a tired breath before pressing snooze and placing it face down on the desk so she doesn't have to look at it anymore. Although she's her own boss, there are some things which still remain out of her control.

Well, only two things, really.

The alarm, and what the alarm represents.

With the removal of her temporary face, Cynthia gazes at her reflection in the blackness of her laptop's monitor, wondering fleetingly if that same blackness resides in her, too. If it's a true representation – a shade – of the woman she is now…and of what she's become.

She's still her though, however much the reflection shouts to her that she's now become OTHER.

De-masked, the true Cynthia Wright sits before the mirror. She's no longer <HoneyCynth> her handle on OnlyFans©. She stares longingly at the woman trapped within the glass, the carefree woman Daniel fell in love with, plain old Cynthia Wright. She wonders if people still see the remnant, the ghost of <HoneyCynth> on her face when she's out and about?

However much she tries to scrub her avatar away, she knows they still see *her* on Cynthia's face. A piece of her, at least, always remains.

Cynthia, or is it <HoneyCynth>, has received her fair share of double takers and quickly diverted gazes over the years. Each gawker fearful that she'd catch their eyes lingering at her for longer than was acceptable. She'd witness their uncontrollable blushing, the rubbing of their brow, deep in thought as they desperately tried to place her; frantically attempting to recall where they knew her from as they held hands with their wife, husband, children or significant other in the supermarket, street or pub.

Whenever she catches someone trying to figure out where they've seen her before, she flashes a mischievous and promiscuous smile of her own. One which speaks of a secret shared, a clandestine affair at an office Christmas Party. She wants to hover nearby, allowing them an extra glance. She wants to whisper under her breath,

"Yes, it's me."

"It's the woman you want no one to know about."

"Your sweet little <HoneyCynth>."

She would never cross that line, though. She will never approach a client on the street because she devotes herself – *prides herself, in fact –* on anonymity. And that pride is shared with her subscribers too; there are strict rules to engagement of this type, and she's cleaved herself to them from the very start. Her pair of egos had defined 'rules' early on in their relationship, separating the work between church and state, <HoneyCynth> and Cynthia, and never should the two cross paths.

Her OnlyFans© owned <HoneyCynth> between 9pm and 5am, then after she clocked off, Cynthia was in charge once more. Off the clock and off the cock.

Yet even when she was off the clock, there was nothing she could do about being recognised from time to time.

Husbands...

Wives...

Teenagers...

Priests...

Imams...

Rabbis...

She didn't judge.

Builders...

School teachers...

Accountants...

Butchers...

She didn't discriminate.

Doctors...

Doctors?

That one word conjured such a strong reaction in her. Instantly, her smile withered on her face, and she gripped the edge of the table to ground herself. The reaction was so intense, it felt like a trauma response. She imagined it was the way one might react when they came face to face with an abuser. Her breathing became short and sharp. That word – *doctor* – made her heart race, caused her stomach to churn, her head to ache, and caused her mind to go spinning away from her, as if she were unable to reel it back in. That word summoned the feeling of unwanted, cloying fingers, and Cynthia couldn't shake those feelings once they took hold. All from just thinking the word, let alone saying it.

She felt physically ill.

Cynthia's phone tilled its chimes once more, pulling her back from the edge and the sickness rising in her throat. Picking up her phone – *as Fleetwood Mac sung about going their own way* – her eyes found their way from the mirror to the screen. Beneath the images of animated bells tolling, two words seemed to throb on the screen, and they were another darkness personified.

DINNER TIME.

Silencing the alarm with a huff, she threw the phone down on the desk.

Doctors…

Oh, how she loathed them.

And of ALL the doctors Cynthia distrusted, there was one doctor whose shadow loomed largest in Cynthia's life. The king mother fucker. *Doctor Osman Hasan.*

The funny thing was, he wasn't even Cynthia's doctor. He was Daniel's.

They'd met for the first time four years ago, and with Daniel's declining health in the year that followed, their meetings had quickly become consistent and frequent.

Their first meeting still played on Cynthia's mind like a fetid and blackened tooth you couldn't stop tonguing, because if she hadn't gone with Daniel – *the only reason she went was to show a united front, because men never take their physical health seriously, do they? All macho bullshit about being strong as an ox and nothing will happen, just a waste of time, it'll clear up on its own, I've had worse* – then business owner <HoneyCynth> and client would never have met.

That chance encounter had been what wrecked her life. And then it became what had taken it over.

O, how she hated Doctor Osman Hasan. She despised him with a passion for what he *did,* and for what he *didn't* do, on that fateful day. She detested him for what he *saw,* and for what he failed to *see,* in equal, devastating measure.

Cynthia rose.

She needed to step away from the computer. Needed to get some air, to try and rid herself from that most haunting of recollections. Peeling herself out of her red lingerie, she placed them over the back of her swivel chair before stepping into her grey, fleece-lined jogging bottoms, reclaimed from the floor next to her bed where she'd shed her old skin before stepping into the one she wore for the camera.

Grabbing a jumper from her bed, she pulled it over her head and slid her arms through the sleeves, pulled the hem down over her waist, and placed her sockless feet into her slippers – *which took the form of two large, decapitated bunny heads* – to complete the look. She was her old self again. The *'self'* Daniel found irresistible in whatever she chose to wear.

Appraising the skimpy, red lingerie which hung on the back of her chair, Daniel's voice rose unbidden in her mind.

'Your fans, Cynth, do they really like this kind of stuff?'

She could see him now, holding her skimpy wares between his fingers as if he might contract some venereal disease from them, face puzzled as he contemplated which bits went where. He never really got the fascination with all the dressing when the pudding beneath was so tasty. He was but a simple man with simple pleasures.

'Why don't you ask your dad, he seems to like it?' She'd shot back with a wink.

As she recalled the moment, she remembered the pause, that long, pregnant pause as Daniel pondered the enormity, not to mention the depravity, of her words. She'd laughed to break the tension, and finally they'd both fell about on the bed in a fit of giggles.

'That's a good one, Cynth.' he'd said once he caught his breath. His breath which, after that first appointment with Doctor Hasan, had become harder and harder for him to catch.

It was 'a good one,' she'd said, and it was so good because it was the truth. Daniel's father *was* one of Cynthia's subscribers. He hadn't had the forethought to use pseudonym. She hadn't even known Daniel's father knew how to use a computer, let alone sign up to her Only-Fans© page. His computer had apparently elected – *she assumed* – to use the autofill option from his Apple® keychain which also filled in his credit card details too, the silly old sod.

So, on Wednesday nights, when Daniel's mother was at her Church bible study, 'Women of the Word' – W.O.W. *Everything it would seem has an acronym these days* – Stanley Keegan, religiously – *in his own right* – logged on. He never stayed long. An hour at most, likely worried his wife would catch him in the act of bashing his own bishop; yet every Wednesday without fail, *he* was watching <HoneyCynth> doing what she did best.

Cynthia never overtly told Daniel his father was a pervert. Rather, she chose to instead allude to the fact in jovial conversation and a bit of friendly banter from time to time. Why shatter Daniel's long-held picture of his father, especially when everything else in his life was going to shit?

Her fans paid well for their anonymity, as if it were *AA* or *NA* or *CA* or *ACA*, and Cynthia prided herself on keeping those confidences; given all the GDPR crap she'd had to sign her life away to when she set up her account – even if she wanted to blabber about who was watching her, she couldn't without getting sued to kingdom come.

The alarm chimed yet again, and turning her phone over, the words jumped off the screen at Cynthia.

DINNER TIME.

"I'm coming…for crying out loud, I'm coming!"

With phone in hand, she made her way to the top of the stairs and paused.

Doctor.

A shake of the head, but the word flowered this time, blooming large and ominous.

Doctor Osman Hasan.

She hated that cocksucker with a never-ending passion.

On that first appointment she'd attended with Daniel, he'd recognised her. And there was a knowingness to his eyes. He'd seen what she looked like underneath her Cynthia Wright garb. She didn't know him from Adam though, he'd obviously elected to change his name and opted for some digital avatar when he'd subscribed to her OnlyFans© page, unlike Daniel's father.

So there was nothing Cynthia could do as she sat down holding Daniel's hand because church and state had become entwined, despite their best efforts to keep them apart. She could tell by the way Doctor Hasan eye-raped her as she sat in his office that he knew exactly who she was, and to his credit – *although it pained Cynthia to give this piece of shit any credit whatsoever* – he didn't mention it. He was the consummate professional during the entirety of Daniel's appointment

As she replayed that first appointment in her mind, as she did often, she struggled to recall anything he'd said of note during the entirety of their allotted five-minute slot. He just sat there either oblivious, or outright ignoring Daniel's pain and discomfort, not to mention his startling loss of weight. She recalled Hasan passing the symptoms off as indigestion or IBS, stress or the re-emergence of his adolescent asthma. Although Cynthia didn't remember much of what was discussed and imparted, she had noticed one thing; Doctor Hasan hadn't even looked at Daniel for the whole appointment. He didn't even look him in the eyes when he welcomed them to his office in that harried way Doctors' do – *which instantly causes you to feel as if you're putting them out* – with a limp and sweaty handshake. She knew he didn't give a diddly about Daniel because although he didn't have eyes for him, he had eyes for her and the only time they left her was when he tapped something on his computer – which Cynthia had a sneaking suspicion was: OnlyFans© <HoneyCynth>.

They'd taken Doctor Hasan's silence for ineptitude. However, Doctor Hasan more than made up for his silence when he called the house the following day, and it was Cynthia Wright, not Daniel Keegan, who answered the phone.

CHAPTER 3

'This is Doctor Hasan, from The Green Medical Practice, with whom am I speaking?'

'Cynthia, Cynthia Wright.'

'Good afternoon, Miss Wright. And how are we today?'

'I'm fine thank you, is everything okay? Shall I get Daniel for you?'

'No, no. No need to bother him, it was you I was calling to speak with actually.'

'Me? I don't underst–'

'I just wanted to call and say...' there was a pause, and Cynthia wondered if he was weighing his words, wondering what might happen should he spilled them, what kind of repercussions could come back to bite him in the arses. But in the end, he was a proud man and spill words he would, because he foolishly believed that he had all the power in the tryst.

'Your eyes, they're brown...it threw me at first.'

'My eyes?'

Church and state.... church and state... church and state... church and state...never should the two meet, mix, coexist.

She pressed on, a little flustered. 'I'm really sorry, Doctor Hasan, but I think you must've got me confused with someone else… let me get Daniel for you.'

'NO!' he blurted out. 'As I already said, I didn't call to speak with him. I called to speak with you.'

'I'm sorry, but–'

'Sorry? Why should you be sorry? I hope you're not apologising for what you are…for *who* you are?'

'And who am I, Doctor Hasan?'

'Are we playing one of your little games? I know you like your games. Okay, I'll play along…'

Heavy breathing down the phone. Panting, as if he were doing something he shouldn't be doing, *especially* on what she assumed was a work call from his sterile working environment.

Church and state…church and state…church and…

'Listen, I don't think you should call this number again–'

'And why's that?'

'Because–'

'But I haven't answered your question.'

'What question? Look, Doctor Hasan, I'd really appreciate it if you–'

'The question of who you are? And please, call me Osman.'

'Right, maybe not. Who is it you think I am, *Doctor*?'

'Oh, you know…you know damned well who you are…'

'I don't appreciate being spoken to like this, *Doctor* Hasan. Believe me when I say, when we've finished whatever *this* is…I'm going to ask Daniel to call the surgery, to speak with the practice manager and to lodge a complaint about your conduct, about your harrassm–'

'You'll do no such thing…'

'What makes you so confident about that?'

'Because no one will believe a word you say.'

'And what makes you so sure?'

'In my world, a *whore's* word doesn't count for shit. Doesn't hold much weight when it comes to accusations against health professionals. People like *you* making accusations like that. Sex workers…' the way he said *sex workers* sounded as if just saying the word had left a bad taste in his mouth. "…are an occupational hazard. I'll tell you what they'll think.'

'Actually, no. I'll tell you what they'll *know*, because I'll tell them what to believe…I'm a very powerful man, Miss Wright. You'll come to understand that sooner or later. I'll tell them you're only complaining because I turned you down for prescription drugs, that you're using your partner's ill health to try and line your own pockets–' The rest of his words faded as she fixated on only one of the words in his exhaustive diatribe.

'*Whore?*' She replied belligerently at his assessment of her.

'Oh, do keep up, Miss Wright. It's not fun unless you keep up with the conversation.'

'Did you just call me a…a…*whore*?'

'Yes, a dirty, filthy, lying…WHORE!'

Flustered by the outburst, Cynthia couldn't string one word to the next.

'Cat got your tongue? Truth hurts, doesn't it…you diseased little slapper?'

'Doctor Hasan, I'm…I'm…I'm going to hang up now.'

Cynthia hated how her stuttering made her sound weak before the bully.

'Wait…wait…please…'

'I'm going to hang up.'

'I feel we got off on the wrong footing here, Miss Wright…Miss Wright…'

Cynthia should have hung up, yet she found herself clinging to the line, her hand vibrating with the anger she had boiling within her.

'Wrong footing? Wrong footing? You are certifiably insane, do you know that? I'll make sure you lose your fuc–'

'Or should I call you <HoneyCynth>?'

Cynthia couldn't talk.

Think.

Breathe.

Her mind was screaming the same words over and over again: CHURCH AND STATE…CHURCH AND STATE… NEVER SHOULD

THE TWO MEET…CHURCH AND STATE…CHURCH AND STATE… NEVER SHOULD THE TWO MEET…

'I love what you've done to your hair by the way.' Doctor Hasan continued, his words a hushed whisper down the line. 'I barely recognised you…although, after a while the whore shone through, as it always does…'

'Goodbye, Doctor Hasan. If you know what's good for you, don't EVER call this number again.' And with those parting words – *part threat and part promise* – she slammed the phone down.

Daniel came in looking rather ill. Or, maybe he could have been tired, although Cynthia knew more than likely it was a bit of both. Daniel asked if everything was okay. He said that he heard raised voices and thought she was arguing with someone on the phone.

Cynthia should have told him the truth, but their rules were pretty clear. Church and state should never mix, never cross over. She hadn't wanted to trouble him, not when he looked so ill, and so she decided to tell him when he was feeling better, and stronger.

But better and stronger never came.

They were words which had been wiped out of his stars as if they were chalk words on a blackboard.

She'd opted to tell him it was a *Chugger – one of those charity muggers who usually call when you're having dinner or just about to get in the bath or watch a movie; the ones who give a sob story about people not having access to clean water or food and that dogs and cats and birds and flipping dolphins were dying* – knowing full well that Daniel understood how much she hated those calls and that it would put an end to his prying and the conversation.

Doctor Hasan, however, elected to refuse Cynthia's parting message, that of her veiled warning, because he called again the following day…and the next…and…the…next.

"I love what you've done with your hair…"

"Goodbye." She hung up on him.

"I prefer you in the black thong…"

"I'm warning you, stop calling this number." She slammed the phone down before picking it back up to place it on the side, off the hook, so he couldn't call back.

"We should meet..."

"Piss off." She slammed the phone down so hard she heard the plastic crack on the mouthpiece.

Doctor Hasan was a pest of the worst kind: a bonafide *sex pest*. He did stop calling, eventually, although that came more down to Cynthia's intervention than him being a decent human being. She had the landline disconnected two years ago, after she was inundated with well-wishers and family members offering platitudes and sympathy slogans for Daniel. Each apology they offered *'for her loss'*. It all got to be too much, and Cynthia preferred the power she had in screening her calls on her mobile and speaking to who she wanted to, instead of the torturous *Russian Roulette* the landline had become.

Recalling those conversations with Doctor Hasan had her operating on autopilot.

She'd successfully navigated her way down the stairs, through the hallway and found herself in the kitchen, hand resting on the worktop where she discovered, to her delight, that she had remembered to get the poached rabbit out of the braising liquid. It was waiting for her on the kitchen side.

The trick to rabbit risotto – *which she'd discovered though much trial and error* – was to poach the rabbit gently. Because it was a very lean meat, cooking it too fast turned it into the tongue of an old leather boot and it quickly became chewy and inedible.

Cynthia had a love/hate relationship with cooking. The love of it came from having a mother who was a chef, and a damned good one at that. Seven restaurants bore the family name, and at the last count, two of those boasted Michelin stars. But last count had come before Cynthia and her mother had drifted apart over the past few years, and before Cynthia lost interest in her mother's success.

When cooking, Cynthia always remembered her informative years fondly. Stood on a rickety old chair at the kitchen counter, with her chubby hands holding a knife, hacking at carrots and onions; the longer she remained at her mother's side in the kitchen, the more adept and confident she became in dicing herbs and frying shallots on the hob with butter.

Over her adolescent years she had displayed a knack for cooking, every inch a sous chef in the making. They were fond times whilst they lasted. But in her late teens she had discovered boys, and that her body could get her all kinds of things she'd never thought possible.

Time spent learning the family trade at her mother's hip became somewhat irrelevant after that.

Cynthia's hatred of cooking – *maybe a little strong. Her* dislike *of cooking* – had its roots in the union of her and Daniel, and how in some unspoken law between the sexes – *displayed in homes across the country, hell, the whole damnable world for that matter* – the responsibility of cooking dinner had fallen squarely on her shoulders. Cynthia, woman of the house, jack of all trades, master of none, and now the resident chef. There wasn't even a discussion about it. She had just been bestowed the grand title and mantel of cook – why? Because she had tits? It was a woman's job? To hell with that.

She knew full well if she hadn't, no, didn't take the lead, they'd have grown emaciated rather quickly, that or survived on cereal and toast. It never seemed to enter Daniel's mind that the food which magically appeared each evening had to first be planned, a varied menu curated in painstaking detail – *because no sane person likes eating the same shit week in and week out*. Also, the ingredients that made these meals a possibility had to be sourced and purchased, cooked and timed to perfection.

She hated Daniel for his obliviousness whilst despising the world for establishing that *this* was the way things were in households all across the world. However, although Cynthia hated him for it, she couldn't blame him for the situation either. He'd never overtly expressed to her it was her responsibility. They'd just fallen into that rhythm, and if she thought about it for a prolonged portion of time, she ended up realizing that she hated herself for allowing it to happen more than she hated him.

Cynthia looks down at the rabbit.

Aside from her gripes around gender roles, Cynthia does miss the act of cooking for Daniel. Although she's still cooking for him in some strange way, she supposes. And in doing so, she's been keeping that candle – his memory – burning in a peculiar kind of way.

People will never understand the choices she's made and the

things she's sacrificed to make the things she does now work. In all honesty, Cynthia doesn't give a rat's arse what people think about her life, they could all take a long walk off a short pier for all she cared.

Opinions are like arseholes. Everyone's got one and they're usually full of shit.

Was a common refrain often heard leaving her lips when she got off the phone or read an email or lost herself in doomscrolling her OnlyFans© chat.

Placing the frying pan on the hob, next to a number of assorted stainless-steel pots, she checks on her ingredients; they're all there, ready and waiting for her gastronomical creation. Each one sits in a little dish, arranged neatly on the marbled sideboard, in the order of their use in her recipe.

'*Preparation is the key*' her mother's voice echoes in Cynthia's head. She smiles wanly at the recollection, yet doesn't get lost in it. There isn't time to delay longer than she has already.

She begins by sweating off the shallots before adding chopped garlic. As they cook, the combined smell infuses the kitchen with one of her favourite, hedonistic scents; causing her mouth to water and her soul to ascend. She's a child once more, cooking and laughing at her mother's side; transported, albeit momentarily, to a time before her life imploded and she was left shuffling around in the perpetual wasteland which has become her world.

Time and circumstance have robbed her of so many special occasions.

Leaning over the pan, inhaling deeply of the aromatic scent of the gods, a groan of pleasure escapes her lips. Standing straighter, she reaches for the bowl of rice, adding it with a flourish to the pan. She keeps the rice moving, never allowing it to settle, wanting it toasted and not burnt, and to ensure this happens, she lubricates the pan frequently with hot chicken stock, one ladle at a time.

One.

Two.

Three.

The trick to a good risotto is to flirt with it. And if Cynthia knows anything, it's how to be a great flirt. Her bank balance is living proof of how good she is at it.

With a few flicks of the wrist, Cynthia lets the risotto flirt with the tantalising possibility of boiling, removing the pan from the flame just in time. She'll let it believe it's reaching boiling point for just a moment before dashing its hopes, dreams, and chances – as she'd done with a man or two before she started dating Daniel.

Having learned all she knows at her mother's hip – *about cooking that is, not leaving someone blue-balled* – she knows that if you allow the risotto to boil, to reach its climax before its time, the risotto will lose its creaminess.

With a pinch of salt and pepper she seasons the risotto, lightly, before adding a sprinkling of grated parmesan cheese. A little chopped parsley soon follows – *fresh, not the dried stuff out of a jar* – and she stirs her creation as she watches the parsley begin to darken the risotto.

Wild garlic soon follows. It's stronger than the garlic she used at the start, and since she doesn't want to overpower the dish, she adds a small amount at a time, tasting until she's happy. To this concoction, she adds the sliced, poached rabbit to heat through before adding a little extra butter, a liberal dollop of crème fresh and a touch of lemon before stirring it through.

Using a wooden spoon, she works the risotto into a creamy texture, and when she's sufficiently satisfied with her creation, she begins plating it up; opting for a white plate with a duck-egg, blue flourish around its edge.

EGG! Shit, I forgot the bloody egg!

She hits her forehead with an open palm in mock stupidity, yet she doesn't let it phase her. She just cracks on and starts to boil the kettle. Once the water has boiled, she adds the bubbling water to a pan with a pinch of salt and gently lowers an egg into the simmering liquid with a ladle – four minutes and it'll be done.

Returning to her steaming risotto, Cynthia adds a nice drizzle of olive oil over its steamy, creamy goodness before turning to the kitchen island and pulling an antique tray with ornate silver handles from one of the cupboards beneath. Setting it down on the island, she places her plated risotto, silver cutlery, and a red napkin on to it. She adds the small, silver candleholder from the island's marbled surface to the tray also, as a final touch.

Removing the egg from the boiling water, she plops it into an egg cup with blue and white stripes swirling up its sides and adds that to the tray too.

Wine?

Shakes her head at how forgetful she's being this evening. She's an ardent supporter of the phrase 'life's always better with a glass of wine'.

White or red?

Red or white?

She settles for a bottle of red, as usual, knowing it'll compliment her meal.

Removing a wineglass from a high cupboard, she finds a space on the tray and places the glass down. Opening a bottle of *Penfolds*, Bin 169, Cabernet Sauvignon 2018 – from the Barossa Valley, Southern Australia, Cynthia pours herself a glass. It's a £230 bottle of wine, but Cynthia doesn't care. She's been making progress, and if she wants to treat herself, then by God, she'll treat herself. As the wine trickles into the glass she can't help think its blood. The hue is so rich, so similar.

And she'd know. She's seen enough blood in the last few months.

With her diligent work displayed before her, she marvels at its glorious presentation, knowing it wouldn't look out of place in one of her mother's restaurants – *she did, after all, learn from the very best* – and Cynthia nods her approval.

She picks up the tray and walks slowly towards the basement door before placing it on an antique dresser; the one Daniel purchased for fifty pounds in a quaint little shop in Petts Wood a few years back. It's a hideous thing, really. Too much mahogany, full of woodworm and with an excessive number of brass handles for her liking. But Daniel had loved it, and so Cynthia, over time, grew to love it too, even more so in his absence. She observes the tray resting on its dark, smooth surface, and she can't help see how poetic it is that Daniel should still have a part to play in all these nightly – *well, morning in her world* – proceedings.

Turning from the tray, Cynthia begins to undress.

She slides her slippers off first before teasing her jogging bottoms down and, once those are discarded, she finally removes her jumper. Cynthia collects her clothes and she places them neatly on the padded seat of a chair that's positioned to the side of the basement door; another of Daniel's projects which he'd reupholstered in some hideous aubergine fabric that clashed something cruel with the aesthetic of the kitchen. Yet she couldn't bear to throw it out, given the care and love he'd shown in bringing that tattered old thing back from the brink of becoming firewood.

On tiptoes, she reaches up to reclaim a pair of paint-stained overalls from their hook. The overalls had once been Daniel's. They were the ones he'd worn through all of his restoration projects. He'd always been good with his hands – *although that's another story for another time.* The overalls are large, huge things made out of denim and, once buttoned up, their material swamps her, hiding every curve she possesses.

Stepping into a pair of worn work boots, the steel of each toecap peeking through the leather, Cynthia bends over and sets about tying the laces. The last thing she wants to do is trip and break her goddamned neck. She stands and lifts her feet up and down, marching on the spot, checking to make sure the boots are fastened tightly and won't slip off her dainty ankles. Once happy, she lifts her gaze and stares in awe and wonder at the last adornment she'll add to her look. The thing which hangs on the second of the two hooks by the basement door.

She reaches for it, and the feathery face of the mask tickles at the pads of her fingers as she absently strokes the mask one way, then the other. It's smooth on the downward movement, then sharp and bristly when brushed the other way. Lifting a hand, she taps a nail on one of the two large circles, clicking against the black glassy eye nestled within the faded, sandy-coloured feathers.

Her finger lingers and she traces the feathers from the corner of the eye to the mouth, where the prominence of a small beak resides. Hooking the pad of her finger under the tip of beak, Cynthia pricks it on the sharp hook and winces. She shakes her finger off, then holds the mask before her in both hands, smiling before turning it over and slipping it over her face.

The back of the mask is hooded by a cream-sand coloured shawl which is almost the exact colour of the feathers around its eyes. It's not perfect, but she'd like to see a blind person spot the difference.

Manoeuvring the shawl takes a great amount of time, care, and attention to ensure that her hair is tucked inside, hidden from prying eyes. She doesn't want any of it spilling out and ruining the surprise of who lurks behind the mask.

Finally, wrapped in her new skin, she approaches the basement door.

Laying hold of the brass key, she turns it.

CLICK.

Twisting the knob, she pulls the handle, and the door swings wide on rusty hinges.

SCREEECH.

Collecting the tray, she slowly and carefully begins to descend into the darkness, one steady step at a time.

Leaving one world, one existence, for another.

CHAPTER 4

The basement was darkness personified. A wall of obsidian.
There were three long windows which sat horizontally near the ceiling, seven feet from the basement floor. They would have afforded a slim view of the garden, if Cynthia hadn't painted them black a year before; wanting, no, needing to shut the world out. In doing so she'd transformed this already dank place into a den of perpetual darkness. A place where shadows bred and where secrets could be hidden. Disorientation had been her aim, and deception was the game.

Descending the rickety wooden stairs, the smell of dampness creeping through the feathered filter of the mask caused her face to screw up. It was pungent and earthy. Food waste left to rot in black bags in the sun. The basement was a gulag, a dungeon where darkness was the convict, and a place where light feared to tread, knowing that if it ever did, it would illuminate things best left unseen.

The air was fetid. Pungent in its assault, the notes of flyblown meat and curdled milk– *it was all of those things and more* – caused her stomach to roil. The mask helped in some regard with filtering the stench but still it assailed her each time she came down here, and she was sure there wasn't a mask on the planet that could stop its invasion of her nostrils. The candle would help tamper down some of the stink, scented with bergamot and vanilla. She just had to make sure she was done before the candle went out.

The staircase turned to the left near the bottom, where the room, veiled in darkness for the time being, opened to a space which mirrored the house above, minus the walls. Just a vast expanse – *for now at least* – of infinite black. Cynthia took her time navigating the turn in the stairs as she balanced everything on the tray.

Glancing down, through the huge glassy aspects of her mask, she willed her eyes to drink in the remnant of dim light sneaking through the narrow gap under the closed kitchen door behind her. Her vision improved slightly and she planted her foot securely on the first step of the bend.

From this point on, after she turned the corner, everything would have to be done from memory, as any modicum of light which dared to venture further was feasted upon by the ravenous maws of the dark.

Slowly, she descended the last four steps to the dusty basement floor.

One.

Two.

Three.

Four.

She casts herself adrift.

There was a sudden crunching underfoot as her work boots trudged across the gravelled floor, scraping over the solid foundations the house was built on, but which had never been rendered. Charting her course for the table, Cynthia slinks further into the darkness which welcomes her with open arms.

She's counting her long strides in her head.

One.

Two.

Three

Four

Five.

Cynthia pauses before a tentatively shuffled sixth step, half the previous long strides. The table's edge presses up against her hips, the legs screeching a little as they bark across the floor from her body's momentum.

She places the tray down gingerly, insuring it's wholly on the table and won't upend to the ground once released – *her perfectly planned meal ruined in an instant*. Letting go of the tray, her fingers trace the smooth wood of the tables surface. Gripping its edge between her fingers, she slowly and methodically, slides her way around it. Feet scraping once more on the ground as she shuffles.

When her fingers run around the edge at a ninety-degree angle, she removes one hand, ensuring the other holds firm – *not wanting to be sent further adrift in this place of ruin* – as she reaches out into the darkness and her meal grows ever colder. However, there's a ritual to the proceedings and she must follow it, regardless.

'*The secret of your future is hidden in your daily routine.*'

She'd read that somewhere once, a powerful sentiment, and so she stringently keeps to her routine. Nothing has changed one iota in the past year; day in, day out, rinse and repeat. Although, it isn't the secret of her future she's desperate to discover. The thing she's searching for is the secret from her past, which would have – *should have* – defined her future.

With her arm still pawing, groping into the dark, her fingers finally connect and lay claim to the chair, a buoy in this dark ocean. It's always a tense moment as her hand searches the dark, imagining another hand closing around her own, taking what they want, again; it doesn't matter that she's repeated this action over three-hundred-and-twenty-five times and never discovered anything before – it's the thought that one day she *might* which scares her.

Pulling the chair closer, the legs scrape over the rough, concrete floor.

Once the chair is in place, her hand travels its way down the wooden backrest, her fingers rising and falling over the latticed, wicker back before finding the plump coolness of the leather padded cushion – *another of Daniel's reupholstered jobs. This one though, Cynthia adores.*

Circling around, she gradually sits down, the foam within the cushion letting out a small huff of air, like her Grandma discretely passing flatulence after a Sunday roast whilst watching *Last of the Summer Wine*.

Bunny hopping the chair closer to the table by reaching one hand between her legs and gripping the seat of the chair, Cynthia's other hand anchors her to the table and pulls; two hops later and she's in position.

She marvels at the smoothness of the table as her hands glide across its surface in search of her tray. Delicate fingers crawl over its edge before sliding it carefully, inch by slow inch, towards her, positioning it in the dark like all the other times before; so many times, before.

Drinking in the dark, she waits, listens to the silence; allowing the room to settle, and the darkness to wash over her. There's the pattering of rain against the blackened glass, the wind outside causing the panes to rattle ever so slightly in their insecure frames, as a bad tooth shifts in a gum.

Outside, morning is coming, and with it the light. But darkness reigns in here.

Inclining her head to the right, she stretches her head back slightly, leaning towards the sound behind her. The sound that's almost hidden beneath the storm outside. The steady beep of the machine.

BEEP... BEEP... BEEP...

From the same place, the slight rustling of sheets. Cynthia's breathing quickens. Each exhalation of her warm breath causes beads of condensation to form behind her mask and she starts to feel the dampness, and the humidity on her skin.

Beneath those sounds is another presence, a person breathing over her shoulder, frantic as ever, frantic as always. She imagines the rabbit she braised for her risotto to have had snatched breath like that, right before it was caught and butchered.

Short, sharp, and scared gasps – until it breathed no more.

Reaching a hand into the pocket of her overalls, she finds the lighter, Daniel's lighter; an heirloom passed down to him by his Uncle Vic, a salt-of-the-earth kind of man, abrasive, called a spade a spade, but kind-hearted. The lighter is gold plated – *real or fake, it's hard to tell* – and embossed with a fine filigree pattern. A delightful and fascinating object to hold and run your fingers over, which Cynthia does in the dark, wondering how many times Daniel had run his own fingers over it.

She flicks the lid open.

Instead of the usual wheel to run a finger over to generate the spark to ignite the gas, this particular lighter has a rolling mechanism down one side, one in which you roll the pad of a thumb over and it births.

It's an exquisite thing of beauty, and tactile too. An arsonist's wet dream.

Holding the lighter in one hand, she rolls the pad of her thumb over the mechanism, and after a small grinding noise the flame blooms to life in the darkness.

Leaning forward, flame held out before her, she lights the candle. It flickers for a moment before the wick finally blackens and the yellow-white glow illuminates the tray, the meal, and the table before her.

Snapping the lighter closed with a flick of her wrist, Cynthia deposits the heirloom back into her pocket for safe keeping.

She takes her time to remove each item from the tray.

Firstly, she places the wild rabbit risotto in front of her, the cutlery on top of her napkin just to the right of the plate. She picks up her wine glass, swills the contents, then holds the glass before the mask, inhales its delicious aroma which sneaks through the two tiny holes under the masks nose, hidden beneath the feathers. The smell of wood and cinnamon acts like a tonic to her senses. She sighs with a wanton desire to guzzle it down, although she'll wait, like she always does. The glass of wine is deposited on her designated coaster, and she leans back slightly, the chair creaking as she inspects the wine in the candle-light, remarking once more how it resembles a receptacle full of dark, arterial blood.

Plucking the egg cup from the tray, its solitary egg nestled within like an old man's, speckled, bald, and tanned head, she reaches across the table. Her bottom rises from the plush cushioned seat as she stretches past the flickering candle and places the cup opposite her, in the place for her esteemed guest. Falling back onto her cushioned seat, the air puffs out again.

Finally, and carefully, Cynthia lifts the candle holder. Her movements are slow and precise, not wanting the flickering flame to go out, for her to be dropped back into the darkness she holds at bay with its illumination. She places it gingerly in the centre of the table, pride of place, ensuring not to besmirch the tables' French polished surface with spent candle wax.

With the tray cleared, she lifts it from the table and rests it on the ground against one of the legs before picking up her glass of wine and listening to the sheets moving behind her and the subtle panting of her guest.

A gentle rotation of her wrist causes the wine in her glass to swill around like a whirlpool whilst her other hand plays nonchalantly with a switch mounted on a red and green box to the left of the table, now illuminated by the candlelight.

The switch is not part of the original features of the table. Cynthia placed it there for ease, so that she doesn't have to get up from her seat when the time comes. Its black wires trail off the table's edge where they're quickly consumed by the darkness that swarms around the dining tables edge. The blackness is so absolute that if feels as if the table is a raft floating on the River Styx, although Cynthia's guest isn't Charon. There's no soul to carry across the river, although there's one which she desperately hopes to bring back – *and she's close, so close to doing exactly that* – and it causes her heart to flutter in her chest at the prospect.

Momentarily relinquishing her hold on the switch, she tilts the chin of the mask up and takes another sip of the wine. She doesn't swallow, instead opting to swill it around her mouth before lowering the mask and placing the wine glass back on its coaster. She lets the wine settle in the recess of her mouth, behind her teeth, where it bathes her tongue. Opening her mouth slightly, she takes a long breath in, allowing the air to move over the liquid before swallowing. She'd seen the odd procedure in a wine tasting video, the process apparently allowing the richness of the wine, and the tasting notes, to become fuller.

The wine coats her throat with its lusciousness and Cynthia slowly lifts her gaze from the table to the oval mirror placed upon a cabinet behind her dinner guest's vacant chair. The cabinet is yet another salvaged antique of Daniel's, although this one hasn't been repurposed. He never had time to complete its transformation. The sight of it causes an aching despair in Cynthia's chest, and a thickness forms in her throat as she thinks about what transpired and the cruel twist of fate that robbed her of the man she loved so deeply, so completely.

As her eyes linger on the mirror, adjusted now to the dim light, the patina of dust and time on its surface go some way in obscuring her, appearing almost ghostlike within its reflective, dull surface. Both there and not there at the same time. Her image softened, portent-like in the ethereal glow of the candlelight.

Tilting her head, she smirks, finding humour in the obvious as the reflection does the same, but it's not Cynthia staring back at herself, it's the barn owl. The way her head is inclined makes it look as though the owl has spotted a rodent in the dark, dinner skittering its way through the basement. She stares intently at the reflection, taking in the pale, feathered-face and the black, sleek beak. The brown fringe of feathers at the masks crown and the same brown tracing its ways from the eyes to the beak make it look as though it were crying sandy tears.

It's the eyes which hold her rapt attention, and she finds herself leaning closer, head hovering over her cooling dinner as she takes in the hugeness of them staring back at her. The glassiness of their reflection. Held within those dark, convex disks, the whole room pools at the centre of its flame.

In this moment of reflection, she wonders – *ponders, deeply* – as she does most nights when taking in her masked reflection, if the flame reflected in those dark, glassy lenses is the same flame she still carries for Daniel.

They had great plans for this basement. Her studio. His restoration workshop. Perhaps their unborn children's playroom. None of those plans came to fruition, though. Although whatever this place would have become, Cynthia knew she would have eventually persuaded him. It was her job, after all, which kept them afloat; it was her nightly romps and her OnlyFans© who footed the bill for their exuberant, expensive lifestyle.

The disagreement never got to an argument, yet somehow, they both lost.

Her gaze left the mirror and Cynthia tilted her head up, following the beam above the mirror to over her head. There, in the wood, was the first signs of her getting her own way. Four silver anchors gleamed above her, installed for the sex swing, although that was as far as her takeover of the basement had got because when things happened, they happened quickly. And there was nothing sadder than a swing with no one to push you.

And so, the basement remained as it was, pieces of her and pieces of him

The only reason she still came down here at night – *every night* – over the past year was to be close to him. Over the last few months, especially, there'd been a breakthrough, and the closeness Cynthia had been desperate to reclaim had become imminent. Almost tangible. So close she could taste it, the same way that she could smell her food on the table.

Being a recluse – *from the real world at least* – had its benefits in bringing this moment to fruition. And she hailed the advent of Covid as her enabler. Before Covid someone had to leave the house, step out and into the big bad world to gather sustenance and work and friends, the world before the pandemic had folks scrambling to survive, and being *seen* made people feel valued, that they were, for all intents and purposes, part of society.

During, and more importantly after Covid, the world; so big and so vast, came to you.

Deliveries of all kinds and number arrived hours or days after being placed and no one batted an eyelid. Amazon™, Uber™ and Deliveroo™ became embedded in our vernacular, whilst also raking in a fortune as their share prices rocketed through our fear of leaving the house, profiteering on our basic need for *things* and *sustenance*.

You could literally order anything, and nothing was too impossible to source; medical equipment, sex toys, and other suspicious items could be ordered and delivered, no questions asked, no dodgy look from a checkout girl or boy. Everything was delivered with anonymity and security, and it was this anonymity Cynthia craved for her twisted and dark desires.

Jobs went the same way as our habitual consumerism.

Working from home – *or remote working* – had never felt so sweet;

allowing a new an ever-insular population the option of never having to toll the company line, or having to suffer the stupidity of lonely and annoying work colleagues or the constant, banal drivel of office banter.

However bad Covid was, it helped make some people Kings and Queens of their own fortune.

No one batted an eyelid if you didn't emerge from your self-made pit for months on end. It quickly became a new normal, a *good* normal, to isolate; and for Cynthia and her plans, well, it wasn't a *new normal* or a *good normal* as much as it was a *stupendous and welcome normal*.

And so, Cynthia became ever more insular. An island in the stream of the world; a stream in which family and friends floated away, following the current from her safe harbour, knowing if she needed them, she was more than capable of throwing a rope and pulling them in, but otherwise she was happy to watch them drown.

Their family and friends gave her space and time to grieve and to be alone. The space they'd afforded her though, turned into a gulf over time – *three years and counting* – and yet they were still waiting for the rope to be thrown, not knowing that it would never come. The thing was, Cynthia didn't need them as much as they needed her. She was happy in her isolation with the distance she'd forged between her family and friends because all she needed, all she had *ever* needed was Daniel, and he was almost present again, as he was, before.

She glanced up at her reflection, the barn owl, its face wide and open, fire still burning within its eyes stared back at her.

"I love you, Daniel. I've *never* stopped loving you."

Gripping the silver switch between her thumb and forefinger, she flirted with the idea of flicking it.

"You're almost returned to me, and when you finally come back, we'll have that meal, and that special evening you'd planned which never came to be. The one we both craved, and have been hungry for ever since."

Glancing down through the orbs of the mask, she observed the switch hungrily.

The power it had, nestling between her pinched fingers. She was Dr. Frankenstein, and with the flick of a switch she could bring Daniel – *or the essence of Daniel* – to life in an instant.

METAMORPHOSIS   37

It was time.

Her risotto was moments from becoming lukewarm and ruined.

Raising her gaze once more to the mirror, she stared intently at the darkness over her right shoulder, where a small green light moved in a straight line before blipping up and down, then continuing in a steady line and winking out.

It appeared again.

Straight line.

Blip.

Up.

Down.

Straight line.

A hypnotic light show, flashing over and over again, playing out in a steady rhythm.

Breathing deeply, she finally flicked the switch.

From the dulled reflection in the mirror, Cynthia observed the fluorescent strip first humming, then flickering to life. It strobed at first, teasing with illumination before finally settling and casting a clinical light on the basement's proceedings. The light highlighted a square space in the far corner of the infinite black. A dark sea of obscurity had formed between the safety of the table's candlelight and that other, harsher island of light.

With the sudden illumination came movement.

Then a groan.

On the hospital bed – *which she'd snapped up for a measly £1,194.00 minus shipping, thanks to Opera Beds© for their discretion* – was a wasted figure, its bony arms laying at its sides, each wrist cuffed to the guardrail by a large, wool-lined restraint.

The figure struggled for comfort, squinting their eyes and turning their head under and against the harsh glare of the lights. The leather ball gag was still in place. The brownness of the leather and the startling red of the ball clashed shockingly with the wan, pale skin of their face.

The gag kept them quiet. It had been Daniel's once, but since Daniel was gone, the toy had sat in a drawer collecting dust. Until this current situation. Silence was needed whenever the figure got excited –

angry – and well, Cynthia had the exact thing needed to fit the bill in that dusty drawer.

From the waist down, the figure was covered in a dirty blue sheet, which was pulled and tucked under the mattress, pinning the figure's emaciated body to the bed. She'd elected not to use ankle restraints anymore. She had relied on them for a time – *she didn't want him running out on her* – however, after six-months of inactivity, the power those legs once contained had wasted away, and they were nothing but phantom limbs now.

It had amazed her – *and it still did in a way* – how quickly the withering of their lower limbs had occurred. It was astounding what starvation, bad nutrition, and a lack of exercise could do to a person.

Lifting her wine from its coaster, she raised it to the mirror.

"Bon appetit." The words were muffled by the feathers of the mask, she didn't care. She always toasted her esteemed guest.

'*The secret of your future is hidden in your daily routine*'

Using her free hand, Cynthia tilted the mask up from her chin, took a sip, swilled it for a moment, savoured the bouquet and the mouthfeel of it, and then swallowed it down with a gulp.

"Delicious."

Allowing the mask to settle back in place, she set her glass on the table and picked up her napkin, snapped it in the air to her side – *a practised routine which had the red napkin unravel all at once* – and she placed the silky material over her lap, over the already stained overalls. Redundant? Maybe. But it's the thought, the routine, that counts.

Scooping a forkful of risotto from the creamy pile on her plate, ensuring the mouthful has a bit of everything, Cynthia once more peels the bottom of the mask away from her face. She slides the fork towards her mouth, and her tongue emerges to greet the tines, where it guides the fork slowly into her open mouth. Her lips close around it and she pulls the fork free, her lips removing any of the stubborn risotto from each tine, savouring the taste-sensation in her mouth.

She's eaten the same meal every night for the last year, yet still finds it heavenly. Or is it the thought of perfecting the meal, the night, the possibility of the question and her unspoken answer which tantalises her so greatly? She doesn't know, however, the tastes exploding in her mouth have her groaning with pleasure.

"Mmmmm...heavenly." She simmers, adjusting her mask, ensuring it sits perfectly in place, hiding her true self.

Glancing in the mirror, at the island of light in the distance, she discovers the pale face staring back at her, eyes wide with the thought of food.

"How silly of me," she mutters. "You must be starving."

Sliding her chair back, she stands, checks herself one final time in the mirror before leaning over the table and reclaiming the egg cup. Holding the cup aloft for a moment, she inspects it, then plucks the egg out of the receptacle, and gripping the egg between her thumb, forefinger and middle finger before discarding the cup the table.

She turns to the darkness splitting the room in two, her gaze travelling over the river of blackness absolute. Her observations rove higher, drawn irresistibly towards the hospital bed and its withered occupant.

How small you look now.

A year ago, this figure had seemed larger than life. A colossus standing in her way, a looming tower of judgement which had cast her life in perpetual shade.

Even towers fall.

A wry smile behind the mask.

Stepping away from the table, relinquishing the candlelight for the stygian dark, she plods onwards, towards the white light from the humming fluorescent strips, the egg held before her as if it were a precious gem. Peering past the offering in her outstretched hand, towards the bed, she registers its sole occupant again and the wry smile crumbles from her face. Her lip curls up in a snarl of hatred.

"Dinner is served, my love."

CHAPTER 5

Swiftly emerging from the dark, and swooping into the light like her mask's namesake, Cynthia descends on her petrified prey; her shawl billowing out behind her as if she's trailing wings.

Suddenly she stops, hand outstretched, egg held steadfastly before her as if it were some reverent thing to be worshiped and adored.

The body in the bed's eyes grow wide and white above the ball-gag. They worship the egg and have, over time, grown to also worship Cynthia.

The bed's control is hooked over the side, and she reaches for it. With the remote in one hand, and the egg held aloft in the other, she presses the grey button with the embossed, up arrow.

There's a hum, a whirring, as hidden mechanisms begin their laborious task and the head of the bed begins to rise, slowly. It brings her specimen to a more comfortable, seated position, folding their emaciated body to a 60-degree angle.

Through the harsh glare from the fluorescent strips overhead, Cynthia observes scalp peering through their thinning hair. Tiny pink worms stand out amongst the grey, brittle wisps that still cling to his skull which, four months ago, had been thick and black. Dye and malnutrition helped her achieve the look they wear now; the same visage Daniel had worn near the end. '*Distinguished hobo*' he'd called it. She loved that about him. How, even in the midst of all his pain and suffering, as his body circled the drain, he was still able to laugh at himself.

O, how she missed that laugh.

Sometimes she still hears it, but most of the time she doesn't. Just echoes of his pained wailing.

Cynthia smiles at her work, the emotion hidden by the feathered mask.

Her shaping, her sculpting, her remoulding.

With each passing day she can see everything panning out just the way she wanted it to. He's returning to her, piecemeal by piecemeal.

She could fold the figure before her in two if she kept holding the button down. But this time she'll show restraint, *mercy*. She hooks the remote back on the end of the bed before sliding around it, moving as if she is floating or flying.

Placing the egg carefully on the bedside table, ensuring it won't roll off and crack on the floor, she checks the heartrate monitor. There's the steady green blip she'd seen before in the mirror, continuing on its merry way across the screen, however, instead of the usual one blip, there's two now. An elevated heartrate.

You're excited, blood pressure is on the rise.

Her hand moves towards their face and they flinch away. They always flinch, although she hasn't given up hope that one day they won't; that *one day* in the not too distant future they'll lean in to her touch, instead of shirking away from it.

Do you think I'm going to hurt you, again?

Their scared – *blue now instead of brown, given the contacts she's forced him to wear* – bulbous eyes stare back at her, sunken within a now angular face. She always gets a kick out of how defeated he looks, like a beaten dog looking up at its master.

Before, near the beginning of their time together, his face had been pudgy. Not through an unhealthy lifestyle per se, but rather one full of entitlement and greed. A life of fine living and fine dining, opulent in whiskey and red meat, gouts' dream travel destination.

Three blips on the heartrate monitor now, and the promise of a fourth.

Her fingers clamber over his greasy, flaky scalp in search of the strap at the back of his head. The ball-gag is yanked taut, the leather biting into the skin of his face and back of his head, and Cynthia has to ratchet it tighter before she's able to get enough wiggle room to slip the teeth of the buckle out. The jerking movement causes him to groan in pain.

With the straps loosened, she pulls it away, the red ball almost popping out of his mouth, trailed by a silvery string of drool, momentarily connecting man to ball before snapping and dribbling down his chin, hanging there like some leftovers from a bukkake party. Dropping the ball-gag on her esteemed guest's non-existent pelvis, she notices the sheet tented tightly across his lap from the emergence - *over recent weeks* – of his prominent hip bones.

He doesn't speak. Only stares up at her, wondering what will come next. Will it be beauty, or the beast? She often wonders what he's thinking as he takes in her mask. Wonders if he thinks he's dreaming or high or drunk, pondering when this will all end and when he'll wake up at home. She hasn't the heart to dismiss his possible thoughts with words, or to tell him this will all end when he finally accepts *who* he is and what she desperately, achingly, *wants* him to become: *then* and only *then* will it end. Not a moment before.

A sideways glance to the bedside table, and then back at her.

The egg. Of course.

His eyes have lost some of the fear they held, although it still resides in him, written plainly on his face, contained within the creases of his raised brow, pleading with her, begging her without words for food. For sustenance. For the egg.

Plucking the egg from its resting place with three immaculately manicured fingers, Cynthia obliges his silent request. She taps it on the bedside table, lightly, manoeuvring it in her hand until its entire surface is covered in cracks, fissured like parched soil.

All the King's horses and all the King's men, couldn't put Humpty together again.

The nursery rhyme is lodged in her head, her lips mouth the words behind the mask as she peels the egg, dropping each piece of shell in the bin between the bedside table and the heartrate monitor, where they join the countless other peelings of broken shells.

A mound, no, scratch that. A ~~mound~~ growing pyramid of the stuff – formed from hundreds of eggs. Once done she holds the warm, white egg aloft. And the expression on her distinguished guests face? You could imagine she were holding a Fabergé Egg before him.

Awe.

Wonder.

Hunger.

How could she blame him for his uncensored yearning? For the basic desire to not go without? It's human nature after all, yet the desire he's exhibiting is almost carnal, and Cynthia observes all his yearning through the two large eyeholes of her mask. It reminds her of her own desire to have Daniel back, returned to her, so they can finish what was almost started.

Soon, soon I'll have you back.

She shakes her owl head.

Focus, focus, focus.

"Dinner…is…ready." She says with a flourish.

He doesn't speak, only nods his head enthusiastically. He looks like a heroin addict before a scorched spoon, the smack a glorious puddle within its oval head. She brings the egg closer to his lips, teasing him as she brushes its warm, waxy texture against his cracked, dry lips, but she pulls it away so he can't take a bite.

"A, ah, ahh…" she says, with a wagging finger.

His lips quiver, from fear or from the words he desperately wants to sling at her but fearful of the repercussions.

"What do we say, Danny?"

A test.

Will he pass?

Or will I have to correct him again?

They shake their head, no.

"Come on, Danny. I know you want it… just say so and it's yours…"

Tilting her head, peering at him through the mask's lenses – *the huge eyes of the barn owl, which take up so much of the mask* – Cynthia focuses on the nose she broke.

She didn't break it out of spite. No, she's not a monster. She broke it to make it look more like Daniel's.

There was a kink to Daniel's nose – *across the bridge* – from where he'd broken it playing rugby. It was one of the first modifications Cynthia had made to her guest's body, she used a hammer and a blunt chisel to carry out the deed. Once she'd broken it – *pulverised it* – she used her bare hands to manipulate it, pressing it in at all the right angles, the cartilage crunching and grinding, pliable beneath her roving fingers as if she were pressing her thumbs into wet clay. She needed it just right, to bring an essence of the face she loved so much, back.

The nose which could be Daniel's, on a face which – *over time* – has gradually become his, has her swelling with pride, but a sudden bark from her guest sends her reeling.

"That's not my name."

Lips quiver slightly before drawing together in a thin line as if they've said something they shouldn't have. The crease between their brow deepens.

Concentration?

Anger?

Confusion?

Betrayal?

It's hard for Cynthia to discern.

"What did you just say?"

The words are offered in mock surprise and Cynthia waits. The egg is now held within Cynthia's softly closed fist. If her guest has backslid to who he was before, he'll go without. She can't waste any more time on this.

"I. Said. That's. Not. My. Name."

Each word its own sentence.

The hand holding the egg forms a tighter fist, another correction imminent.

Say it, I dare you.

Say it…say you're…DOCTOR OSMAN HASAN.

I fucking **dare** *you to say it, you piece of shit.*
Say it and see what happens to you.
The thoughts roar in her head.
"Danny…" he blurts. "That's not my name."
There's petulance in his voice.
She waits.
A cloying silence falls over the room before *he,* whoever *he* is in this moment, is brave enough to fill it with words.
"My name… my name…is…Dan. Or Daniel. Never…ever…call me Danny!"
Good. You passed the test.
Daniel hated being called Danny. He said it sounded like some character out of a *Roald Dahl* book, and he didn't need to be fictionalised to be the champion of the world. He *was* the champion of world, Cynthia's, and that had been enough, until it wasn't.

Uncrossing her arms, Cynthia opens her hand, revealing the egg with a flourish as if she is a magician performing a sleight of hand trick. Buoyed by his statement and his progress, she smiles, yet can't help but recall the dark times before today and the many corrections she'd had to inflict. Not to harm him, no, but to *teach* him and to *encourage* the Daniel she once knew back into this new body.

There were times when she'd had to lay heavy hands on him. Not in a praying sense, but more the abusive kind. There had been one time where she'd broken his leg. It was an accident, sort of. She'd had no idea his lack of calcium would cause such a weakness in the time he'd gone without proper nutrition; but it had, and she had, well, broken his damned leg. However, he shouldn't have tested her as he had. His refusal to adopt his name came across as belligerent and entitled, and the only thing his entitlement brought him was the privilege of a beating.

"Good. Well done, that's right."
She placed the egg to his lips once more, and he tentatively leaned forward to nibble at the white. Then, confident he wouldn't be hit, he took a larger bite. The yolk trickled from inside, dribbling over Cynthia's fingers. He's soon licking them, lapping up the yellow, and Cynthia lets him, Daniel, lick the goo from her.

As his wet tongue licks at her fingers, she closes her eyes, remembering what a generous lover Daniel had been, with her needs in bed always placed above his own. As his tongue continues to lick now, his lips persistent in their slurping, his mouth suckles at her fingers, and Cynthia imagines his tongue, not on her fingers but her neck, her breasts her–

"Ow," the sudden, sharp pain pulls her back to the present, tearing her unceremoniously away from the fun they'd shared between the sheets. Some of that exciting echo remains, a warmth radiating through her body, originating from between her legs.

"Did you just bite me?"

He looks at her, mouth full of egg, eyes reduced to slits, squinting as if already fearing what's to come.

She looks at her empty hand, the egg gone, consumed, but in its place four indents mar her finger, two on the top, two underneath. Teeth marks.

"Forry...I couffun't...helfp...myselpff..." spittle and egg, yellow and white fly from the paste in his mouth. Larger, unchewed chunks tumble down his hospital gown and disappear under the sheet.

The owl head shakes side to side.

No...no...no...this won't do. THIS WON'T DO!

Suddenly, anger is rising within her, and the bellows of rage begin pumping her wrath from the pit of her stomach. Her hands close into tight fists, the nails of her fingers biting into the fleshy palms of her hands, her arms quiver and shake, and her shoulders rise up and down with each heavy, rage-filled breath.

The mask becomes unbearable; her breath -*warm, angry breath*- steams up the concaved lenses. She's about to boil over and *he* can tell. Suddenly he's pulling at his restraints, trying to squirm away, yet he can't. He's trapped. A butterfly in a Lepidopterists collection, only without a pin securing him in place through his thorax.

The way Cynthia clubs him with her fists, two fleshy hammers, it's as if she's trying to drive a large, sharp, metal pin right through his body to pin the fucker to the bed for all of eternity. Her clubbed, cudgel of a fist connects with his pelvis.

The restraints snap him back as he attempts to protect his soft, malleable innards, and there's a desperation about his frantic but restricted movements. An innate need to preserve what little of his wasted body is left.

Cynthia raises her hands again, for another pre-emptive strike.

The barn owl mask snaps to face him. Huge, serine eyes peer down at his torture, as if he is a rodent ripe for the taking.

"Daniel would never…*ever*…speak with his mouth full!"

Hand hanging in the air.

"I'm forry…I…"

More egg and spittle fly.

Those three mumbled words are all he manages before Cynthia slams her fisted hand down again. This time she misses her intended, repeated, target of his pelvis, and her fist clashes against the sharpness of his hip bone with a crack.

He yelps in pain, and Cynthia wants to yelp too, because that one hurt her more than she believes it did him.

"I'm sorry," he mumbles. "Please, I didn't mean to… I was just so hungry… please… Daniel's sorry. I'm sorry…" His wrists rattle against the restraints, and Cynthia can tell he's desperate to hold both hands out in a warding off gesture, but he can't.

There's a growing desire to hit him again. To really destroy him this time. However, she needs to show restraint, because if she destroys him – *now and completely* – it would set things back drastically; her carefully laid plans would be forfeited in an instant. She's not prepared to wait another year, to be forced to keep *him* for another year, a prisoner down here, just for the perfect time to come around again.

She lifts the ball-gag from his lap and snaps it tight before his eyes.

He flinches briefly before freezing, like prey before a predator.

Cynthia doesn't pause. She strikes with ruthless aggression, wrapping the gag around his face. The ball clacks against his teeth as it finds its way forcefully into his mouth and stifles his cries of pain. Forcing the buckles closed, she latches the gag one notch tighter than needed, just to be a callous bitch, and she flings his hanging head back in disgust.

He's crying, and the owl watches him sob uncontrollably.

Tears trickle freely from his eyes, soaking into the straps of the gag, staining the brown leather dark before running its length to the pillow, and dampening the material around his defeated head.

The shawl billows out behind her like sandy wings as she turns in one swift movement. She reclaims the remote for the bed and presses the button with the embossed down arrow.

The bed hums, and mechanisms whir, as it begins lowering its cargo once more until horizontal. She drops the remote and strides into the dark once more, his sobs echoing around the basement.

Sitting down at the table once more, with her back to the bed and the lights, and the mumbling, bumbling, sobbing thing, that was Daniel, but which is not Daniel, she places her finger to the switch. Checks her reflection in the oval mirror again. He can't see her, although she can see him, and for now that's all that matters.

"We'll try again tomorrow. Goodnight, Daniel…pleasant dreams."

With a flick of her finger, the light behind her extinguishes.

Lifting the bottom of her mask, she slips another forkful of risotto it into her mouth, but it's cold, spoiled, ruined now. She swallows, then replaces the mask.

"Utterly ruined,' she scathes before reclaiming the tray from beside the table leg to set about tidying the dinner things away, leaving the candle burning, for the moment, solely to aid her retreat.

Replacing the chair to its original position so it'll help her navigate her way back safely in the dark tomorrow, she picks up the tray and shuffles slowly to the bottom of the stairs. The darkness swarms in behind her retreat, growing thicker and bigger as she shepherds the light away, a swarming nothingness that conceals a somethingness.

Cynthia climbs the stairs, one rickety step at a time, and she notices the light crawling from underneath the kitchen door, highlighting the lips of the stairs above her.

She pauses, takes one heavy-laden breath.

"I love you, Daniel…"

Just words, a sentiment she's longed to whisper and have answered in return.

Her lover doesn't answer.

Maybe tomorrow?

Blowing out the candle, she continues to climb the stairs, mulling over her hope that's flagging, yet a hope she'll cling to nevertheless.

Or the day after that…

…or the day after that…

…or the day after that…

…or the day after…

…or the day…

…or the…

…or…

…

PART TWO
CATERPILLAR

CHAPTER 6

The coffee machine slowly hums, dripping her espresso drop by delicious drop into her Utopia™ double-walled Espresso glass. It's the morning after the night before, or the late afternoon of the morning before Daniel bit her in the basement. Her concept of time has altered, shifted significantly with her online presence and her nocturnal pursuits of resurrecting Daniel from the ashes of Hasan.

Cynthia's early morning rise is everyone else's lunchbreak and as she rests against the marble countertop in the kitchen, humming along to Fleetwood Mac's 'Everywhere,' she wonders when her life became *this*.

She's contemplated how her life differs from those in the real world a lot over the past few years, and she can't stop thinking about Daniel, trapped in the basement, where every waking moment; scratch that, every ~~waking~~ moment, every human interaction he's had – *with the owl lady* – happens at night and over dinner.

Does he think he's sleeping through the days?
Is he wondering if he's slowly lost his mind?
Or does he think he's only awoken at night by the owl lady of the house because she's a nocturnal creature?

Do bears shit in the woods?
Of course he does, and of course they do.

The last drips of coffee splash into the glass receptacle and she immediately swipes it from the counter, holds the glass below her nose, and inhales its goodness – *nothing beats that smell.*

Coffee is what keeps her functioning. That, and her desire to sculpt something beautiful from the flesh-bag in the basement. It's the first cup, that initial hit of the hard stuff in the morning/afternoon, which energises her flagging soul for the long day ahead. It also helps her bowels regulate. If she misses her cup of coffee in the morning she's usually bound up for the rest of the day, and she can't let her fans see her bloated – *although some might like that, and she's sure a few might pay to watch her deposit it too.* The thought makes her shudder. She's never been a bodily fluid kind of girl, it all makes her feel queasy, and not to mention the damned laundry.

She sips her coffee.

'Black Crack' she calls it because it kicks like a mule and she always takes it black.

"Milk?" she mumbles to herself questioningly before taking a larger swig of coffee. The heat of it lances down her throat and she places the glass on the marbled kitchen-top, smiling, because the coffee matches her mood. It's bitter, just how she likes it.

Padding her way to the fridge in her bunny slippers, she opens the door and rummages through its contents.

'Milk…milk…milk…" she murmurs.

Her gaze falls to the shelves in the fridge's door, where it's usually stored. It's not there. She moves some of the bagged-up rabbit in the heart of the fridge and finds a two-pint, plastic bottle on its side.

"Phew." Relieved she won't have to buy some for tomorrow's working day and risk the chance of it not arriving in time. Her Only-Fans© have requested that she drink milk for them. Slurp it. Guzzle it. The messier the better, apparently.

They also mentioned in the poll last night that should she spill milk down her chin or on her t-shirt. She knows that's what they're expecting – *hoping for* – this isn't her first rodeo, and it doesn't take a rocket scientist to work out why they keep returning, with requests that are becoming more outlandish and perverted. They're hungry for her, for her flesh, for her breasts, for her lips, and for her to disgrace herself for their amusement; they're banking on it and for her shirt to become see through.

She understands this delicate dance, as she knows the sun will rise in the morning. They (her OnlyFans©) also know that she knows, and they know she'll do their bidding because, after all, they'll be paying for it

Pathetic little creatures really, but what does that make Cynthia?

Cynthia will oblige – *she's not proud or a prude* – as she always does, because if she doesn't, she knows they'll find someone else who will. So why shouldn't it be her? She's not hurting anyone, and the money is good, helping to cover a multitude of sins. So why shouldn't she get rich off the backs of her fan's stupidity?

It's not like what they're asking her to do is taxing or illegal.

Cynthia's been drinking all her life, like every other human being on the planet. Hell, she's would even regard herself as good at it. She's never spilled a drop in thirty years; even when she's been off her face, back teeth swimming in booze, trolleyed, totalled, trashed – she can still handle her drink. She's proud of this fact, but she doesn't think they give out certificates for that kind of achievement.

At the end of the day Cynthia will be paid to drink a glass of milk, albeit in front of a live audience and in her underwear, but how hard can it be?

It doesn't matter to Cynthia how she drinks the milk.

Fast or slow, seductively or messily, it's just milk to her. But she knows the milk she'll drink, blow bubbles in, gag and choke on, and which she'll eventually dribble down her chin, making her top translucent so her nipples show through the fabric, represents something else entirely to her viewers: the sick little puppies they are.

Before closing the fridge, she pulls a bag of poached rabbit from within, deposits it into a bowl on the countertop. She needs the meat room temperature, ready for tonight's meal. As the fridge bangs closed, she notices the marker pen – *attached by a string* – whip out before clattering against the outside of the fridge.

Following the string higher reveals a calendar, hanging from the door by a large magnet, the shape of a butterfly. The calendar's slipped slightly, revealing another calendar behind it.

The song changes, and now Stevie is singing about landslides bringing shit down. Cynthia hums along to the song, it's one of her favourites, and she tears up when Stevie sings about handling the seasons of her life. The seasons of her life – *which both calendars testify* – for her at least, all look the same now, bleached with the same torment and sorrow.

Wiping the wetness from her eyes, she stares at the squares on her current calendar. All of them, each day of the month – *barring the first day of the month, which represents yesterday* – have a big, red, X drawn in them. With all that happened in the basement last night, she'd forgotten to add her mark for yesterday.

Unfastening the lid of the marker, she makes two quick slashes, as if she's a mugger wielding a knife in a darkened alleyway, carving red without a care. She stands back, observes the wet, red X splitting the box into four triangles.

And just like that, the month is done. October is all but buried.

She drops the pen and it bounces on its string as she removes not one, but both calendars, placing the hidden calendar down first on the countertop. She holds the other in her hands, taking a moment to process October's end before she turns it over.

Not forwards, but backwards.

October turns into September.

A smile graces her lips as she places the calendars side by side.

It's September to Cynthia now, whilst outside this house, it's another month entirely, and she can't remember which month it is to everyone else. As Stevie sings about *being afraid of changin'* it strikes a chord with Cynthia because she's been afraid of changin' too.

She used to keep track of the months that other people lived by, but now she's no idea. There are other pressing things to contend with, and isn't time just a construct we give too much credence to, anyway?

Cynthia's stuck. Living her life in reverse, battling her way through each month one red cross at a time, always heading backwards, retracing her days and weeks and months back to *the* day, *the* night, when her life could have gone in a different direction. To her fork in the road moment.

But she didn't get to choose which fork she took, did she? Instead, she was rather bundled down it by cruel circumstance, and even cruller negligence, from the shitty doctor who didn't do his fucking job; the doctor who Cynthia is slowly transforming in the basement with the sole purpose of getting a smidgen back of what he stole from her.

She desperately wants the time he stole from her back, and the only way she can see for getting it back, is to go back herself; day by day, week by week, to the day when her choice of path was presented to her. The day on the calendar marked with doodles of flowers and hearts, and in the middle of the square – *the twelfth of September* – two words, written not by her hand but his, her Daniel.

'Date Night'.

Beyond the twelfth, further into September, and filling every month afterwards, or previously, all a case of how you look at things, are more of Daniel's scrawled words; reminders of meetings, dates, birthdays, shopping-list items, notes, hearts and doodles.

Cynthia had loved that about Daniel, how even with the busyness of their daily schedules – *when they were often ships passing in the night* – he still found the time to leave her notes on the calendar, touching base with her. A heart here, and an *I love you* there.

Sometimes there were even double hearts, code for their special nights of planned intimacy. The planning of said intimacy never took away the romance as one might have thought, it just ensured they made time for one another. If anything, the double hearts built their excitement, knowing that a night of unbridled passion was on the horizon.

Reclaiming her espresso, she knocks it back, tepid now, but still nectar from the gods.

Her gaze returns to the squares on the calendar and her heart throbs, aching with each beat in her chest as if she's been lanced, with a red-hot poked shoved into her innards, sizzling, bubbling, steaming in place. Cynthia grips the edge of the marbled countertop to ground herself as the room begins to spin. A sheen of sweat breaks out across her skin, and her shirt suddenly feels as sprayed on as a wave of light-headedness rocks her and she clutches the counter tighter, her fingers numbing with the exertion.

Releasing one hand, she wipes sweat from her top lip, and ponders if the disabling pain and the tightness fanning out across her chest is due to the fact she skipped breakfast – *hunger can do the craziest of things. Just ask Doctor Hasan about that* – or if it's perhaps, instead, an undiagnosed cancerous tumour eating away at her lungs. She's a strong feeling though it's just the mule-kick-buzz from her Kopi Luwak Coffee™ on an empty stomach causing her heart to thud harder and faster.

The brand-name coffee is strong, and expensive, and not to mention very, very exclusive, but she can afford the luxury, and the money she makes affords her the ignorance of not giving a shit how her coffee's sourced. Ethically or unethically. If blind children working their fingers to the bone had to harvest it for two-pence an hour, she didn't care. It was her little slice of heaven, in a world of Hell, and she wouldn't give it up.

Screw the blind children.

The fact that Cynthia's coffee consists of partially digested coffee cherries, cherries which had been eaten and defecated by a collection of Asian Palm Civets in captivity was of no concern to her. She didn't even know what a Civet was, so why should she care. If it was a poodle or a cat, something like that, something she knew, then maybe she'd give it up. But a Civet?

You can't just make animals up to pluck at people's heartstrings.

She didn't care how many Asian Palm Civets lost their lives producing her bag of coffee, and she'd plead ignorance to the Civets plight because there was no way she was going to drink '*Bronze Blend*,' or some other generic shit like a heathen.

Cynthia did look into the sourcing of her coffee, thinking if she had guests round she'd be able to enlighten and wow them with how exclusive it really was, not just some run-of-the-mill stuff you know. It had yielded a double advantage. Knowledge, firstly it would help to reinforce to her visitors how rich she was, whilst secondly showing how poor her guests were.

The cherries became fermented as they passed through a Civet's intestines, whereupon after being defecated – *along with other faecal matter* – were then collected, washed – *she hoped* – packaged, and then sent across the world to folks who required their coffee a little more exotic and who were willing to pay for said exoticness.

Cynthia doesn't have guests to chat and gossip with over a coffee and a slice of cake, but being forewarned is forearmed, as someone once said. Although Cynthia knew if she ever *did* entertain someone, other than her resident guest in the basement, she'd have one hell of a story to tell them about the coffee they were drinking. She'd also enjoy the look on their faces when she'd tell them they were drinking defecated coffee, instead of decaffeinated.

O, how she'd laugh.

And she smiled at the thought, as the tightness in her chest waned and her dizziness faded away. She'd always thought she had an odd way of making a living, as she placed her cup under the coffee machine once more, clicking the button down for another cup of tantalising Civet shit. Watching the blackish-brown liquid drip into her cup, she mused that clawing through shit to refine coffee made her line of work seem tame in comparison.

The coffee aroma filled the room with its aromatic charm, and she wondered if Kopi Luwak Coffee™ had an OnlyFans© page too? She felt pretty sure that, if it did, it would float someone's sick and twisted boat for sure.

With her Utopia glass in hand, she turned back to the calendar and realised instantly that the ache in her chest hadn't been from the *'shit-coffee'*, or from thinking about small mammals being force-fed cherries in captivity. No. Her heart's ache was for the words and doodles that were never added after the twelfth of September, and the reminder that the twelfth had also held a double heart.

The ache slowly returned, and Cynthia picked up the second calendar, a mirror reflection of the other calendar, and Cynthia began thumbing through its pages, front to back.

January, February, March, April – every day crossed off with a red X.

May, June, July, and August – again, crossed off.

Turning over August, she knows what she'll see; September, yes, but also, the twelfth of the year following their date night. Their would-have-been anniversary. It was also the day she had decided to take her life back, the day which became the advent of her life in reverse.

Half the month was crossed out, red X's starting on the twelfth.

But from the twelfth onwards, there was nothing. No notes, no appointments, no birthdays or anniversaries. Nothing. It's as if her life stopped on the twelfth, and in a way it did, it stopped and began running in reverse. Placing a finger to the date, she reads the words that are just legible beneath the scratched and re-scratched X:

Today's The Day.

Knowing she couldn't leave a trace of what she was about to do, because *what if* someone saw it, *what if* they found her calendar in the recycling and, and what if that *someone – heaven knows who that someone might be that gave a shit about Osman, the pig of a man* – came looking for him. Caution was the reason she still kept the useless thing tucked behind the other calendar, not just because she couldn't bear to throw it away, but because it was evidence and what would happen if one of the nosy recycling people riffled through her rubbish – *one person's trash is another person's gold* – and found it? What would happen if they saw **Today's The Day** and read between the lines, put two and two together, and came up with five? Or worse:

Today's The Day We Abduct The Bastard.

Although she'd wanted to write that, she'd thought better of it.

As her fingers flitted across the other crossed out squares, they highlighted the true reason behind keeping the calendar. They showed intention. Pre-meditated thoughts of seize and capture, without directly or overtly stating them outright – the clues were there for anyone with half a mind, if they had the inclination to look.

Sliding her finger from the twelfth to the ninth.

Delivery: Hospital bed.

A red X over scrawled over it.

METAMORPHOSIS   61

Can something be pre-meditated, if you're living a life in reverse?

It was an interesting concept, because instead of Cynthia's choices being pre-meditated, maybe she was shooting from the hip now. Working back through days which *have*, and yet also have *not*, happened. A cosmic glitch – *the way of the masses* – each day already having been lived, items having been purchased and installed in the past, as the future continues to march on.

If anything, living a life backwards just throws up a great many coincidences. Not motive, though. Surely not motive. Turning the calendar backwards instead of forwards is more like regressing into a past which has now become days of a future past.

Thinking about such things for a prolonged period of time usually gives Cynthia a headache, and what with her current heart palpitations, she opts to let it slide, for now, and she takes another sip of her coffee.

Each day crossed off brings her closer to *that* day, *the* day, which she plans to relieve again, fresh and in person – it's all she really cares for, and in the grand scheme of things, all that matters.

A moment to return to the day she never got to live.

The meal she never got to eat.

And she hopes when the day finally comes again – *and come again it will* – she'll get to answer the question which was never asked, and maybe, in some weird and wild way, her answer can mend her brokenness, eclipse the total-permanent-eclipse of her heart and mind.

Maybe they *can* be together; forever, for all time, as it should have been.

Her finger shifts to the eighth.

Order: Bed-sheets.

The second.

Order: Hair dye.

Flipping the calendar over, back, reveals August.

The twenty-second.

Pain-killers, bandages, replenish first aid kit.

Nineteenth.

Heart-rate monitor, delivery.

Seventeenth.

Order: heart-rate monitor.

She flips the page over again, July, more of the same; provisions, equipment.

Fourteenth.

Order: Chemicals.

Third.

Training: Chemical peel.

Flipping back through the months – June, May, April and March.

On the third of March there's a picture of binoculars. It's an icon, the legend in her head remembers, and she knows, either in her sanity or her insanity – *isn't love often referred to as a temporary madness?* – what the binoculars represent.

Surveillance. Stalking.

There are others before and after this date. The same squiggle on countless days, all leading up to the twelfth of September, or away from it, depending if she was living her life forward or backward. She was methodical in her observations. She had to be. There had been too much riding on this, and if she was going to be apathetic in the task ahead, well that's when she would have gotten caught. And she wasn't planning on getting caught.

Not then. Not tomorrow. Not ever.

Planned, or unplanned?

Reactionary, or progressive?

Luck, or coincidence?

The coffee's got her riled up, her pulse a steady thrumming beneath the skin of her temple, breathing rapid, sweat beading on her brow as her anxious mind dives down rabbit holes she doesn't want it to.

If someone asks about the binoculars on the calendar, what are you going to say?

The reply to her posed interrogation comes instantly.

I'll tell them I took up Ornithology, how would they know any different?

Another question rises in her mind.

What about the hospital bed, the medications, all the other purchases?

Not even a moment's pause before she rattles off the answer.

A prepper. I'll tell them I'm a doomsday prepper. The simplest answer is usually the correct one, Occam's razor, *always sharp, never fails.*

With her questioning mind speeding up, she ponders a smoothie to counteract the huge caffeine hit that her body is working through. Anything to stop the anxious thoughts which percolate in her mind like her black crack, mammal sludge.

What about the body on the bed?

The man in your basement?

Cynthia thrashes her head. No.

What about the body on the bed, huh?

There's a crack as she slaps herself in the face, open handed, and she takes a few deep breaths, feels her face fill with pins and needles, her vision narrowing.

No... it won't come to that.

If the authorities do kick in her door, slap handcuffs on her, and interrogate her, she won't falter or even quiver under their barrage. She'll look them square in the eyes and spill her truth because she won't be lying; it'll be the god's honest truth. Because, regardless if this is an imaginary future, or the nightmarish past – *whatever path it is she walks now* – the man in the basement, tied to the hospital bed, *will be, is and forever will be,* Daniel.

In mind, body, and soul, returned to her as he once was.

He's in the bed because he's ill.

That wouldn't be a lie because he'd been gravely ill. She even had a death certificate to prove it.

How do you explain the cuffs? The restraints?

With a flutter of her eyelashes she'll smile demurely at them. She'll say he's been hurting himself, that he can't handle the diagnosis, the medication makes him have off days. She'll tell them she's caring for him, because she is. However strange it looks to the outside world, he's *hers* and she is *his* and...and... I'M CARING FOR A SICK LOVER, A DYING LOVER...AND YOU SHOULD JUST LEAVE US IN PEACE, LEAVE ME IN PEACE; YOU NEED TO RESPECT OUR PRIVACY AND KEEP YOUR NOSES OUT OF OUR BLOODY BUSINESS – WHAT A COUPLE DECIDE TO DO BEHIND CLOSED DOORS IS OF NO CONCERN TO YOU...THANK YOU VERY MUCH, NOW KINDLY GET THE HELL OUT OF MY HOUSE.

September stares back at her.

September.

The voice in her head sounds defeated.

Date night.

Two words tinged with an aching depression.

Placing two fingers to her lips she touches them to the calendar, presses them longingly to the square which reads *'date night'*. The day which once *was* and *will* be again.

Beans?

The thought comes from nowhere.

Baked Beans…that's it.

And she's off, shuffling from the fridge to the cabinet above the sink, opening the dark-wood cupboards. Rows and rows of beans are stacked neatly within, all labels facing out, positioned exactly the same way.

"A prepper," she mutters, and a coy smile dimples her cheek.

Removing tin after tin of Baked Beans, Heinz™ – only the best will do – she removes a battery operated can opener from the drawer and, grabbing a large glass bowl from the drying rack, Cynthia begins simultaneously opening and decanting the beans into it. Her disdain for beans is clearly visible by the pinched look on her face. She hates everything about them, from the way they look, taste, and smell.

If the Devil had sperm, I bet it would resemble Baked Beans.

Shuddering as she scoops the persistently clingy, gelatinous filth from the cans into the glass bowl – more frogspawn than edible treat that's for sure – and she has to swallow hard to stop her coffee rising from deep down.

Job done, she doesn't even wash the cans before throwing them out the window and into the recycling bin in the garden. She doesn't want to get its filth-juice on her fingers. Filth-juice on her feet is one thing, a thing she's paid handsomely to endure, but on her fingers? That icky tackiness on her hands? No, no, no, she won't abide that.

Tonight though, she'll be cashing in on the lesser-known Podophilia, which is not, repeat *not*, to be confused with Pedophilia. Switching out that first E with an O is really important, especially if one wants to keep the thing in their basement concealed and hidden from prying eyes; she doesn't need the police raiding her house because she made a faux pas with her vowels in a search engine.

Podophilia is the term used to describe individuals who find feet, legs, or even clothing that covers those areas sexually arousing. Cynthia doesn't mind the weirdos, she more often than not encourages them. She's become versed in many a *philia* over the years. That's where the big money is, and because Podophilia brings in a substantial chunk of funds to OnlyFans© accounts, she's more than happy, albeit a little disgruntled and disgusted, to be doing her bean-foot-thing again.

Dipping her feet in the bowl, she'll squish her toes in its cold, gooey texture. The beans will stay cold. She won't warm the foul contents of the bowl, having discovered over time that it only makes the stench worse.

Once she's dipped her feet in, she'll lift her dripping feet to the camera, wet and slick; juice dripping off her attractive feet – *because Cynthia does have attractive feet* – and when they're inches from the screen, she'll fix her gaze upon the camera and ask demurely: '*Are there any* naughty boys *out there who could lick me clean.*'

When the money bags appear – *because they will* – and when their replies start pinging and the hearts start floating to the top of her monitor and begin exploding – *because they'll be clambering over themselves to be the one she mentions, the one that she's talking directly to, because everyone wants to feel special, even if only for a short while* – she'll titter and laugh, giggle like she's being tickled. She'll exclaim in equal parts joyous-delight and rancour at their imaginary licking of her feet, telling one special viewer – *each of them still thinking it's them she's singled out* – 'I love having my toes sucked like that.'

Not resting on her laurels, she'll then snap at them for biting her. She won't discourage them, oh no, she'll say: 'DID YOU JUST BITE ME?' leaving it a beat, before purring with desire and smiling at the camera in that *I-know-what-you-like-you-dirty-boy* kind of way which gets them riled up and then she'll say: 'I like it, bite me harder next time.'

They'll be made to feel special and naughty. She'll even dominate them if she has to. Some of her viewers like the good cop, the wholesome girl next door vibe. Others prefer the mean bitch, not able to get enough of 'Cynthia the Dominatrix,' and she won't discriminate against either group. She'll play all the roles that are asked of her like a professional, because that's what she is.

Cynthia leaves the beans on the side, then turns off the steady rolling drums of Fleetwood Mac's *'Tusk'* before downing the granular silt in the bottom of her coffee glass. Once cleaned up, she heads upstairs to take her morning shower, in the early hours of an afternoon, in a month she no longer remembers, or -come to think of it- even cares about.

CHAPTER 7

A plate of wild rabbit risotto steams in front of her.
The candle flickers gently over proceedings.
Overalls, on.
Work boots, on.
Mask, on.

Before sitting down for her evening meal in the basement, there was a great deal of scrubbing that had been needed to rid her feet of the stench and presence of her baked bean session with her fans; diligently checking her feet for rogue beans, finding a great many squished between her toes and mushed under her pedicured nails.

After removing all traces of bean – juice and all – she'd used a lavender scented scrub, really worked its grittiness into her feet and toes and heels. The soapy suds it produced were tinted orange, from the beans, but she persisted with reapplication until the bubbles ran clean.

Lifting her mask to sip her wine, she could smell the faint, lingering odour on her hands; lavender, not the rancid stench of bean-funk, and she sighed with delight. She was pleased with how the evening – *which was all hers and the morning which was others* – was progressing. With her legs crossed at the knee, one work boot bounced up and down before her ankle began to rotate in a small, concentric circles as if she were a conductor leading an orchestra.

There had been no tell-tale signs of Doctor Hasan returning, yet she knew the night was young and the meal even younger, with Cynthia having only managed a nibble of her meal before deciding the risotto was too hot to fully appreciate just yet. The richness of the wine lingered. It had coated her tongue like a satin sheet. It was that initial sip which had her in good spirits, the wine was delectable, and she gave considerable thought to the prospect of getting a little drunk.

Why shouldn't I? Things are progressing so well.

Shifting her gaze from the plate to table revealed the ball-gag resting next to her wineglass. On discovering it again, Cynthia raised her head to the chair opposite her, where her guest, her beloved Daniel *should* have been seated, but wasn't. Her eyes raised higher, and she took in the grimy mirror and the reflection it contained.

Her missing dinner guest was lurking over her shoulder, sitting up, still restrained by the straps on his wrists to the hospital bed within the island of light at the other end of the basement.

Tonight, she'd decided that he could watch her eat, and she had raised the bed to ensure and unobstructed view. And if he behaved? If Daniel stayed present for the duration of the meal, then maybe tomorrow he'd be brought closer.

If he was really good, if she didn't lose her temper or have to correct him in any way, then maybe, just maybe, she could have him join her at the table, in his rightful place.

But before any grand gesture would be decided upon, there was a dinner to get through, and a quiz. She needed to quiz him often, to make sure that if he ever did make it to the table, he'd be him and not *him*, that other inconvenient shit stain.

She needed to trust him, to know he wouldn't ruin the meal completely. Because if he did, he'd force her to ruin him completely, and if she did – *destroy him* – it would put their much-heralded date night – *which was quickly approaching* – into jeopardy.

And Cynthia couldn't stand for that.

Beating him, or, as Cynthia preferred to call it, *correcting him*, would cost her time and energy, and she had very little of either left in that moment.

Yes, he'd slipped up yesterday, speaking with his mouthful, but once she'd cooled off and the ache in her hand had subsided from where she'd hit is bony-as-fuck hip, she'd forgiven him for that small misstep along his long road to recovery – *his emergence* – because she put it down to him being starved for so long. It was almost like telling a man dying of thirst that he couldn't guzzle the bottle of water you were handing him. That he had to just sip it. It just wouldn't work, and so, she cut Daniel some slack yesterday and forged on with what today would bring.

Regarding his reflection, he seemed somewhat compliant, and that was all she really wanted. Companionship over a meal, in preparation for the meal to come. A dry run of the most anticipated, most important, meal of her life; which *should* have, *would* have, would *still*, change her entire life.

After they would have their delayed meal, and she gave her answer to the question she'd longed to answer, Cynthia had no idea what to expect, or what was to come, but also, she didn't really care what happened afterwards. She was living her life – *albeit in reverse* – for the chance to change her past, and in doing so, she prayed in some weird way, her answer might – *would* – change her future, depending on how she looked at it.

In a strange way, she was a time traveller, and the choice she'd make on that fateful day, when it resurfaced again, would drastically change her past-self and future-self because once she finally had everything she'd ever wanted, she'd never be the same again.

Complete.

That had been all she'd wanted to be, ever since the meal-which-was-never-a-meal happened. Fate carved up the playing field, swapped the Italian Restaurant for a trip to the hospital. Substituted a romantic candle lit dinner for a picnic in the family waiting room. Exchanged her wild rabbit risotto for a stale, warm, tuna fish mayonnaise sandwich and a packet of salt and vinegar crisps.

What Cynthia had wanted from that date night was to feel complete.

She'd almost had it all, everything she'd ever wanted, everything she'd ever dreamed of; but instead, she'd lost it all as she ate that tuna fish sandwich in one of the most depressing rooms she'd ever had the displeasure of sitting in.

Since that day, she'd only ever felt incomplete, having no clue how her mind, body, and soul fit together without the glue of her beloved, Daniel.

It wasn't until she'd grieved, until she'd climbed her way out of that pit of despair, that she finally found a way to make it right. It was simple, really. To make it right was to squeeze justice from injustice, to make a wrong finally right, to trace it all back to its source.

Doctor Hasan was both the wrong and the source, and she would see to it that he made things right. However long it took, however much she had to break him, hurt him, to achieve that goal, she would; she pictured the calendars on the fridge.

A year…it's taken almost a whole year to get to this point.
Eighteen days left and he should be perfect.

Her Daniel would finally be able to step free from the husk of the man who'd taken everything from him and finally be able to join her at the table, fully returned: mind, body and spirit.

Eighteen days until their anniversary meal.

Four-hundred-and-thirty-two hours until a question would be asked and an answer given.

Twenty-five-thousand-nine-hundred-and-twenty minutes until the annals of history would be re-written.

Changed irrevocably: forever.

Her gaze shifts and the huge vacant eyes of the owl stare back unflinchingly into her soul from the mirror. Cynthia wonders, if someone could see into her soul, what would they find? Tilting her head, she observes the man behind her again.

"Danny?" she offers, tilting the chin of the mask up, exposing her mouth as she brings the fork and its yield from the plate to her lips; warm and creamy, just as she likes it.

"DANIEL!" He shouts back.

She places her fork on her plate with a clatter.

Good. Good boy.

"Or, Dan," he utters, meekly, clearly scared about his voluminous upsurge of irritation, knowing he's been beaten for much less before.

"Please." He shuffles uncomfortably on the bed. "Don't call me Danny…I can't abide that name; it makes me sound like some kind of tosser."

Good, but not great, Daniel.

"I'm…I'm sorry…for shouting. For raising my voice…"

Better, much better.

Daniel would never, NEVER, have raised his voice to me.

"I won't do it again, promise. I just really dislike being called that…"

"Not a problem, my love. I was distracted, I'm sorry, it won't happen again."

Forking more risotto into her mouth, she finds a piece of tender rabbit and chews. It tastes divine, and as her taste buds scream out in ecstasy, she knows she's almost perfected the meal.

"Y-Y-You've nothing to apologise for, darling," he offers. "I'm the one who should be apologising. *It's my fault, all of it…*"

Slipping the mask in place she lifts her head sharply, birdlike in its inquisitiveness. Something about those words doesn't ring true to her, a small fluctuation in his voice, a warble from another voice desperate to break free of its shackles and speak some half-truth.

Is that you, Doctor Hasan?

Her huge owl eyes peer into him, probing his face for any tell. She studies his visage closely, looking for any perceptible shifts, as if a person – *a face* – ripples beneath the face she gazes upon, as if Daniel's face were some cheap Halloween mask, a mask much like her own, concealing a hidden beast lurking beneath.

Is Doctor Hasan looking at me now through Daniel's eyes?

Speaking to me with Daniel's tongue and mouth?

It's inconclusive, yet she will remain vigilant.

'I'm the one who should be apologising…' the man who has become Daniel utters.

Leaning forwards, elbows on table – *all table manners forgotten* – Cynthia rests her masked face against her palms, unflinching in her appraisal of him.

Nothing.

"Is there something the matter?" he questions, eyes wide, brow raised, the pallid skin of his brow wrinkling as if a farm of giant pink worms wriggled beneath his skin.

He's questioning, worried, scared.

The owl shakes its head at him.

"Nothing," she replies, nonchalantly spearing another piece of rabbit with her fork.

"Good. I'd hate to have offended you. It's just…it's just I hate that name… Danny."

The word leaves a bitter taste in Daniel's mouth, evident by the way his face screws up like a chewed-out arsehole.

"Where did you go to school?" She changes the subject quickly, with the aim of catching him out as she places the speared rabbit in her mouth and chews.

"Burnt Ash Primary, in Downham. Then Ravensbourne for secondary…"

The owl nods. *Good.*

It was very good. He didn't even pronounce the H or the A and lost the O and the W, replacing them with a U and a double A, making it sound more like *Daanum*, just like Daniel would have said it.

Swallowing the food in her mouth, she smiles, pleased that her nearest and dearest is present.

"Where did we meet?"

The question hangs in the air for a moment, and he coughs, clears his throat.

"You know where we met, why do you ask?"

There's something in the way he deflects the question which has her a troubled. She can't tell if he's forgotten, or if Doctor Hasan has forgotten, because Daniel *would* know, she's sure of it. If it *was* him lying there in that bed, he'd revel in regaling her with that particular story.

Could the same be said for Doctor Hasan?

Did she have more work to do? More correcting to make the memory stick?

"I was just curious to see if you remembered the day as clearly as I did. That day changed my whole life. I just wondered if it meant as much to you as it did to me?"

"How could I forget? That was the day I finally started living, started–"

Cynthia interrupts with her eagerness to get to the point.

"Then...tell me. How. Did. We. Meet?"

Placing another forkful of food in her mouth, she leans back in her seat, adjusts the mask to hide her vulpine snarl at his delay in recall.

He doesn't know...he doesn't know...he doesn't remember...fuck...fuck... fuck...

"Well, it's silly really–"

"Go on..."

Cynthia doffs a hand in the air, beckoning him to continue. She lowers her hand to her lap, her fingers closing into a fist, ready to correct him should he falter in his response; poised to wreck him should she find it's Doctor Hasan threatening to poke his head out from behind that thin veil of a face; lying dormant like the cancer he never diagnosed, which ate Daniel with toothless-aggression, piece-meal by piecemeal, until there was nothing left.

Speak your truth you bastard.

"Well, it's not the best story..."

He's stalling. He can't remember.

He shouldn't have to try, this is his life, we've gone over this again and again and AGAIN. He should *know the ins and outs of everything. It's not going to work if he can't remember...he's going to ruin everything.*

EVERYTHING GODDAMNIT.

"I don't really cover myself in glory..."

OUT WITH IT.

Behind the mask, her teeth squeak and crunch as she clenches her jaw. Her three fillings – *white because she can afford it* – ache in her gum with the pressure.

"...I was..."

"Yes?"

Her eagerness to get an answer practically pulls her from her seat, poised to strike.

"I was on the floor of a pub. Some guy had taken offence at something I'd said. For the life of me, I can't remember what it was though..."

Funny that you don't quite remember...isn't it...Doctor Hasan.

Don't think I can't see you there, behind Daniel's eyes; your pathetic weak face peeking through his. I can see you lurking there, trying to deceive me, you little piece of–

"I'd said something about him barging into me, I think? Something about him spilling my drink and that he should get me another..."

That's right.

A smile from the recollection graces her face.

"How'd he take that?"

Cynthia was probing for the truth, expecting an untruth.

"Well, not very well. As I said, I was on the floor and bloodied. He'd broken my nose, again. As you know I've broken it a few times over the years playing rugby. Fifth time I broke it was the night I met you."

This is true.

Although I broke it again, didn't I? Sixth time's the charm.

"You broke something else that night too..."

Expects him to say *'his heart'* because the Daniel she loved would usually say soppy shit like that. All that lovey-dovey stuff had made her cringe, but in the gaping year of his absence, she'd actually grown to miss hearing those words of affection. Realized that she'd actually grown to love them, and in their absence, in *his* absence, she'd longed to hear them uttered again.

"You broke that bottle over his head, remember?"

Yes. Yes, I did. And I'd do it again in a heartbeat.

"Yes, I remember."

"Well, he'd hit me and then I'd hit the floor, and then you hit him. I remember you helping me up. I was bloodied and crestfallen at the fact that the woman I was trying to impress had to come to my aid...what a hero, right?"

"I gave you a napkin to wipe the blood from your face–"

"No. It wasn't a napkin, it was a handkerchief."

Good catch.

The mask conceals the look of approval on her face at his recall.

"It had roses or some flower pattern embroidered down one side. Cath Kidston©, I believe."

Correct.

"It was…yes, roses. I can't believe you remembered that."

"Do you remember what we did next?" Daniel questions.

"We ran. It was raining, wasn't it? Pissing down and we got soaked."

"I've never stopped running since that night."

"What do you mean?"

"I mean that I've never stopped running into your arms. Grazed my knee bad, too…"

"How?"

"Falling for you."

That was something Daniel – *the real Daniel* – would say, and it takes her breath away how it sounded so natural.

"Oh, Daniel," she titters. "You're a silly sausage sometimes, but you're *my* silly sausage."

Daniel shifts on the bed before looking up at her again, his eyes wet.

"I…I…I…love…you," he stutters.

At the sound of those three words, Cynthia's smiling face grows slack.

The barn owl's head tilts to the side and she stares at the man in the bed.

The man who she loves?

Loved?

The man she's growing to love all over again, after so long apart.

There's something odd in the phrasing which sends a dagger of doubt into her heart.

"Is something wrong?"

There is and there isn't.

"Did I say something wrong?"

Confusion muffling his words.

It takes her a moment to place her concern as she recalls the way he phrased those three simple words, and suddenly it all falls into place. They weren't uttered from the heart. They were spilt into the world from the mind. They weren't a statement of his love. They almost were, and she'd almost been duped by him. Recalling the words in her mind, the way they were formed, it wasn't a statement of his love, it was more a question of it. Not overtly or out-rightly so, but she'd noticed the slight pause and upward inflection on the 'you' as if the words leaving his mouth hadn't been vetted by his brain before they'd passed his teeth, and by then it was too late.

Whose mouth is that now?

Daniel's?

Or Doctor Hasan's?

As those words were leaving his mouth, a question must have arisen in his mind to the veracity of the sentiment he'd so dearly wanted to impart.

Whose mind is pulling the strings in that body?

Daniel's?

Or Doctor Hasan's?

With her hands balling into two meaty cudgels in her lap, Cynthia repeats the phrase again and again, pulling at it, testing its truthfulness.

This won't do.

No, no, no.

He needs to mean it for this to work, otherwise they were both fucked. And in that moment, he doesn't mean it. He might, later on, but for now it's a lie. He's just telling me what I want to hear.

More than anything, Cynthia needs him to believe in *his* truth, otherwise what were they doing here but wasting precious time.

What is there to gain from this if he doesn't remember our love…he'll ruin everything…if he doesn't feel those words with his heart, then what's the point? Do I have to break him again?

Do I have time to break him again, and then remake him?

"Nothing."

Cynthia painstakingly relaxes a fisted hand before waving it dismissively in the air. "It's getting late and we've a busy couple of days ahead. You need your rest."

The risotto is once more ruined, not because how it was cooked, but because of the bitter taste she has in her mouth now. Although there is a *small* light in the ever-present dark. She's making headway in perfecting the recipe. The rabbit was delectable, and she knows that by the twelfth she'll have the rest of it nailed, and it'll be perfect, just like they served in the Italian Restaurant they were destined to dine in, but which they never made it to their reservation with.

"Are you sure? I…I…I…lo–"

"DON'T!" She shouts, standing up sharply. The backs of her legs knock her chair over, and it clatters to the ground. Her eyes dart to the mirror. Daniel's scared. Or is it Hasan? There's the jangling of his restraints over her shoulder as fear runs rampant through his veins at what is about to happen.

She won't come for him, though. Not tonight.

Instead, she turns, picks up the chair and places it neatly back in place for tomorrow night. Glancing up at him now, not in the mirror, but rather across the darkened room, the fear he has of *her* is written on Daniel's pale, gaunt features; the prominence of his distress displayed in his bulging, screaming eyes.

The owl shakes its head at him. Slowly. Dismissively. The shake of the head from a disappointed lover.

"Not now," she offers quietly. "Tell me tomorrow, I'd much rather hear it then…now isn't the right time".

"I will. And every other day too…"

He's trying too hard now, the silly fool.

Stepping through the dark, she reclaims the remote from the foot of the bed and presses the down arrow, lowering him again for another night. Once Daniel's horizontal, his head raises from the pillow and he fixes her with his pleading, glassy eyes, the tears they'd held now spilt, and the tracks they've made on his face shimmer under the lights like slug-trails.

"You did well tonight, Daniel. Maybe tomorrow we'll see if you'd like to join me for dinner? How does that sound?"

He nods. "I'd like that very much, thank you."

"Now get some rest, you'll need it for what's next, and don't forget…" Cynthia turns and begins to walk away. "It's *date night* on the twelfth, and I'm really looking forward to it. So, rest up and we'll try again tomorrow."

Placing the remaining items on the tray, she clicks the switch on the table and the lights around Daniel's bed go out. He's lost once more to her. Candlelight reigns in the basement as she heads to the stairs, taking the radiance from the room along with her.

Out of the darkness, Daniel's voice, yet it could still so easily be Doctor Hasan impersonating him. Although the words warm her heart, she senses an unspoken threat in the two words he speaks.

"I'm looking forward to it too," he says.

Climbing the stairs, Cynthia's buoyed by the thought they made *some* progress tonight. That Daniel's recall was almost perfect, and his diction had been spot on. It had taken a great many months to change the way Doctor Hasan spoke to the way Daniel did. *Does*. There were many a corrective procedure in getting him to lose Hasan's Scouse twang and to instead pick up Daniel's London lilt. However, those corrective procedures seemed to have done the trick – *however much they pained her and him* – because, based on tonight's conversation, there wasn't any evidence he was born and raised anywhere but the southeast of London.

There still wasn't room for complacency though, and she wouldn't get over-confident about the inroads they'd made yet. There was still some way to go before Daniel would be fully returned to her, and time was ticking. There'd been many times they'd made a breakthrough, yet as she reached the turn in the stairs, she remembered solemnly that however many breakthroughs or break-ins they'd experienced, there were an equal – *if not greater* – amounts of time where he'd backslid; where Doctor Hasan had raised his ugly head again, or spat his spiteful rhetoric at her.

It hurt Cynthia to see his leering face stretching through the confines of the face she'd changed so completely, and modified so expertly.

Eyes, changed with contacts.

Hair, changed with a cut, die, and a poor diet.

Teeth, which Cynthia had ripped from their gummy moorings; molars mainly, teeth you couldn't really see, even when he smiled. She'd removed them anyway with a pair of rusty plyers because she would've known they were there, lurking in the back, hidden imperfections lurking in the perfect visage that she was diligently honing. They had to go, there was no way around it, and she had enjoyed the pain it caused him, because she removed them in the early days. The days when moulding Daniel from her captive were just an imagined possibility, instead of now, when her dreamed vision of her transformation had so nearly become an actuality.

Halfway up the stairs she blew out the candle.

The words Daniel had uttered still plagued her: 'I…I…I…love…you.'

No, that wasn't right.

'I…I…I…love…you?'

Do you, Daniel?

Do you love me?

CHAPTER 8

There was a vigorousness to her actions as Cynthia pumped her hand up and down.

Each stroke, each pump, had been harder, firmer than the last. Her breathing had become laboured, as if her lungs were two punctured sacks in her chest that would never inflate completely.

Perspiration slicked her brow from her rigorous exertions, hair stuck to her forehead underneath the mask as small rivers of sweat trickled down her face and collected at the bow of her lip, her tongue flicking out to taste the saltiness of her body's own creation.

With one hand holding tightly to the shaft, the other busied itself with gliding up and down in a fluid motion. Long strokes. Up and down. She'd twist her wrist slightly on the up stroke before plunging it down deeply to the base, before starting the same movements again.

She paused in her relentless pumping. Glanced up at Daniel.

His face was a picture of joy, excitement and pleasure all rolled into one broad grin of exhilaration. He knew what was coming, and so did she, and she couldn't stop now. Not when her actions promised so much.

She pumped the shaft three more times.

One.

A soft murmur of breath escaped her mouth behind the mask.

Two.

Biting her lip, a small groan of pleasure, her exertion reaching its climax.

Three.

There's a guttural exhalation of breath as she slams her hand down to the base of the shaft and Daniel, still reclining, wears a grin of pleasure, as if he fell asleep and someone left a coat hanger in his gob. Cynthia, no, the owl, scowls back at him. Zero emotion displayed on its feathered face, however, behind the mask excitement reigns. He continues to smile at her like a simpleton after a pat on the back and the telling of a job well done.

Pulling away, she finally disconnects from her furious labours.

Pinching the soft tip of the protuberance between her thumb and index finger, she leans forwards, pulls it closer to her face, her lips. Lifting the bottom edge of her mask with her other hand, peeling it away her sweaty chin, she places her exposed, moist mouth – *moist through a mixture of lip gloss, saliva, and sweat* – to the tip of her fussing and the object of her desire.

Lips close around it, her mouth a wet cave.

She lubricates the tip with her spit, licks at it a few times before she starts to blow air into it. Lightly at first, then harder. Her cheeks puff out as she keeps eye contact with Daniel through the lower-half of the large apertures of the the owl mask.

Three longer blows and Cynthia knows she's finally done.

It's hard.

Rigid.

Plumped up and erect in all the right places.

The proportions feel as they should, and so Cynthia squeezes it just to make sure, runs her manicured fingers over its form, caressing it freely before Daniel's gaze. She teases at its firmness, praying it will stay the journey and not grow limp before they've finished.

Stretching her arm out, she strokes and squeezes it with her fingers, works her way down its engorged length. No dents, no folds, or bumps. It's smooth sailing down the entirety of its sides – *it's got a great girth, too* – and she raises an eyebrow at its surprisingly warm feel, given the circumstances and location – *and the fact that the heating has been turned off in the basement for the entirety of Daniel's re-emergence.*

Must be all the hot air and friction.

Thumb and forefinger squeeze the opening closed, the plastic slippery from her greased mouth. Using her other hand, she flicks the cap up, slipping it in the opening; teases it in, the tip of her tongue emerging from between her lips again as she concentrates in getting the knob of plastic into the tiny hole.

Once it slips home, snug and tight, she presses her thumb to the top of the cap, forcing it deeper into the plumpness of the whole, until the cap is subsumed by the rubber once more, as if there were nothing there.

Slipping the mask over her face again, Cynthia disappears into the darkness of the basement, leaving Daniel in a state of heightened anticipation. Walking away, Cynthia imagines him thinking her a tease – *a prick tease as some folks like to call her* – although she's not finished with him yet; far from it. The fun – *as people tend to say* – is still yet to come, and with it: the pain.

Clomping her way through the obscurity of the basement, but not towards the table, where her empty plate resides, she wanders evermore into the deep, stygian-black in search of what she needs. She'd been able to eat her whole meal that night, although she realised that something was missing. A seasoning of some kind, which she'd try to perfect in the coming days and weeks, because *everything* needs to be perfect.

Over dinner, Cynthia had quizzed Daniel again. She hadn't felt comfortable bringing him from the bed, given the previous evening's shenanigans, knowing there was still work to be done in ensuring Hasan stayed the fuck away. The words which had been said, not as a statement, but as a question, had plagued her dreams.

'I…I…I…love…you?'

However, the quizzing this evening went without a hitch. He was perfect in every way, showing great aptitude and recall; his speech pattern, his accent, his phrasing, all of it was as if Daniel was in the room. Even down to the way he paused and licked his lips from time to time, when asked something he needed to think about, digging out the implanted memory; it was exactly how Daniel would have behaved. One of his many little tics.

He didn't even falter on the more obscure questions fired at him, instead he just powered through, answered everything as *her* Daniel would have answered:

'If you could be half animal, what would you be?'

'Half eagle. Not the legs half, though.' That had made her giggle. The humour was uncannily *his*, and even his facial features mirrored her lovers; the cheeky raised eyebrow and the sly smirk creasing the corner of his mouth. '*I'd want to be able to fly.*'

'What colour is the word happenstance?'

'Mint-green.'

Daniel had always associated words with colours – *Synesthesia* – an oddity she loved about him.

'What's your niece's name?'

'I don't have a niece.'

She'd tried to trick him with that one, yet he just batted it away.

'If you could be anything in the world, what would you choose to be?'

There were three things she'd expected him to say; rich or a writer – *heaven knows he'd tried* – or even a father. They'd discussed all three of those on numerous occasions, but instead he said:

'Happy.'

That last answer had earnt Daniel his supper, and he didn't even have to sing for it. The way he'd been so obedient – so *Daniel* – he probably would have sung for his supper if she'd asked him to. He'd have done anything she'd have asked of him in that moment; a few bars of *Fleetwood Mac* were not out of his repertoire, should she ask him, and he wouldn't deny her because he knew Cynthia's love of the Mac came from him. It had been one of his many gifts to her over the years.

As much as Daniel wanted to be happy, the Daniel *she* knew found *his* happiness in *her* happiness – and she knew he would do anything for her, and likewise she – *would-could-is* – doing all she can to bring him back to her again.

She'd peeled his egg for him at dinner and let him eat it from her hand; as if he were a goat and her palm contained a handful of grain –

they'd fed goats at Christmas Tree Farm in Down once and it had felt just like this – his lips busied themselves with hoovering up the egg as his hot breath and whiskery chin – *a week's worth of growth* – tickled her palm.

Towards the end, his tongue had been lapping at the errant crumbs stuck in the creases around her fingers as his lips and mouth sucked up all the crushed bits of crumbly, yellow yolk. He'd literally licked her clean – *it wouldn't have been the first time.*

Within the folds of darkness she traversed, Cynthia quickly stumbled upon what she'd been searching for and she began to gently tease the rubber through her fingers until she discovered the end, where the loose metal rings chimed together.

Searching the darkness before her with a free hand, she found the wall. Crumbling mortar and cold, damp bricks scratched the pads of her fingers as she trailed her hand down in search of her prize. She found it moments later and began the difficult task of attaching the thread from the thing in her hand to the thread hanging from the attachment on the tap of the small butler sink that's connected to the basement's wall.

Once completed, she turned on the right tap for warm water and began trailing the hose back through the darkness, towards the light which hung from her hand like a dead snake. A snake with no end, apparently, as she uncoiled the hose foot after foot. The water now rushing through it, made the thing difficult to manage as it twisted and turned; at one point it snagged her wrist, wrapped around it as if it *were* a boa constrictor. She managed to free herself and struggled the rest of the way back to the island of light that Daniel was nestled in.

As Cynthia swam closer to the light, she observed Daniel almost flinch back into his pillows, his arms pulling weakly against his restraints. But he soon relaxed as she moved fully from the veil of darkness around her, manoeuvring herself to the foot of the bed and to the inflated paddling pool where she dropped the hose into its empty innards. Bending down, she turned the attachment on its end, cycled through its many functions. Spray. Mist. Jet. She continued in this manner until she found the correct function for the job which allowed the warm water to pour unhindered into the paddling pool.

"Would you like bubbles?" Her voice was pitched high in her excitement.

From the foot of the bed, she picked up two bottles and held them aloft.

One was lavender, the other, summer berries.

It was obvious which one Daniel would choose, because right now, in this most sacred of moments, *he* Daniel, and *they* had shared a life together, and she knew him like no other person on the planet.

"Lavender, please."

"Good choice. That's your favourite, right?" She placed the other bottle on the floor and began opening the cap on the chosen bubble bath.

Daniel nodded excitedly, mumbled a "Mm-hmm."

"I know how much you love that smell, and I have to say it's grown on me too over the years. What does it remind you of?"

Another test, let's see if you get this right?

"My mother's house—"

Perfect, you're still with me.

"Yes, exactly," she crooned. "I'm sure Freud would have a field day detangling that strange tryst?" Cynthia was giggling at her joke as she poured the silvery liquid into the now frothing water.

"It's not like she shared a bath *with* me." His face screwed up in disgust at the thought as he pondered his next words. He's busy racking his brain as Cynthia screws the cap on the bubble bath and places the bottle on the ground. Standing again, she observes him, transfixed at each and every facial movement as he tries to recall an implanted memory. His eyes raise to the ceiling, desperately searching for the conversation they'd had.

He levels his eyes at her.

There's a sparkle in those eyes, and she knows he's found it.

"It was the smell of the drawers…at my house…my mother's house." Pauses for a moment, checking the veracity of his statement in the body language of Cynthia, who claps her hands together in a *good-golly-gosh* he's got it gesture.

Cynthia nods her head for him to continue and he does without further prompting.

"All of the drawers in that house stank of the stuff whilst I was growing up. They still do, as I recall. Last Christmas, or the one before, I've lost track a little..."

"It's understandable. You've been through so much. It was actually three Christmases ago."

"Really? That long? Wow…"

The owl mask dips up and down.

"Time flies when you're having fun, right?"

He says it with a smirk.

They both chuckle and it feels warm, and right.

"You joked about it on the drive over there. You said your mother had socks of lavender in every nook and cranny around the house, and if I slept with my mouth open, then I might wake up one morning to find a sock full of lavender stuffed in my gob!"

Daniel laughed heartily and the sound, so sudden, so unmistakably *his* laughter, brought tears to Cynthia's eyes.

"That's right," he said breathlessly. "And, as I recall, you didn't snore once that whole trip."

It was true, and Cynthia snorted as she laughed.

For a moment, for the first time in many months she finally felt as if she'd gotten something back which had been stolen from her. Something which, if she was being honest with herself, she'd thought had been lost forever: her best friend, and their companionship.

The laughter – *soothing as it was* – soon died in her throat, and her joy at being reunited once more with her soulmate slipped from the face behind the mask as if she were having a stroke. Her eyes grew wide as she observed Daniel's expression grow ever more maudlin, his eyes clouding over with doubt.

Is that bastard coming through again?

Why can't he just let us have this one moment?

The possibility of losing him, again, to the beast which lived below the dermis she'd altered, was ever-present. She feared the re-emergence of the monster she'd vanquished. The one who still – *it would seem* – lay dormant under the veneer which had become, over time – *and her diligent torture no less* – her remoulded version of Daniel. His brow knitted together above his wonky nose. Breathing deeply, she throttled her hands.

It was all she could do to stop herself rushing him.

To break the mind, one had only to ruin the body, and she'd ruined *his* completely. Although, she preferred the term '*remodelled,*' instead of ruined. Surely there was nothing left of that phantom, that leviathan, from their past.

What is it that's troubling you?
Is it despair?
Judgement?
Anguish?
Betrayal?

"I...I...I..." Daniel was struggling to form his words.

Concern grew within her, swelled into a darkened storm cloud which promised rain. She couldn't afford for Daniel to slip, to regress into Doctor Hasan again, not if she were to untether him from the bed for his much-needed sponge bath. He was weak. That much she knew to be true. Although what strength remained in his flagging body and spirit had yet to be *fully* tested, outside of the binds which restricted him, he looked like a stiff breeze could blow him over.

What if I untie you and you try to leave?
If you overpower me, try to hurt me, try to...escape?

Placing one of her hands on his blanket covered, rail-thin legs, she squeezed gently.

"What is it, darling? What's troubling you?"

Eyes darted from her face – *the owl mask* – to her outstretched hand, the process repeating a couple of times as if he was deeply troubled by the small act of kindness from his personal 'Bird Woman of Alcatraz,' though Cynthia thought he appeared lost and scared, drowning inside of himself, unable to shake the riptide of Hasan.

Are you ashamed of what you've become?

"I...I...I didn't go to her funeral, did I?"

At a loss as to whom she was speaking with, Daniel, or that dastardly fiend Doctor Osman Hasan, Cynthia grits her teeth.

It could be either of them. Neither had been present at Joselin's funeral.

It was that small doubt which stilled her desire to loosen the restraints. If she was wrong, even a little, what could she do if he decided to bolt. Could she do what needed to be done to stop him, if stopping him meant she'd have to kill Daniel?

Could I physically, let alone mentally, do that?

Taking a life and *taking a life* were two very different things.

If he'd deceived her with how weak he'd been all along – *which she contemplated* – and he somehow overpowered her, escaped, then everything – **EVERYTHING** – would be lost. Not only her long-held and heralded *'date night'* – *which loomed large on the calendar* – but also the opportunity to answer the question of a lifetime that she'd never had the chance to answer.

If *he* got out, she wouldn't just be forfeiting her sacred and revered *'date night'*, in the ensuing mess – *because it* would *get messy* – she'd forfeit her freedom too. It wouldn't take long for the police to turn up. Kidnapping, imprisonment, and torture weren't something the authorities usually overlooked.

Cynthia realized that she'd been stationary too long, the owl mask cocked to the side as if in contemplation, and at the sound of her voice Daniel flinched.

"No one made it to her funeral, darling. It was during Covid, remember? Right at the beginning when the shit was well and truly hitting the fan. Do you remember when we watched it on the news? All those mass graves in the States?"

His dry and cracked bottom lip began to tremble.

"Thank God we didn't have some bumbling lunatic leading the country and telling us to inject ourselves with bleach..." she offered before Daniel cut in.

"Well, the bumbling lunatic we had did his fair share of damage too, don't forget."

"I guess he did."

"It's just so, so sad."

The person in question lowers his head.

"What is sweetheart?"

"That she was alone, at the end."

Turning away, Cynthia noticed the bubbles had formed a fluffy mound atop the water. Reaching in, she pulled the hose out and turned the water off from the attachment before dropped the hosepipe to the floor with a clatter. Movement from the corner of her eye drew her back, and Daniel peered over the edge of the bed at the bubbles and water with what Cynthia took as an intrinsic longing.

With her hands on her hips, she shook her head slowly. There was a choice to be made, and it boiled down to *who* was the *him* she was staring at.

Daniel, or Osman?
Osman, or Daniel?
Osiel or Danman?
Namdan or Leiso?

"Could you bathe me, like before?" He asked the question, head still bowed.

"Before?"

Scepticism in the word, knowing full well this was the first time she'd bathed him since his capture, and a spark of hope ignited in her chest.

"When I dislocated my shoulder," his head lifted, eyes focusing on the mask. "Don't you remember?"

The thing was, Cynthia did remember. It was one of the first things she'd impressed on Doctor Hasan, at the very beginning of the transformation process. The weeks in which she'd rattled off the extensive list of all the medical issues/procedures Daniel had gone through, to ensure that Daniel 2.0 had an intimate knowledge of his new/old body. She'd quizzed him relentlessly in those early days, and if he failed to answer correctly, she beat him. Scratch that. She ~~beat him~~ bludgeoned him until his face was the colour of petrol on water, bluish-green and yellow.

Daniel had dislocated his shoulder slipping in the bath.

He'd also had his appendix removed when it burst when he was fifteen.

He'd broken his femur as a child when he was knocked off his bike riding down Victoria Road, by Old Man Roger who lived next door, driving drunk again and shit out of luck.

Cynthia didn't need to inflict those injuries. All she had to do was brainwash him, gaslight him into believing he *had* indeed suffered these injuries, and with Daniel's recall of the bath and the bathing, how he clearly remembered something that hadn't happened to the shell of the man she'd transformed; she finally realised how perfectly those lessons had been learned. Sparing the rod had spared the child, apparently, which was why Cynthia had beaten him every chance she got.

"I remember, but that was so long ago, I'm surprised you remember it so clearly."

"How could I forget? Do you remember what you used to call the smell?"

"The smell?" Her faced screwing up under the mask.

"Yeah, the smell under my arm. Where they'd strapped it to my body. You used to call it *The Bog of Eternal–*"

"*Stench!*"

Joy cracked her voice at Daniel's recall of a memory even she had begun to forget.

"That's right…you bathed me then, could you do it again? I don't smell half as bad now as I did then…well, I don't think I do."

It was either the biggest, most elaborate ruse ever constructed, or it was actually Daniel in that bed, and her heart overruled her mind which, moments before, had been flooded with trepidation; she stepped closer, placed her hand on the cuff of the first restraint.

"Of course, my love."

"Thank you, because I don't think I'm strong enough to do it myself."

"You'll never have to do anything by yourself, ever again, Daniel. I'm here for you, always."

The first strap fell away from his wrist and Cynthia leaned over the bed to undo the other. Leaning over him made her feel exposed. If Hasan was going to make a move, it would be now. He could grab her throat with his free hand and strangle the life out of her.

She pulled on the other restraint, making it tighter before slipping the teeth of the buckle free, and she paused, waited for the crushing grip around her throat. However, as the restraint slipped down the side of the bed, she realised it wasn't coming. She had been wrong in her estimations. A smile worked itself on her face at her error of judgement, not because she was wrong, but because she realised how good a job she'd done at changing him.

Putty in her hands.

Daniel rubbed his thin fingers over his wrists as Cynthia observed him. The skin where the cuffs had been were dry and cracked. There were places – *she noted* – where the skin of his wrists had split open; red, angry fissures appearing across his dried skin as he rotated them in ways they'd not been moved in months. Daniel hissed at their emergence.

"Right, let's get you to the edge of the bed." Her voice soothed as she pulled back the cover.

Reaching her hands under his withered legs, she shuffled Daniel to the edge of the hospital bed. He helped as much as he could, using his hands and elbows to shunt his body across the mattress, wincing from the opened, split skin on his wrists, until he finally sat, hunched forward and whimpering on the edge of the mattress.

Each moment, it looked as if Daniel might have toppled over from the weight of his sagging head, to land headfirst in the paddling pool. Cynthia didn't want him to drown – although she had waterboarded him previously – and so she stood before him, rested a hand on his shoulder, kept him upright as she struggled with untying the knot of his stained hospital gown with the other hand. Once unfastened, she slipped the garb from his body.

There was a sharp intake of breath which whistled past his teeth as the oozing bedsores on his back were exposed to the air, the gown having covered a multitude of sins. This was the first time Cynthia had been able to bask in the complete transformation of the man that was – *Doctor Osman Hasan* – into the man that once was and will be again – *Daniel*. Tilting her head at him, as if the owl she projected to the world were investigating its next meal, she let herself drink in her creation.

He was emaciated, skin an alabaster white. He was everything he should be at this stage of transformation. Of metamorphosis. Utterly broken, and with the threshold of death's door yawning open before him, ready to welcome him home.

Her smile broadened behind the mask.

Lifting one of his arms, she slid herself next to him, to prop his body, and to start the laboured process of getting him from the bed, into the paddling pool.

"You're going to have to help me a little bit."

"I'll take most of your weight, but you'll have to step into the pool and then we'll lower you down gently, okay?"

He winced at her touch but nodded.

As Cynthia's hand slid around his back, bony protuberances – *his ribs* – made themselves known to her fingers as she pulled him to her and hoisted him up from the bed. He let out a groan of pain and stumbled on his weak legs. She kept him upright, digging her fingers under the bottom of his rib cage for purchase, as if it were a handle, and Daniel let out another yelp of pain.

They shuffled a few feet, to the edge of the pool, where Daniel lifted one of his legs, his body shuddering against her with the exertion like a baby deer taking its first tentative steps in the world. Shortly, both feet were in the paddling pool and Cynthia began lowering him, inch-by-excruciating-inch, until he sat slumped like a sack of bones amongst the bubbles and warm water.

"Th-Th-Thank...you." Like his body, his voice was broken, sounding exactly as it had before the end. Before *his* end.

Each bedsore on Daniel's back shone wetly under the light. Some wept, others contained a whitish-yellow mess. There was fresh puss trickling down his back from a large sore where she'd torn the gown away, opening up an old scab, the wound glistened ghastly in the harsh overhead lights, making it appear as a raw and wet hole in his back, more burn than wound.

There were four areas on his pasty looking back which were worse than the other blemishes: the base of his neck, both shoulders, and his lower back. Cynthia knew that when it came time to wash those areas clean, he'd howl like a wolf with its leg in a hunter's trap. She looked at his sheets and saw the same arrangement of pussy-blood smears displayed on those too, as if it were a dot-to-dot awaiting completion.

"I'm so sorry, Daniel. I should have treated you better. I should have changed your sheets, tended to your wounds, got you up and about more...why didn't you tell me–"

"–It doesn't matter–"

"–It *does* matter. *You* matter. I've neglected to look after you, and for that, I'm truly sorry."

"You *have* looked after me. Not a day goes by that you don't check in on me, that you don't bring me food–"

"I should have, *could have,* done more. You're the most precious thing in this world to me, and I've let you get like this." She waved both of her hands in front of her, defining the *'this'* she was speaking of

"I am what I am..." he said as his hands splashed around in the water.

"You deserve better."

"I deserve what I deserve." He glanced up at her. "Could you bathe me now? I don't want to catch a cold."

"Of course." Cynthia grabbed the sponge from the end of the bed.

"I'd do it myself–"

"You'll do no such thing. I got you into this mess, the least I can do is help get you out of it."

"Bless you. Thank you. I don't even think I could manage it on my own if I'm honest, but it kills me having you dote on me so much, to depend on you as much as I do."

Tears welled in her eyes, and Cynthia was glad the mask covered her trembling chin, and the shame she felt eating her alive.

"I'll never have you do anything for yourself again. I'm here, Daniel, and I'm not going anywhere. I promise you that. I'll be here with you until the end."

"Thank you. The end is coming, I can tell, but it's great to have company for when it finally comes."

Dipping the sponge in the water, she lifted the waterlogged item and pressed it against Daniel's back. The water trickled down and over his open sores and he winced, his tired body shuddering with excruciating pain, yet he didn't flail about like she thought he might; he just remained where he was, a glutton for punishment.

Near the beginning, she'd given him a flannel wash and he'd fought her the entire time, bucking around on the bed like a madman. He'd pull at his restraints, watching on as his skin came away in clumps and strings of flesh with each hash scrub of the flannel. His flesh, once alive and healthy and bronzed, had peeled away in dead, crispy strips like dried parchment. It felt like a lifetime ago when she recalled it now, and in a way it was. He was another person entirely, and after the deep chemical peel she'd given him, he'd slipped from his old skin to put on another. One where, with each passing day, as his dermis healed, he began to look more like Daniel and less like Doctor Osman Hasan.

There'd been no other option. She'd had to burn him, to rid his body of his olive-coloured skin, peeling it away layer-by-layer from his body until not a remnant remained. It was a torturous occasion. One which she'd had to repeat numerous times before she began to see fruits from her labours as the whiter skin rose up from beneath those darkened layers.

The process had set Cynthia's schedule back a few weeks. And during those weeks as she wet the flannel and scrubbed Doctor Hasan's burnt and peeling flesh from his body, it was always Doctor Hasan who stared back at her. Daniel had yet to make his appearance at that point.

Every day, for two weeks, it was Hasan's eyes, Hasan's thoughts, Hasan's words, and wrath, that answered her interactions. It was as if the excruciating pain he endured was the thing which anchored Hasan to the present, keeping Daniel at bay.

And in those dark weeks she'd wondered and pondered and fretted endlessly over her dilemma, deliberating darkly if Daniel would ever return to her after the hideous process had run its course. All of her worrying was for naught though as, in the end, he did return to her, setting up his new home in the husk of Doctor Hasan's fried and crispy remains.

By the time Daniel emerged, she'd successfully peeled Hasan's entire body. It had taken numerous procedures, where she'd had to repeat the process again and again until Daniel had a skin to call his own once more, the milky-pasty-white he'd always been. If she'd not been able to change Hasan's skin tone, there was no way this metamorphosis would have worked, because Cynthia knew that whenever she would have looked upon him with his tanned flesh, she wouldn't have seen Daniel, she would have seen an imposter.

The process hadn't been perfect by any means. There were still a few patches where the peel hadn't taken and as she stared down at him in the pool of water, she inspected those areas again. The folds in his neck, the creases in his elbows, and the backs of his knees still possessed the skin of the man he once was. There was also a darkened ring of flesh around his gut, which was more apparent now, given his considerable weight loss. Yet all those small blemishes, those chinks in his otherwise new and flawless suit of armour, could be overlooked and covered up, she was, afterall, a magician with makeup brush and concealer.

Pressing the sponge to the crown of Daniel's head, she watched as the water trickled down his face and back, repeating the process again and again.

Waterboarding.

It had less than satisfactory outcomes, she remembered. One of her biggest concerns was secondary drowning, a thing she'd become aware of after hours spent watching the show *Saving Lives at Sea*. Daniel had blubbered and spluttered as she held a towel over his mouth and poured water over his mouth and nose, similar to what was happening now.

Daniel's body hitched with each spongeful of water deposited on his head.

Still, she continued with the drenching.

Soon he was shaking, shivering.

Dropping the sponge into the water, she dipped lower and placed her hand into the water.

Warm.

Why's he shivering?

Cynthia leaned forwards and peered intently at his bowed head. He sensed her closeness and turned his head to her. It became apparent, very quickly, that he wasn't shivering.

He was crying.

Sobbing his heart out and biting his bottom lip to stop his whimpers from escaping his mouth. Placing a hand to his bony shoulder to comfort him, Cynthia shuffled closer, her feet pressing up against the edge of the paddling pool, the owl mask just inches from his ear.

"What's wrong? Does it hurt?"

A shake of the head.

"Are you cold?"

Another shake. No.

"Then what is it? Please, tell me so I can help?"

There was a moment of stillness as Daniel tried to compose himself. An attempt at speech, yet the words were lost in a juddering exhalation of breath.

"It's okay, take your time." Cynthia enthused.

And he did.

They stayed that way for what felt like hours. Daniel with his head bowed and Cynthia with her hand resting on his cooling back. She noticed his features screwing up every now and then, as if he had some sort of nervous tic. But she knew there was a battle going on in his mind. Unspoken words rattling around in his head.

The question, though: Whose words were they?

Daniel's or Doctor Osman Hasan's?

The only thing Cynthia could do was wait. Deal with whatever came when it arrived.

"I…I…I…" Daniel stuttered, his body visibly shaking, causing ripples to appear in the water.

A squeeze of his shoulder, gently, affectionately.

"It's okay, I'm here."

Taking a deep breath, he turned his face to hers – *well, to the owl* – and swallowed. She couldn't help but notice how pronounced his Adam's apple had become as it darted up, then down, causing a gulp to escape his dry throat.

"I…I was wondering. If it's okay…" He was staring down at his emaciated legs, then his jutting hips, and lastly at the wrinkled manhood between his legs.

"Go on, please," she encouraged, wanting to know which of the two men in her life she was talking to.

Again, Daniel swallowed before lifting his timid eyes to the mask.

"I was wondering if…if you'd hold me?"

"Hold you?"

"Yes. If that's okay, I just want to be held."

"Well—"

"Not in a sexual way, of course. You probably find what I've become abhorrent anyway...I know I do. How could you love this...this *thing* I've become?" And with his last words, Daniel – *because Cynthia had no doubt it was him speaking now* – thrust his hands into the bubbles, splashing water over the floor and wetting Cynthia's overalls.

She didn't flinch. Just remained there with him, hand resting on his shoulder, silently appraising the ruined man before her; every inch the broken man she'd set out to create. A proudful smile crested her lips.

She'd finally done it.

She'd broken the beast and turned him into the man, the lover, the soulmate who was no longer, but who now sat, resplendent, reincarnated, resurrected, before her.

"I love you, Daniel," Cynthia enthused. "I've always loved you... at your best and at your worst."

"At my worst...sure..." a snigger of contempt. His hands disappeared into the water where he struggled to pulled his stick-thin legs up. Once raised from the water, he hugged them, rocked slightly, desperately looking for comfort where there was none. As his body hunched forward, the knots of his spine soon emerged, rising up from his back; each vertebra poking looking like a pebble slipped beneath his skin, each seemingly testing the elasticity of his skin.

"Daniel?" His name was a question.

With a free hand, Cynthia pulled his chin to face her, whilst her other hand squeezed gently, lovingly at his shoulder. "I've always loved you, and I never thought I'd get this time back with you. But I have, and I won't ever leave you again. Ever. Do you hear me? I promise you, there's not that much longer to go before we finish what we planned to start so long ago. We've got a second chance, a chance to make everything right, a chance to rewrite our future, and our past, and we're not going to squander it this time."

"I'm a monster...look at me. How could you love this? I don't want your pity..."

"I am looking at you, Daniel, and it's like I'm seeing you for the first time. How I've longed for this moment. How I've craved it with every fibre of my being. I. Love. You. And that should be enough.

"Is it enough?"

Daniel nodded his head.

"It is."

His voice was weak.

"Thank you. I don't know what, or where, I would be without you looking after me." He pulled his head away from the grasp she had on his chin, and she let him; she'd said her piece, and she hoped those pieces had stuck.

With his head hung once more, chin touching his knees, Daniel continued to rock himself, though slower this time.

"I just want to be held. To be loved. Could you do that for me, please?"

"Gladly."

With her shawl trailing in the water, Cynthia hugged Daniel to her.

Water from the pool trickled over its edge as she leaned her knees on its edge, a growing a puddle spreading around them on the floor, but Cynthia didn't care because she was with *him* and he was with *her*, and in that moment there was nothing else she wanted, craved, or longed for any more. Nothing, not even the growing puddle around her knees, could have dampened the moment.

She soothed Daniel as if he were a child who'd done a terrible thing, stroked a hand over his head, down his neck and softly across his back. Her fingers rose and fell with each vertebra, her fingers rippling as they rolled over his ribs, and she remembered him.

Oh, how she remembered him.

This was how *he*, Daniel, had felt beneath her fingers before the end; his end. As his body wasted and his time grew shorter with each passing day. The many nights they sat on the edge of their bed, her hugging him, him hugging her, crying, laughing, hoping, kissing and cuddling.

It hurt her heart to remember those times now, and the utter cruelness of the world. The atrociousness of the cancer which had fed on him and the wrongfulness of his missed diagnosis which had caused all of this, all of *his*, and all of *her* suffering.

There was hatred for herself in the bitter reflection, too.

Despising the fact that her job, her online persona – *fucking <Honey-*

Cynth> – had played a part in all of this, because if Daniel had gone by himself to the doctor, as he'd asked to do all those many moons ago – *a request which Cynthia had denied him, telling him she wanted to be there for him* – Maybe, just maybe, Doctor Hasan would have been more focused on his job rather than trying to get into her knickers. Maybe then, things would have been different.

Something wet tickled at her face, pulling her back to the present and away from her spiralling thoughts.

A wet, bony hand had snuck under the mask. His damp, wrinkled fingers were stroking at her face as his thumb rubbed gently at her cheek. She'd expected herself to instinctively pull away, but instead, she leaned in towards his touch, permitting his hand to transgress the boundary of the mask because it felt, at long last, that *he, Daniel*, had come home.

"I love you," he uttered, head resting against Cynthia's chest.

"I love you too, Daniel." Cynthia whispered, wondering if he could hear how hear heart thudded for him.

They remained that way until the water grew cold. Hugging and loving and whispering to each other, both praying their time together would never end. However, all good things must come to an end, eventually. Their end was racing towards them, and there was nothing either of them could do to stop it, for they were always predestined to be:

Ill-fated courtesans…

Bedevilled devotees…

Star-crossed lovers….

Their fate, however much Cynthia longed to change it, would forever be etched in the stars. And regardless of how much she tried, and strived, and struggled, one thing was certain for Cynthia.

She can't out-run destiny.

CHAPTER 9

The computer was on, and Cynthia was busy darning a pair of Daniel's socks in her bedroom turned office. The light of the screen gave her just enough illumination to do the task at hand, whilst the laptop's camera was busy recording and streaming the session to her fans.

What her fans paid to watch really beggar's belief sometimes.

Flicking her eyes up to the camera, she observes the top left corner of the screen, the headcount for tonight's stream. It's in the low forties, a quiet night in general, although she'll still make a killing.

I'm darning a pair of socks…come on folks, get a fucking life.

She was darning, true, although the allure of the matter was that she wasn't just anyone, she was <HoneyCynth> and not just 'Big Bertha' from the laundromat down Chatterton Road who would sit in the window in her grubby, cream coloured tabard with stains down the front from a quickly scoffed egg and cress sandwich, and with her hair in rollers.

Cynthia, unlike Bertha, darned her smalls – *and Daniel's smalls –* whilst wearing the most revealing of negligees – and it was that small, yet aching difference, which her fans were paying handsomely to observe.

I guess they can have a bit more.

With an absent-minded tug, she opens the front of her negligee to reveal the shelf of her cleavage, all lifted high and pressed together by the Wonder Bra™ which came in the mail the previous day, a little red number with lacy straps which perfectly present her voluptuous cargo to her paying audience; the little flash of flesh earning her a few new comments and deposits.

Popeye <Oooo…that's nice, I could park my bike in there>
Creepy4U <That's a chest I'd love to use for target practice>
Slut4Hire <Very nice, fancy showing us a bit more?>
HungLikeADonkey <R U takin da botums off, cum on, I need 2getoff b4 werk?>

Smiling demurely at the camera, she lowers her eyes back to her work, ignores all their pestering messages, and slips the needle through the fabric once more. She hits the wooden darning-mushroom and, instead of the needle being guided – *sliding smoothly on* – it gets lodged in the wood, and when she tries to push it with brute-force, the needle skips and shoots sharply across its polished surface, stabbing her in the soft pad of her thumb.

Wincing, she drops the darning mushroom where it clatters to the floor, entangled within the sock. Inspecting the damage, she notices a small pinprick of blood which has bloomed on the fleshy pad of her thumb. Watches it bead and swell before it trickles slowly down the length of the digit. Moving her thumb to her mouth, she first licks the blood up, all the way from the webbing of her hand to the thumb's tip, before slipping her throbbing digit into her mouth where she sucks on it like a toddler at a barren teat.

This innocent action – *although she knew her viewers wouldn't view it that way* – causes another spate of messages and monetary deposits to chime on her computer.

PaperCuts <I've got something you can suck if you get bored.> (a winking emoji)

Hilarious. Haven't heard that one before, you cretin.

FemmeFatale1973 <Can you look at the camera whilst you're sucking; I'm imagining you doing the unimaginable.>

What's the unimaginable?
    Clopping?
    Pegging?
    Beastiality?
    Nanophilia?
    Apotemnophilia?
Whatever the unimaginable was, she had a sneaking suspicion a philia would be involved because someone's *unimaginable* was, well, someone else's guilty pleasure.

'Rule 34' means anything can be pornographic. She'd read that somewhere, what rule 34 was, though was forgotten where. *So, the unimaginable doesn't even exist anymore, my dear FemmeFatale1973.*

GhostPuffin <Can you do it again? I like to see you bleed.>

There's always someone that brings the mood down.

Leaning forwards – *still sucking her thumb* – Cynthia goes in search of the sock and mushroom, absentmindedly giving her fans another glimpse at her heavily reinforced cleavage, and as her fingers alight on the wooden darning tool a moment of clarity strikes.

Mushrooms?
That's it!

With darning mushroom in hand, she pulls her thumb from her mouth and sets about locating the needle and thread before continuing where she had left off. Operating on autopilot, her mind runs away with the variety of mushrooms at her disposal and how foolish she's been up until then for neglecting them.

I've been using the wrong damned mushrooms for the risotto.
Stupid. Stupid. Stupid.
You daft cow, you silly prat, you miserable excuse for a vagina.

Leaning back, revealing more of herself to her fans, she reclines on the edge of her bed onto the many throw pillows behind her, continuing her dutiful work of darning the pair of socks Daniel will wear on their date night. They're the pair he'd been wearing on the night he shuffled out of the house and, well, shuffled out of the world for good, wearing.

Her mother always used to tell her to make sure she wore '*nice clean knickers*' when she went out, and '*matching socks too*'. On asking her mother why it was so important – *apart from good personal hygiene* – she'd retorted with a shake of the head at her daughter's apparent stupidity: '*So if you're ever hit by a bus, the Doctors and Nurses dealing with you will know you're from good stock and not some commoner.*'

At the time she'd thought the remark was odd. Stupid even, as if wearing odd socks or grubby knickers would be of any concern to the doctors and nurses trying desperately to save your life.

'Sorry Doctor, I can't possibly stop the bleeding. If you hadn't noticed, this woman's wearing three-day old knickers with skid marks in them.'

'Okay Nurse, why don't we just call it now, there's no point in trying. I've just looked at her socks and there's a hole in the heel, not to mention one's black and the other has Tuesday written on it and today is clearly Gin-Friday.'

'Are you sure?'
'Positive. Call it.'
'Time of death...'

A small, demure giggle escapes her lips, which causes another influx of responses on her computer. But she was too busy thinking about Daniel's holey socks to look up.

What if Daniel died because they'd seen his socks had holes in them?

She glanced over at her drawers, wondering how many of her undergarments have holes in them – actual holes, not access holes – and if she needed to throw them out in case she got hit by a bus or fell over in the street and hit her head whilst wearing them. She rubbished the thoughts before they took root because she never left the house anymore, and she doubted she ever would again, once Daniel had been returned to her.

Mushrooms, get back on track woman.

Mushrooms. Mushrooms. Mushrooms.

Button Mushrooms had been her go to option, never once thinking to vary her choice of fungi during the entirety of her gastronomical exploration, opting instead to stick with what she knew and loved; and she loved the taste of button mushrooms, even eating them raw on occasion when finding an open punnet in the fridge as she scanned the contents for a quick snack.

Instead of mixing up her choice of mushrooms, she'd chosen to tamper with the seasoning of the meal, a bit more salt, less pepper, a smidge of Cayenne and a pinch of Italian herbs. She'd even tried marinating the wild rabbit in various concoctions, causing the meal to be different each time, and her enjoyment of said meal had varied considerably with each seating. But the mushrooms. The mushrooms had always been the bloody same.

How could you be so stupid?

It was obvious to her now, with hindsight, as they say, being a beautiful thing.

Knowing the error of her ways, Cynthia was suddenly buoyed at the possibility of rectifying it as soon as possible. As she continued fiddling with the darning mushroom, she decided that tomorrow – *if she could get one of the online, upmarket food establishments to deliver them* – she'd change the damned mushrooms and hopefully unlock the secrets to the meal which had been plaguing her for months.

She began thinking about the various fungi she could use, not even concerned or worried about what her viewers were making of the spectacle. They, like her, lived in a reality television world nowadays.

The Big Brother / Real World generation, where people watched programmes of people watching TV – *such a strange world we live in.*

Maitake mushrooms would be Cynthia's first choice. They were also known as the *'hen of the woods'*, and they'd bring a subtle, meaty quality to the dish, which she believed would pair – *look at her getting all* Gordon Ramsey *with the chef talk and minutia on the details of the dish* – exquisitely with the tenderness of the wild rabbit.

Porcini mushrooms could be another option. They would be perfect for that woodsier flavour, uplifting the gamey taste of the rabbit, making the meal more of an experience. She imagined describing the taste to Daniel over dinner as… *'walking barefoot though a forest after a thunderstorm.'*

You pompous tit.

If she wants to mix it up further, and she does, knowing how everything – *everything, past, present and future* – rides on this meal, she could go for a more outlandish, more luxurious mushroom altogether. And that's where her thoughts run off to.

After pondering it for a moment, she comes up with either the *Chanterelle* mushroom for a much-needed splash of colour. She'd sauté them in butter and sprinkle them over the top of the risotto. Or, there was the *Morels*. She loved them for their deep, nutty flavour and their unique spongy texture, not to mention how they looked like dried-out brains. That would at least be a conversation starter, should their chitchat wither; although she didn't think they'd struggle with conversation. Not with everything they had to say to one another after all this time apart, but one could never be too sure.

What if Daniel was nervous?

Shy about what he had to say and ask?

Decisions, decisions.

Lastly, if Cynthia really wanted to blow this dish out of the water – *and she did, she wanted to be treated like the queen she was* – she could always go for the most magnificent of all mushrooms; either a white, black, or burgundy truffle. She wouldn't cook the truffle – *of course she wouldn't* – as even a fool knows that cooking a truffle ruins its delicate and expensive taste. Rather, she'd shave it over the top of her risotto –

taking her special dinner, their *date night* meal, to a whole new level of delectability.

How could you have overlooked the bloody mushrooms?

'There's not mush-room in here.' Daniel's voice in her head.

Another giggle. She bites her lip to contain it.

'*I'm a fungi to be around, you know,*' his voice croons in her mind.

Now she's cackling, but she quickly remembers where she is and what she is doing, and she places a hand to her mouth to stifle her joy.

RANDYRANDY <Hearing you laugh gets me excited.>

An attachment appears next to the text box.

She clicks on the attachment and the window maximises instantly, its contents displayed – *full-screen* – and she just sits there staring at it, her head turning sideways in concentration.

At first, she can't make it out. It almost looks like a baby chick in a nest of black straw. Leaning closer, her brow knitting together, she realises what it is, <RANDYRANDY>'s un-circumcised penis.

To call it a penis was a kindness really, because this wasn't like any penis she'd ever seen before. It was a stunted and dwarfy-looking thing, resembling an albino dwarf shrew. It was a penis which was dwarfed in size, not of a person with dwarfism, there was a huge difference in that regard. Cynthia had known of a girl who had dated a dwarf once – *or small person, as they tended to say nowadays* – and she'd told and shown Cynthia – *with a couple of photos over a glass of Sauvignon blanc* – just how hung her '*little-lover*' had been. It was enough to make the eyes wince. 'Ouchy-ouchyerson' Cynthia had said to her friend after feasting her eyes on all of his manhood, and they'd both burst out laughing.

Another message pinged on her computer, and Cynthia quickly minimised the oddity of the penis on her screen and opened the text box, it was <RANDYRANDY> again.

RANDYRANDY <*You get me so hot, I'm so hard for you right now.*>

Cynthia laughed aloud, her hand shooting to her mouth to stifle her outburst. She couldn't contain it; it was like laughing at a funeral. The more she tried to stop herself, the more she laughed, because if the squat looking penis, the stunted appendage she'd just seen, was, as <RANDYRANDY> had suggested, at full mast, then he really shouldn't be shouting about it so proudly.

What an embarrassment. Cynthia had seen nipples that reached a higher state of arousal than that silly thing. She assumed the words: '*Are you in yet?*' would have been the constant and most common refrain of <RANDYRANDY>'s life.

Cynthia had seen her fair share of penises over the years, an occupational hazard, and one of the only downfalls of the job really. What was it with man's innate hunger and need to show a stranger his penis. It didn't matter if it was erect or flaccid, long or short, hooded or circumcised, thick of thin, straight as a rod or kinked like a tree branch – Cynthia had seen them all. And men – *it would seem* – never tired of the desire to show her – *and many other women too, she assumed* – their tackle.

However, it wasn't just the men who liked to show what they had in their pants, women did it too, but with more decorum, style, and sophistication.

The women who frequented her site showed more restrain. Usually just sending her a risqué or candid photo of them laying on a bed and cupping their breasts. Sometimes she'd get photos of them reclining with a strategically placed hand or piece of fabric covering their personal glories – somehow knowing that if their personal areas were on show, they might find themselves spread over the internet like a wildfire, and that wildfire would inevitably find its way to their wives, girlfriends, husbands, boyfriends, and perverted bosses.

When a man flashed his shit online it was acceptable, sucked into the vastness of the internet and forgotten, but if a woman did it, the consequences were that much stickier and had further reaching repercussions and implications.

Cynthia dragged the attachment of the *'dick-bird'* to her recycling bin. She had a file on her computer labelled *'Dicks&Chicks'* where she kept some of her personal favourites, but she didn't keep them to look at, no, she kept them as an insurance policy, and for possible use later on should she need them for anything *unsavoury*.

Blackmail wasn't above her, should the opportunity be called for.

'Dick-bird,' however, was nothing to write home about, so she deposited it into the trash, where her computer made the sound of something landing in an empty bin. Once safely deposited, never to be seen again – *with any luck* – she right clicked, scrolled down the options to the word delete and clicked it where her speakers made the sound of a sheet of paper being scrunched up.

Cynthia couldn't lose the smile on her face as she thought about how proud <RANDYRANDY> was of his dick, or more accurately the sorry excuse of a dick he had, more nubbin than penis.

As she reached the end of her darning, holding the rounded girthy lump of wood in her hand, her mind drifted to Daniel's dick.

Daniel had a great dick.

Size.

Shape.

Length.

Girth.

A handsome cock, if cocks could be such things as handsome.

She shivered at the memory of it. A warmth spreading through her body and between her legs. At times, Cynthia had mused that Daniel's penis felt as if it had been sculpted just for her, to fit her insides exactly, one perfect fit.

As Cynthia finished tying off the loose threads of the sock, her thoughts turned to the penis of the man who *was* Daniel – *but who wasn't Daniel* – strapped to the bed in the basement. She remembered catching a glimpse of his shrivelled member the previous night. The wrinkly, withered thing that hung – *well, it didn't exactly hang*– Scratch that; the wrinkly, withered thing that ~~hung~~ perched on his wiry sponge of pubic hair. She'd taken it in her hand and towelled it dry when she was getting him dressed and it barely filled her hands, not like Daniel's would have, even in its flaccid form. No. This *almost* manhood had laid all lifeless and limp, like a worm pulled from the ground and then instantly discarded by a hungry seagull for its lack of appeal.

She'd manoeuvred it in her hand, stroked it, rubbed it dry with the towel, and yet it still hadn't got any bigger, it didn't even twitch, just refused to grow or become aroused. She only had to brush Daniel's penis to get it flooding with blood. Only had to mention sex for his penis to respond like a dog to its owner's call, eager to please.

The lack of arousal wasn't even the worst part of the sorry affair.

The worst part about the withered penis of the man in the basement was that it was circumcised, and there was nothing she could do about it. She'd not given much thought to making love to Daniel after the meal, assuming he'd be too weak, but *should* something happen, should they find themselves overjoyed and overcome by the moment; the enormity of her answer to the question she'd longed to be asked, well, she wouldn't look a gift horse in the mouth. However, she also couldn't reason with putting that thing inside her, knowing it didn't look like Daniel's. It would be like fucking another man, and Cynthia was loyal to a fault.

In the beginning, Cynthia had thought about shaving off a segment of skin from Hasan's thigh and crafting a hood for his penis from his own skin, hoping his body would accept the attachment once she'd sewn it on, rather than rejecting it. She was no Ed Gein however, which for her and for the resurrection of Daniel's penis, was unfortunate. She could darn a sock; but to harvest living tissue, craft a foreskin, sew it on to a penis…that wasn't something you just tried your hand at, regardless of obtaining an A* in GCSE textiles.

There was the possibility of infection.

Rejection of the tissue.

Not to mention the possibility if she did a piss-poor job at attaching it that it might come loose inside her if the mood struck. And Cynthia didn't want to be fishing around inside her vagina for an errant piece of flesh. She'd had enough trouble trying to find a tampon she'd lost when she was a teenager, spending hours digging around inside her for the string, fearing at any moment she'd go into toxic shock syndrome – *which she'd learnt about in a sex education class.* TSS had scared her as a kid, and it terrified her as a teenager, and it stuck with her as a constant worry in the back of her mind as an adult. She couldn't chance some foreign object floating around in her vagina and festering.

No, Cynthia had decided vehemently that she wouldn't forge Daniel a hood of his own flesh.

The risks were too high and judging by the way that she had held it last night – *and the fact that it never even twitched at her touch or rubbing* – Daniel's body was too weak to even contemplate pumping blood to that flaccid organ. His blood was needed elsewhere.

The monitor pinged. Another message appeared from <RANDYRANDY>, thankfully there was no picture this time, just words.

RANDYRANDY <I showed you mine, now you show me yours.>

"You want to see mine, do you, RANDYRANDY?" She purred, before blowing a kiss at the camera and, lifting a hand to her shoulder, she slipped one of the straps loose on her bra, letting it fall away.

DING.

Another message.

RANDYRANDY <YES…YES…YES…> (*aubergine and squirting emoji*)

"Well, strap yourself in…"

She peeled the other strap loose, placing an arm across her chest so it enveloped her breasts, giving them some much needed support for what was to come.

"…here…"

She reached behind her back and unclipped her bra.

"...we..."

Pulled the bra loose, keeping her breasts cupped and hidden with her arm.

"...go!"

She held the bra up to the camera before dropping it, letting it fall out of shot, landing on her keyboard with a clatter. As she began to remove her arm, Cynthia pressed a finger to the delete key with her other hand, ending the live stream just before she exposed herself in front of <RANDYRANDY>, the internet, and the whole damnable world.

They'd come back for more, she was sure of it. She wasn't called the *'Grand Prick tease'* for nothing. It had been a label given to her by her male fans because she wouldn't flash her flesh for the world to see. Of course, she always got close to the mark – *as she had tonight* – but those special places were reserved for one special person, Daniel.

Pulling her negligee around her, covering her nakedness once more, Cynthia picked up the socks and the darning mushroom from the bed and strolled across the room to the chair where Daniel's *'death clothes'* hung. Placing the socks on the seat of the chair, nestled on top of his folded trousers and clean boxers, she observed the jacket and shirt hanging and sighed.

Daniel's *'death clothes'* were the only items of his clothing that she had left having buried him in his finest suit and packing the rest of his clothes into various boxes to send to charity shops.

She'd kept these few meagre items because they'd still smelt of him, carried particles of him in their very fibres. His other clothes smelt of detergent and softener, but these that were piled on her chair still smelt of his very being, his musk, his life, and ultimately his death.

In the beginning, days after he'd left her, Cynthia had laid them out on her bed and cuddled up alongside them, placing a hand across the jacket and shirt, imagining it going up and down as Daniel breathed. A wish that never came true.

His *'death clothes'* had been delivered to her in a plastic bag at the hospital, yet they weren't the only present she'd been given at his death. She'd also been handed a much smaller bag with a bunch of the things that the hospital staff had found in Daniel's pockets when they'd stripped him down, trying to revive him to no avail.

It was that same bag she went to now. The one that was tucked away in her top drawer.

Opening the drawer to her dresser – *another of Daniel's restoration projects* – she riffled through the various skimpy pieces of underwear, a few sex toys and a couple of pairs of woolly socks – *strictly for comfort, not pleasure* – and she found the ziplocked bag nestled near the back. It crinkled when she claimed it. Inside is Daniel's wallet, keys, signet ring – *which he wore on his little finger, it had been left to him by a grandfather* – and a chunky silver number which he wore on his thumb. There was a St. Christopher necklace in there too, the patron saint for travellers, but based on its inclusion here, Cynthia guessed he didn't escort souls to the afterlife. For that, they must be on their fucking own. There was also pack of chewing gum – *Cherry Delicious* – and a handful of change.

None of the small pieces mattered to her; what mattered was the velvet-covered box with a ring inside.

Cynthia hadn't looked in the box. She'd wanted to, of course, but Cynthia couldn't bring herself to see it. She never thought she'd see the ring after what had happened. To peer on it, knowing it represented a promise that would never come to pass, would have broken her. But now? With all the work that she'd done? Soon, if things went according to plan, she might finally see the ring Daniel had chosen. She would learn how he had planned to propose to her, and she would see how he would react to her answer.

She thought about stealing a glance at the ring, yet stopped herself. She couldn't do that to Daniel. It was his to give, and she had no right in cheating him out of her reaction.

The moment needed to be genuine.

Genuine disappointment, or genuine joy, at his choice of ring, it needed to be real, and in the moment, because moments like those only come around once.

Well, twice in Cynthia and Daniel's case.

It was time to prepare dinner for her love, and as she made her way from the room, a joke Daniel once said sprang into her mind, making her chuckle as it was apt in every way.

'What did the grouchy mushroom say to the loud mushroom?'

"Put a cap on it!" She says aloud, breaking into an uncontrollable fit of laughter.

Leaving her bedroom-turned-office behind her, she descends the stairs, making her way to the kitchen where she'll prepare their evening meal and Cynthia will ponder the great mushroom debate before she places her order.

Maitake?
Porcini?
Chanterelle?
Morels?
Truffle?

CHAPTER 10

swear I just heard–
  Pulling her eye mask up, Cynthia frantically searches around her from for the invading, sleep stealing sound.

All logical thought fled her mind when the thunder announced itself and rumbled overhead, as if God has just shifted his footstall. The one his feet will rest on when he kicks back and relaxes whilst Daniel endures his painfully drawn-out end.

The vibrations caused by the ferocity and timbre of the sound shook the panes of glass in Cynthia's windows, all of them were old sash monstrosities due to the house being a listed building. She didn't mind, though. She can afford the extra heating, and there was sod all she could do to change the drafty-falling-apart-windows.

An almighty flash soon follows, as if someone just set fire to the sky. It took Cynthia's sight a moment to adjust to the dimness of her room, observing the muted light of a new grey day creeping in from around black-out blinds which didn't fit quite right. Turning her head to the side, Cynthia will note the time.

11:34am.

It was her middle of the night. The rest of the UK's mid-morning.

What the hell was that noise?

Although still in a state of sleep, and a little flustered by the storm, – *what day was it? How many days until, or since, Date Night?* – Cynthia had no doubt about what she heard. Although, she'd need to hear it again, just to be sure. To prove it wasn't her mind playing tricks on her.

Peeling her sleep-mask completely off her face, Cynthia discarded it on the pillow. Raising herself up on her elbows, she peered around once more before flinging back the duvet covers and sliding her way to the edge of the bed. Dropping her legs over the mattresses side she slid her feet into the decapitated, bunny head slippers which were waiting next to the bed, as usual, and Cynthia sat there for a moment in her silk negligee.

She mulled over the noise, her arms prickled with goose-flesh, not from the cold or the fear of the storm raging outside her windows, but instead unnerved by what she heard. Or, more appropriately, what she *thought* she'd heard.

If she was right, then things had just gone to hell in a handbasket.

The thunder crashed again, and Cynthia flinched from its ferocity, the impending storms arrival announcing itself as rain – *although it could have been hail, given the plonking against her shitty windows* – and began tapping at the glass.

Composing herself, she took a deep, calming breath before standing. Shuffling across the room, she pulled the curtains back, knowing that she wouldn't get any more sleep, and she peered out into the muted, grey morning. The lightening from the previous roll of thunder announced itself in three short bursts, as if someone were outside her window taking candid shots of her in her delicates; creating a strobe effect that left an afterimage of the cross, formed from the wood in the pane, to keep replaying in her sight as she turned back to scan the room.

What she'd find as she searched, she had no idea.

Panic began to set in as she half-expected to see a shadow of a figure in the, behind her open door where the shadows were thickest, or lurking in the reflection in her full-length mirror. A set of eyes staring at her from under her bed.

You're an adult, goddamnit. You shouldn't be scared of things that go bump in the night.

However, the truth of the matter was that Cynthia was still petrified about something grabbing her foot from under the bed. Some fears followed you out of your childhood.

"Is that you?" Her words slurred with fear and drowsiness.

After giving the shadows by the door the all clear – *no crazies lurking there* – she peered into the other corner of her room and froze. Lifting a shaking hand, she rubbed her eyes with the heel of her hand, firstly to lessen the lightening's effect on her sight, but secondly to rid herself of the image of what she discovered.

Opening her eyes again, she flinched. Her breath catching in her throat, the *thing* was still there, and the sight of it made her stagger. Cynthia reached a hand towards the bed post, to keep herself from falling over.

"What do you want?" She uttered, lips quivering.

The thing in the corner didn't respond. It just sat there, looking at her, biding its time.

Two eyes peered at her from afar.

What scant light there was in the room reflected off their shimmering lenses, two pinpricks of light in a hellish black place, as if that particular corner of her room had been decorated with a wallpaper made of tar.

The figure was hunched, crouched in the corner of the room, nestled in near her chest of drawers. Scratch that. ~~Crouched down~~. No, it was coiled. Ready to spring from the darkness to have its wicked way with her.

"How did you get out?" Her voice faltered in her throat. She did and didn't want to know, yet also yearned to hear something, anything, other than her heart hammering in her ears and the rain tapping at her window incessantly.

If it was her time to die, she'd go out fighting, not cowering in the corner or being assaulted by some sexual pervert. And so, one small bunny step at a time, she drew closer.

"We need to get you back downstairs. You shouldn't be up here. Not yet. You're too early." Another faltering step, and Cynthia raised an open palm in front of her in a defensive posture. If the thing from the corner made a lunge at her, then she'd be more than willing to turn that defensive posture into an aggressive one. She'd rake her long nails across his eyes until they bled... whatever fluid eyes bled.

"Listen to me, you need to—"

Thunder roared outside, as if a leviathan had just emerged from its long-held grave, hellbent on bringing about the next apocalypse. A childish, weak, whimper left Cynthia's throat. Turning to face the window, she expected some giant's eye to be peering in at her.

'I'll grind your bones to make my bread'

There was nothing there. Only the rain running a river down the glass.

You're more worried with the fleas at your feet than the wolf at the door, you've been looking out the window too long, he's going to get you!

Spinning back to the room, her gaze returned to the darkened corner and the eyes peering back from the oil slick, sentry, unblinking. The lightening flashed, again, and the brief illumination revealed the thing in the corner for what it truly was. Cynthia's breath shuddered in her chest as she chided herself for being so foolish in believing he'd gotten out.

How could he have escaped when he's chained to the damned bed. Moron.

It was just the pile of Daniel's clothes on her chair. The eyes, those reflective disks from the dark were simply her reading glasses perched atop the chest of drawers. Marching directly across the room, Cynthia swiped her specs from the countertop and deposited them in one of the drawers, slamming it shut.

Cynthia hadn't read a book in, what, a year? And, well, if she never read a book again it would be okay because the last one scared the hell out of her, *Incidents Around the House* by Josh Malerman. In a way, it ruined any other book she might've read afterward that dared to call itself horror, and so, she'd decided that if she never read another book again, she was fine with it because she knew that nothing else could or would damage her that way again; it would haunt her to the grave, she was sure of it.

What she was doing now was testament to the terror trapped within its pages, imagining things in her room when there was nothing. But, no. That wasn't right, was it? There had been *something*. It had called out to her, much like Bela, the young protagonist in that hellish book. However, nothing lurked in the corner of Cynthia's room. Of this she was sure now. There was no *other mommy* or *other daddy* or *other Doctor Hasan* – but there was *other Daniel*, although she was adamant, assured even, that he was still restrained in the basement.

How in the fuck would he have escaped?

The man she'd bathed and held and rocked to sleep couldn't raise his voice, let alone his emaciated body from the bed.

So, what the hell woke me up?

I heard him, didn't I?

Daniel?

Or was it Doctor Hasan?

Setting her course for the open bedroom door, her slippered feet scratched their way across the hardwood floor as she was too frightened, too exhausted, to lift them.

Thunder rolled again and she felt the vibrations through the soles of her feet, working their way up her legs, past her knees and hips, until the seismic quaking found its way to the pit of her stomach and made its home there, rocking her very core with its deep resonance.

We're in the eye of this storm now.

Thought was silenced like a screwdriver rammed through her ear as she heard the sound again.

"HELP ME...SHE'S A FUC–"

A flash of lightening, followed immediately by another rumbling of thunder which briefly cut off the distant, scathing words. It subsided, and the banshee was screaming again. Cynthia wasn't just imagining it.

"GET ME OUT OF THIS SHITHOLE!"

It was the voice same voice which had reached into her sleep and pulled her unceremoniously from the land of nod, with its fingers gripped tightly around her throat.

O, how those fingers want to crush my windpipe.

In her wakefulness, Cynthia could almost feel those fingers squeezing her throat again, and suddenly she couldn't catch her breath. She placed a hand to her throat, relieved that no other hand was there – *other hand*, from *other Doctor Hasan* – and she rubbed gently at her throat, soothing the tightness before gulping a huge lungful of air.

"SHE'S A FREAK, HELP ME, PLEASE. I'LL KILL YOU, I PROMISE YOU THAT…YOU WHORE!"

The voice was relentless in its frustration and its desire to be free. They sounded like a raving lunatic about to be given shock treatment.

Although Cynthia could breathe again, she still found herself short of breath because the voice she could hear, the words, the anger, and the hatred, wasn't the voice of Daniel. It wasn't the weak and pathetic Daniel she'd put to bed after bathing and holding him tightly to her. It wasn't the scared, placid man he'd become over so many months. No. This was the sound of a raving madman, the soundtrack to her nightmares where her abductee reigned supreme. It was the voice of a deranged patient who'd escaped whatever godawful asylum they'd been committed to, rightly or wrongly: It was Doctor Osman Hasan, back – *it would seem* – from the brink of death.

"GET AWAY. NO, DON'T TOUCH ME, PLEASE STOP. STOP IT, YOU'RE HURTING ME."

His voice echoed up from the basement, filled the entire house, battled with the thunder, two waring resonances.

"WHERE AM I? WHAT HAVE YOU DONE TO ME? HELP. HELP ME. I'M TRAPPED DOWN HERE, SOMEONE, ANYONE… PLEASSSSSEEEEE!"

Shuffling her way out of her bedroom and onto the upstairs landing, Cynthia flinched as the thunder roared and the lightning flashed, the rain hammered harder at her window and rattled the roof tiles with its plinking and plonking. It was an auditory assault, a steady rolling din of noise, which thankfully overpowered – *for a brief moment at least* – the clamouring from the basement. The elements had won this battle, but they wouldn't win the war.

As feeble as it was, she tried to listen between the sounds of the storm and the house for the awful sounds rising from beneath it, trying desperately to decipher if Daniel was still tied up, or if *he* was roaming free downstairs; lucid and angry, knife in hand and revenge on his mind.

There was screaming now, no words, just the incoherent, guttural bellowing of a desperate and dangerous soul. Cynthia descended the stairs, one careful footfall after another. There had been a time like this before, a long time ago, a phase of the abduction she'd thought she'd seen the back end of: The Witching Hour.

Although those night terrors had actually been morning terrors, given Cynthia and Daniel's upside down and back to front way of life under this twisted roof, it had been a blessed relief not to have them for the last six months. And in their stretching absence she'd forgotten about them entirely, which was neglectful to say the least, but she didn't have the mental bandwidth to deal with how forgetful – comfortable – she'd become right now.

She'd been so excited with the progress she'd been making that she hadn't even contemplated the possibility of another emergence of the night terrors, or, more appropriately, a *de-evolvement* of this magnitude, or how the night terrors could cause the wailing-bastard who'd taken everything from her to return so suddenly – *she'd taken her eye off the ball, and she knew it.*

How long the old Doctor Hasan would remain was anyone's guess, however, the swiftness, butthe veracity of Cynthia's response would surely determine how long this interloper stayed. She had to be ruthless and, luckily for her, she'd grown more comfortably into that role the longer this ordeal had gone on. She now wore her callousness as a second skin.

Entering the kitchen, Hasan's grumbling voice reached her from the basement; his pained, confused timbre rising above the creaking of the house as it did battle with the elements of the storm.

Before her abduction-imprisonment-transformation became an actuality, she'd done a lot of research and read up on Stockholm syndrome; one of the coping mechanisms for a captive to survive an abusive relationship. In it, the captive would develop positive feelings towards their captors or abusers over time.

She had longed for Stockholm syndrome. Pined for it, if truth be told, because it would help bind Daniel to her all the more, and any help she could get to ease Daniel's metamorphosis from within the husk of the beast that'd been responsible for Daniel's short and abbreviated life should, and would, be welcomed – she needed him to love her, and whether that love was real or shipped in from Stockholm, she'd take it, as long as he loved her when the time came.

Brain washing and gas lighting were other researched topics that she'd put to good use over the time of Daniel's captivity. But what was happening to Daniel in the basement, at that very moment, wasn't a factor of either mind altering phases. It was what she'd learnt from detailed case notes of nurses working in asylums or mental institutions: *'The Witching Hour'*.

It was quite a common occurrence, where the patience within a hospital's charge would often become riled or enraged, posing a danger to themselves or those responsible for their care, usually at a specified point of the day when the sun was going down, or in some instances, when a storm was rolling in.

Cynthia couldn't pick and choose what mental afflictions forced their will on her captor – whether that be *Stockholm Syndrome* or the *Witching Hour* – all she knew was she *had* to put an end to the screaming.

She made her way into the kitchen, stood before the door to the basement, and breathed deeply as the house breathed around her.

Standing in front of the basement door, she could hear his enraged cries.

"I'LL KILL YOU, LET ME OUT OF HERE…NOWWWW!"

Removing the overalls from the hook, Cynthia slid out of her bunny slippers and climbed into the baggy outfit. There wasn't time to remove her negligée, but since it was silk, it clung to her body instead of rucking up in the paint-stained outer garments. Cynthia stepped into her work boots, then she quickly tied the laces and glanced up at the owl mask.

A thunderclap, so loud that it felt as if it were the bugle call for the end of days, crashed above the house, and Cynthia could hear the cutlery and plates – *in the drawers and cabinets* – rattle with the storm's intensity.

"SHIT!"

The exclamation was loud, but she was sure the thunder covered it as she reached out a shaking hand for the mask, her movements underscored with a low rumble of thunder, quickly followed by the flashing, strobing effect of multiple lightning strikes happening all at once.

The feathered face of the mask tickled her fingers as she pulled it free. Turning it over, she slipped it over her head, taking time to ensure that the shawl covered her hair and hung around her shoulders and neck correctly. She couldn't afford a mistake. Not now. Not when she trapesed down those stairs to confront Doctor Hasan.

She peers over at the candle, and thinks of taking it with her, but stops herself from reaching for it. The darkness will hide her intentions from him, and who doesn't like surprises?

The rusted hinges of the basement door squealed as she opened it, betraying her stealthy approach.

"WHO'S THERE?" The voice roared.

Taking two steps into the basement, she turned and closed the door behind her.

"I CAN HEAR YOU, WHOEVER YOU ARE.

"IF YOU LET ME GO, I WON'T TELL ANYONE... I... I... PROMISE!"

The pleading tone in their voice irked Cynthia, because although it sounded genuine –*albeit rather shouty* – she also heard the air of entitlement in it. A tone which belonged to the body's former owner.

Creeping steadily downwards she declined to answer.

She was only a few feet into the basement, but already the darkness was all consuming, and her splayed hands pressed up against the wall, searching for what was needed. Her fingers danced over the brickwork, through sticky cobwebs, gliding over the many objects which hung to the basement wall. Gardening sheers, a rake, a shelf of various cans and gardening supplies, poisons – *rat, slug, and insect* – and then her fingers touched a frame which was hung on the wall, containing an old map of the local area.

"Where is it? Where is it?" she whispered.

Fingers slid across the glass of the picture, returning to the brick wall once more before they found their way to what Cynthia was searching for.

Fabric.

Cotton.

It was an old pillowcase, which was also an old friend. They had a history together. The pillowcase was bunched at the bottom due to what it contained, slimmer at the top where it hung from the wall by a hook, a tear drop shape of fabric. She groped at the bottom of it with one hand, and the angular blocks it held shifted around with her investigations. Supporting its weight with one hand, she drew her other hand higher, following the fabric as it tapered to a thin, taut tip where she found the hook. Flakes of rust fell from it as she lifted the pillowcase free, hugging it to her body, cradling it like a baby.

"WHERE ARE YOU?

"WHY ARE YOU DOING THIS TO ME?

"WHAT DID I EVER DO TO YOU?"

You did enough. Soon you'll find out exactly what you did, you piece of shit, and you'll pay, you'll fucking pay for what you did *and* didn't *do.*

Cynthia slung the pillowcase over her shoulder. The blocks inside clattered together and the disturbance within released a clean odour, lavender, and the scent, so out of place in this festering hole caused her brow to wrinkle up in temporary confusion. But of course the contents would smell that way. Soap, twenty or so bars of it, were going to smell.

Soap's generally used for cleaning; however, these specific bars have never been used for that purpose. For the purposes she needs them for, though? They've been used plenty, and frequently, and expertly well.

With the pillowcase slung over her shoulder, Cynthia plods down the remaining steps, taking great care not to misstep in the dark, especially on the bend. Twisting an ankle, falling down the flight of stairs and not being able to get up, *would* and *could* scupper her plans, and she hasn't come this far, done the unimaginable, to fall at the last hurdle and have all her hard work ruined by the beast in the bed who just won't stay dead.

Work boots soon crunch on unhewn basement from each methodical, resolute step she takes towards her captive.

"I CAN HEAR YOU…WHERE ARE YOU?

"SHOW YOURSELF YOU LITTLE BITCH…I'M NOT SCARED OF YOU, OR THAT MASK YOU HIDE BEHIND."

There doesn't need to be light for her to navigate down here, and Cynthia passes the table with ease. Everything is in its place, and she's grown to trust the darkness rather than fear it, piloting the invisible terrain like her mask's namesake.

From the green blip of the heartrate monitor, she zeros in on her prey.

The green luminescence of the monitor isn't strong enough to reach into the room; it's too weak and fleeting to overpower the stygian dark, preferring instead to hang from her captive's features, giving him a sickly pallor, as if he were some deep-sea bioluminescent creature.

Swooping closer, she slips the pillowcase from her shoulder, hefting its full weight in one hand. The blocks of soap clatter around inside as she lifts it up and down, testing the weight, remembering its weight, and rediscovering how to wield its power.

"WHERE ARE YOU?

"I CAN HEAR YOU OUT THERE, WHY DON'T YOU COME INTO THE LIGHT AND WE CAN TALK ABOUT ALL THIS?"

I'm here, she wants to say, but chooses to remain silent. Cynthia shifts her course to the left-hand side of the bed, away from the blipping green light.

"SHOW YOURSELF YOU FUCKING COWARD!"

All in good time.

The pillowcase swings like a metronome by her leg; back and forth, back and forth, hungry to taste his flesh and bones once more.

Daniel, scratch that; ~~Daniel~~ Doctor Hasan, pulls at his restraints, his thin neck corded with strained tendons, mouth drawn back in a vicious snarl as his eyes peer into the darkness like two jaundice-coloured pearls, looking for her, his judgement.

I'm right here, YOU SMUG SONOFABITCH.

Only a few feet away now, his eyes dart one way and then the other, he still can't see her approach. He won't find her for the want of looking; she's one with the darkness, married to it, moulded by it – whereas *he* is only a temporary visitor here, unaccustomed, and shit out of luck.

The pillowcase hangs by her shins as she watches him, judges him, deciding on how she'll break, bruise, destroy and bury him if it should come to that.

Restraint needs to be shown, because she knows that correcting him as she did in the beginning with the soap-sack – *the bloodstains on the fabric wrapped around her fist testify to the many corrective procedures endured* – she'll ruin everything she's worked so hard to achieve; and so she won't swing to destroy him or break him, she'll just swing to bruise him, maim him at the very worst.

The dried blood from the other corrective procedures – *crispy under her inquisitive fingers* – crumbles and flakes away into the dark as she runs a hand over the lumpy contents. Smiling a sadistic grin, she gauges how much energy she should put into the first swing. She's out of practice, and desperately doesn't want to overstep – *or overjudge* – her first swing to leave herself staggering into the green luminescence. She wants to strike hard and fast, a viper from the dark, in and out.

The soap in the sack clacks together with her fussing and Doctor Hasan turns his head to face her, his face becoming a block of shadow as it leaves the light, a darkened mass haloed, no, crowned by the green glow as if he were some goblin king.

The shadowed head is rather fortuitous, because to see Doctor Hasan's face leering at her out of the face she's sculpted anew, out of those eyes which last night had finally been Daniel's, would be an insult she couldn't tolerate in her fragile state; it helps her dehumanise the man before her for what is to come.

"I CAN HEAR YOU, YOU SICK BIT– "

The force of the connecting blow hits Doctor Hasan in the throat/chin on its upswing, silencing him instantly. His mouth comes together with an audible *CLOP* as his head snaps back and his body rises momentarily from the bed from the force of the impact. His shackled wrists snap his body back down to the mattress, and if it weren't for them, Cynthia's sure he'd have tumbled clear of the bed. There's no pause on her behalf. She doesn't rest on her laurels, just winds up and swings again, this time aiming for his abdomen.

The bars of soap clack against each other as they connect with his bony hips, the hard blow landing firmly on what remains of his emaciated stomach. Hasan attempts to double over in pain but the restraints do their job and he's stuck in an awkward half-hunched position as his legs piston up and down the sheets.

Saliva and blood leak from his mouth, dribbling in long, gelatinous cables to the stained hospital gown, and given the green, moss-coloured hue from the heartrate monitor it appears to be more poison than blood.

Just poison leaving the body, come on Daniel. Be strong. Fight him!

"Why…" he moans. "Why are you doing this to me?"

Retreating once more to the shadows, Cynthia leaves Hasan staring into the place the two strikes originated from. But he won't see her there, as she manoeuvres to the other side of the bed, standing behind the heartrate monitor for fear of the green light picking out her silhouette.

With all the cunning of a fox, she observes Hasan from the security of the dark; his hunched body, his head turned away from her, his succulent, bony back announcing itself as a perfect target, just begging to be struck.

The bag whistles in the air before connecting with a solid crunch, robbing the breath from Hasan's lungs and the spiteful, hate-filled words from his throat. Rocking forward on impact, he suddenly thrashes backwards as she pulls the pillowcase away, leaving him horizontal once more – *a sitting duck.*

With his chest heaving, and his body squirming on the sheets, each inhalation of breath makes whooping sounds as he gulps like a fish on dry land, desperately trying to get air back into his lungs.

Like fucks, no mercy is given as Cynthia prepares to strike again.

With her broiling anger at the man robbing *her* of *him*, her Daniel, she unleashes a sickening, unrestrained show of aggression and the bag flies through the air, connecting with his right arm and wrist, clanging and trapping his arm against the guardrail of the hospital bed.

The hue of his face and neck show that he's still struggling for breath, his skin a deathly green, as if he were already dead, corpse-like, but Cynthia doesn't falter at the sight. She just winds up again.

The cudgel of a pillowcase comes down on his shoulder and neck, narrowly missing another sickening connection with his face and he yelps in pain.

"PLEASE…" his words a gasp.

"PLEASE STOP…I…I…"

Again, she swings.

The pillowcase strikes him across his stick thin legs where it cracks off his bony shins; if she'd swung at full power, she knows she would have shattered those legs like a stick of chalk dropped to the ground.

Giving him a respite from the assault, she slinks once more into the shadows, moves around the bed, and the break in proceedings gives Hasan enough time to mumble a few placating words.

"I…I…I'm…sorry."

He mumbles his half-hearted apologies as Cynthia is lining up another swing; this time for the crown jewels, knowing that nothing gets through to a man quicker than when he's having his manhood threatened. This bag, this swing, could just about pop those wrinkly testicles between his legs like a rotten watermelon. Maybe that's how she could work around the circumcision problem. Reduce everything down to a wet, pulpy mass so that the question became irrelevant.

"Please don't…I…I…"

Hefting the pillowcase over her shoulder she pauses, waiting for the right moment to crush his balls, destroy his fun bags, and decimate his personal-gravy silos.

"I don't know what's going on, please don't hurt me any more…I…I…I…"

Fingers tighten around the fabric, her hand a tight fist around the knot at the end.

"I…I…I…"

Shifting to the left slightly enables her room for a better strike, and now Cynthia is ready to crush his scrotum, his lovers lance, his pork sword, the one-eyed bald man between his legs; her body tenses, ready to unleash unholy hell on Hasan, although the words which tumble from his stuttering mouth stop her in her tracks.

"I…I…I love you…"

Those three words – *five if you count the stutter* – are bullets to her chest, a sobering trinity of words. The bag instantly slips from hanging over her shoulder, the pillowcase now swinging idly by her shins, redundant.

"I don't know what happened to me."

"Please, please don't hurt me anymore. I...I love you, I've..."

There's a shift in the tone of voice, not just a pleading, but an emergence – *a re-emergence* – of the person she'd lost – *albeit temporarily*. Daniel was trapped in there. He'd been fighting his way to the surface like a tired swimmer trying to keep their head above the crashing waves, and now he was here, he was back.

"I've always loved you. Please, I can't take any more...please..." a fit of sobbing robs him of his words and Cynthia knows it's him, because Hasan was too proud, too masculine, to reduce himself to tears. Even crocodile tears.

With her work done, she turns from the bed and walks back to the foot of the stairs, leaving the tenderised body of her lover to lick his wounds.

"I love you," he blubbers.

The pillowcase drags along the ground as she passes the table and chairs.

"I've always loved you..." there was a crack in his voice, and he begins wailing again, not in anger, but in utter despair.

With a hand to the banister, and one foot upon the bottom step, she glances back at the bed. Daniel's pleading eyes, and his scared face stare back at her. Not a single shred remains of the monster who, moments ago, had raised his ugly head.

You did it, Daniel.

You fought your way back to me.

Now stay...dear god...please stay with me, Daniel. I need you.

I can't lose you again...

"I love you. Please, don't hurt me any more...please...I wasn't myself; I know that now, but I also don't know how much more I can take."

There's not much further to go, my love. We're almost there.

Just hang on, because if you don't, I don't know what I might do... next time I might not be able to control myself...I might not be able to stop.

As she climbs the stairs, her booted feet signal her retreat.

"I won't ever stop loving you… please…please…plea….ple…p…p…p…" his voice dissolves into sobbing again as Cynthia continues to ascend.

Near the top, she hooks the pillowcase back on the wall, opens the door to kitchen, and steps through, turning back to lock the door behind her. Still, his sobbing and moaning and pleading reach her, and although it *is* Daniel now, she can't help but think of the man who returned tonight, and who she quickly and ruthlessly banished once more.

An echo, or a remnant, of the man she'd vanquished still remains.

She's sure of it.

As she places her ear to the basement door, listening to his incoherent mumbling and pondering her interloper's lingering presence, the night of Hasan's abduction rises to the forefront of her mind.

Finally, it clicks, and the connection between then and now revels itself. It's the terror threading his voice which reminds her of the terror in *his* voice; that bastards voice, when she first took him. The same fear had been present then, is present now, and it fills her with dread.

Is this going to work?

She thrusts her fists against the door.

It has to. Failure's not an option.

CHAPTER 11

The abduction.

Planned for months.

Yet taking no more than the length of a song to transpire.

Eventually, she'd park her car in Norman Park. The place was a regular hang out for Doctor Hasan, and so Cynthia sat behind her wheel, on a stakeout of the slip road that led to the empty carpark. She was staring at his Audi TT, parked in his usual space – *three spaces over from the clothes recycling bins* – facing the open green space ahead.

There were three distinct times of day when Hasan came here.

Early morning, at 6:12 am, early evening at 6:54 pm, and then late at night 11:16pm.

And so, Cynthia worked within these parameters, and she planned her abduction accordingly. Some of the key factors in her decision-making were visibility and footfall. With autumn well in motion, she'd opted to disregard the early evening slot; although the evenings had drawn in, it was still too light for her to do what needed to be done. What needed to be done was best kept in the shadows, and it just wasn't dark enough to go unnoticed before 7.

So, Cynthia had observed the footfall in the park over many months, and although there weren't many people out and about in the early morning, there were still too many for her liking. Too many odd occurrences. It seemed like everyone and their grandmother had a dog nowadays; and many of them were mothers with dead, soulless eyes, unpredictable sojourners at this deplorable hour, as they strolled through the park with a screaming baby in a pram, a bouncing puppy in tow, propelled by the small hope of getting their little bundles of joy to sleep and the furry ones tired out.

Watching those mothers pulling their dogs along reminded Cynthia of a joke Daniel had shared with her once.

'What do you call a Zoo that only has dogs?'

'I don't know, what do you call a Zoo that only has dogs?'

'A Shit Tzu'

There were also early morning joggers, the scourge on any society, especially the ones who didn't exactly run. You know the type. Done up in all kinds of ill-fitting spandex, but instead of jogging they seemed to just be perpetually staggering forwards, a pace just up from a walk, moving slower than an octogenarian heading to bingo.

On further stakeouts, the 11:16pm had become the frontrunner. There was literally no one about. Just him. Doctor Hasan and his stupid little bitch.

Of course he has a bitch.

To people like Doctor Hasan, the whole world was his bitch.

And on this fateful night, the night of his abduction, of course he'd brought the bitch with him. He was a creature of habit after all.

She'd observed him from the approach lane to Norman Park with her headlights off, and her window cracked open to allow the cold autumn air to chill her. Her need to be on the edge of comfort was key. She had no time for drowsiness to set in, because when that happened, when she finally set her plan into motion, she'd need all her wits about her.

Parked in the same place as always, she observed the dome light in Dr Hasan's car, and she witnessed him pluck an errant hair from his nose – *obviously missed from the Turkish barber he'd been to earlier that day* – whilst staring into the rear-view mirror, totally oblivious of what stalked him further up the approach road.

Over the time that she'd been stalking him, Cynthia had discovered that Doctor Hasan always took great care in what he looked like. He was constantly preening himself. For *what?* For *Who?* She had no idea, but she loathed him deeply for it.

"You can't polish a turd."

The utterance escaping her lips, eyes flicking to the time on the car's dash.

Still on schedule.

Her eyes were drawn back to Hasan's car as the internal dome light extinguished and he finally emerged from his mid-life crisis purchase – his *Audi TT*™ – and shrugged on what appeared to be an expensive *North Face*™ puffer coat over his creased suit. He'd not changed since work, and his brown tie hung loose around his neck; the top button open, allowing his hairy chest to sprout out around the opening as if they were weeds in a cracked pavement.

Thankfully, he zipped his coat up as he walked around to the passenger side and opened the door to let his stupid bitch out as he continued fussing with the zip of his coat, wanting it to be just so. The silly bitch hopped out of the car and busied herself around him.

Cynthia observed the scene unfolding, wishing that the zip was a noose tightening around his thick neck.

All in good time...

Her knuckles bleached to the colour of bone as she squeezed the steering wheel and pondered what to do about the dog, because the last thing she needed was for it to start raising all hell when she finally made her move.

Doctor Hasan's chocolate-brown Labrador, Cassie, who, like Doctor Hasan, appeared to be enjoying the finer things in life hopped out of the car and the fat-bitch's belly swung from side-to-side as she ran circles around her master.

A spoilt dog for a spoilt man.

It pained Cynthia to watch him. The agonising weight was back in her stomach and there was a tightness in her throat. She hammered the steering wheel with the heel of her hand, hating how his life was still trickling along, whereas hers had stalled, no, scratch that. ~~Stalled~~ Ended when Daniel had expired due to this man's neglect.

He doesn't even know what he's done. What he's responsible for.

Breath fogged around her in the front seat.

But he sure as shit will soon, I'll guaran-fucking-tee it.

She'd show him exactly what his ignorance, his lust, and his flagrant disregard for the duties entrusted to him as a medical professional had caused; he would be held to account for *everything* in the end. But she knew that the end – *his* end – was still a long way away.

As Doctor Hasan set off to walk his *fat pooch*, which would take him approximately twenty-two minutes – *she'd timed it* – Cynthia turned the key in the ignition and her car purred to life. Releasing the handbrake, she let the car roll down the long entrance road. As she cruised, her eyes flitted from the road ahead of her, to the retreating Hasan, then back to the road again.

Looping around to the right, she pressed her foot to the accelerator lightly, circling the carpark at a crawl, scoping out the area, ensuring there were no kidults she'd overlooked; smoking in the bushes or inhaling nitrous oxide from balloons by the derelict swing set. It always shocked her the lengths children would go to escape their unhappy home lives or to 'fit in', but of course, it had been no different in her day; kids sniffed glue and inhaled aerosols back then, so what was the difference, really?

Once she'd swung her car around, she parked three spaces over, behind Dr. Hasan's car, wanting her own vehicle to face back up the way she'd come. Fate spun on a dime, and she wouldn't have a moment to spare in executing her plan. Once she'd done it, she would need to make a quick getaway. No three-point-turn bullshit, she'd be putting the peddle to the metal and getting the hell out of there.

A calming breath, then another, she sat for a while, clearing her mind and breathing deeply before the storm swept in and consumed her. She knew she couldn't do what needed to be done on her own, and so she slipped one of her ear-pods in. Seeing as Daniel was gone, and it would be some time before he would be returned to her, she needed something, or someone, to comfort her. Someone to bring her an inner peace when the shit really hit the fan. *The Mac* would be her fuel for this fight, and *'The Chain'* would be the blaring battle cry in her ears, cheering her on like the Mickey from *Rocky*.

I'm going to spit lightening and crap thunder.

The song was already queued up on her phone, which was attached to the suction holder on the windscreen, ready for when the time came; for the moment she would strike.

The *'Rumours'* album cover illuminated the dash with a creamy-white glow.

All that was needed was to tap the screen when she was ready, and the task before her would seem less daunting because she wouldn't be doing it alone. In a strange way, Daniel would be there with her, his presence carried to her on the rhythmic beat and tantalising vocal harmonies of his favourite song; a song he'd sung at full volume in the shower, car, even once when they made love – *only the once though, Cynthia had corrected him for that misstep in his judgement afterwards.*

Although she couldn't get lost in the memory now. She needed to remain focused, remember what she needed to do, and she knew exactly what she needed to do.

She'd pictured this moment many times, mulled over all the variables.

When, where, how, what if?

Through all her deliberations and worry, there was one thing which remained a constant; when she swung her tire iron, after reaching the stage of no return, it needed to be when *'The Chain'* reached its iconic bass riff, heading towards its melodious end.

DUM, DA DA DUM, DA DA DA DA DA DUMMM.DUM, DA DA DUM, DA DA DA DA DA DUMMM.

She turned the engine off and got out of the car to stretch her legs. Pressing her hands to her lower spine, she leant back, felt a crack, and then straightened up and shook the stiffness caused by dread from her arms; her head raised towards the dark sky, and a smile crept onto her face as she marvelled at the twinkling stars above.

It was time to set her honey trap.

Closing the driver's door – *she'd return later to hit play* – she walked to the rear of the car, her high heels clacking on the carpark's surface with each step as she attempted to shimmy her skirt down. When it wouldn't fall, she pulled at the skirt's hem with her fingers, untangling it from where it had gotten stuck on one of her suspender clips. There was a time to flash those suspenders, but *now* wasn't that time.

The boot creaked as she popped it open.

She checked her watch.

Fifteen minutes.

She was so sure of Hasan's movements that she could set her watch by them…and she had in a way; not once in her many observations – *stalking* – of him had his movements or routine varied.

Fifteen minutes and he'll be back.

Dipping forward, she pulled a duffle bag from the boot.

It was heavy, and Cynthia carried it around the side of the car with both hands before dumping it on the ground next to the rear tyre. Bending down, and balancing precariously on her haunches, she removed a screwdriver from the bag and began the process of levering off the hubcap. Once completed, she discarded the plastic covering to the ground near the exposed wheel before reaching into the bag once more. She removed a couple of spare wheel nuts, and she scattered them on the ground, a deception Cynthia was proud of, because it would appear to anyone approaching her that she had already commenced removing the wheel's bolts but couldn't finish the job because she was a *'weak and pathetic woman'*.

She was counting on that misjudgement and misogyny knowing Dr. Hasan wouldn't be able to help himself from swooping in to save the day.

Her deception of using spare nuts also meant she didn't have to secure the tyre before hot-tailing it out of there, what with time being of the essence.

Glancing up from the nuts, she checked her reflection in the wing mirror.

No, that won't do.

She shook her head, not at her reflection in the glass, but at what the mirror reflected back at her. Once again pulling her skirt down to cover her arse, she trotted over to the wing mirror and bent it away from the car, retraced her steps, and crouched down once more into the position she wanted to adopt when Doctor Hasan made his grand entrance.

She knew what she'd do to him, and the placement of the mirror would help in that regard, enabling her to act swiftly and ruthlessly once he entered her killzone. She never doubted he would come for her. Because people like him – *predators* – always made a move, especially on poor, defenceless women.

But when he made his move, he'd find out she wasn't a poor defenceless woman; she was a lioness with razor sharp teeth, and she would be ready to tear him apart.

The frigidness of the evening made her skin come out in gooseflesh and Cynthia pulled her coat tightly around her and flicked up the small hood, her hair tumbling down either side of her neck. The hood was to keep her hidden, anonymous, and full of mystique, but the hood wasn't the only thing that would give her the anonymity she craved.

With her hands disappearing back into the bag, her fingers brushed against feathers. She felt their smoothness beneath her fingertips as she brushed them one way followed by sharpness when she brushed them the other way. Turning the object over and pulling it from the shadowed bag revealed a barn owl mask; its two huge, black eyes stared back at her above a small, sharp beak.

She didn't really know what made her pick this particular mask from all the others. Her decision had *just felt right*. All the other masks – *and there were a great many at her disposal* – looked like something out of horror films, or leftovers from Halloween: goblins, witches, deranged clowns and zombies. Cynthia didn't want to look like someone from a second-rate slasher film. She wanted to look *iconic* and *bewitching*. *Eerie* with a splash of *peculiar*. Once she'd stumbled across the mask online, it made all the others she'd seen before pale into insignificance.

Fate. That was the word she'd used to describe her find, deep in the darkest corners of online retail.

Cynthia had never seen anything quite like the mask, and she had to assume Doctor Hasan – *hell, even the world* – would never have seen anything quite like it either.

It was the eyes that gave the thing life, and Cynthia ran a pad of a finger over them, tapping the glass with the tip of her manicured nail before studying her reflection in the two black orbs. She knew, without question, they would serve the purpose she craved; to reflect all of

Doctor Hasan's fear back at him, just as they reflected all her trepidation back at her.

She wasn't scared, per se. Instead, she was filled with an excited, nervous energy, because once the mask went on, once Doctor Hasan made his appearance, things would change forever; the past, the present, and, what she craved most, the future, would be irrevocably reshaped.

A moment passed as she to calmed herself, breath shallow in her chest, although there was no way to stop her rapid heartbeat or the tingling in her extremities as a wave of nausea ran rampant through her body. She was in the grip of a panic attack, yet she didn't falter; just slipped the mask over her face, and as she slid it down, all else faded away. The hunted became the hunter.

The enormity of the moment, of all her plans coming to fruition, was so intense that the sudden rush of endorphins through her body made her feel as if she could do anything, be anything, *kill* anyone.

This was it, where all her planning had led her, the moment Cynthia finally said goodbye to her grief – *which she'd kept in huge storehouses in her soul* – and finally engineered the return of her beloved, of her loved one, of her Daniel. It was the start. Actually? Scratch that. It was ~~the start~~ the restart of their life together, and nothing was going to get between them again.

Moving to the right slightly, she caught a glimpse of her reflection in the wing-mirror again, and took in a sharp breath, a frightful inhalation, because what she saw stole her breath away.

Resplendent.

Magnificent.

Terrifying.

"Perfect." Her voice was muffled from behind the feathered mask.

She remained that way for a moment, hunched over, observing herself. The mask had a disabling effect when viewed for the first time; a smile behind the mask, a cackle of delight, however, the owl-woman stared back at her, resolute, predatory.

All she had to do was remain calm, wait for Hasan to make his move and then: **WHAM. BAMM.** She'd hit him with everything she had bottled up within her. All her pain, shame, and grief; *everything* would shoot out of her like a cork from a bottle of champagne. No. scratch that. ~~Would shoot out of her like a cork from a bottle of champagne~~.

...all her grief, *everything*; she'd hit him like a sledgehammer.

When the time eventually came – *and it would* – she'd aim for his chin, or his temple, knowing from detailed research that those were two weak spots in the skull. Hitting them just right, and with the correct amount of force, would cause a signal to be sent to the brain; a Ctl/Alt/Del which would render the struck individual unconscious in moments. All she'd have to do after that was lift him into the car and make her getaway.

Cynthia pulled the tyre iron out of the duffle bag and hefted it from one hand to the other; knowing that if she let her emotions get the better of her, she might just kill him with the blow. So, Cynthia needed to rein her anger back, hit him hard enough to incapacitate him but not hard enough to crack his skull – *causing swelling or bleeding of the brain* – rendering him brain-damaged goods.

She needed him functional, not a dribbling fool. If life were to return to him, if Daniel was to have a chance at being resurrected from the grave, *he, they,* would need all their faculties intact for the metamorphosis to hold.

Placing the tyre iron on the tread of the wheel, hidden but within reach, easy to grab and swing when called for, she didn't put all her eggs in one basket; she had a backup plan and when planning an abduction, you sure as shit better have a plan in reserve should things escalate or spin out of control.

She had two insurance policies at her disposal, meticulous in her maliciousness, because if the blow from the tire iron didn't render Hasan putty in her hands as she'd hoped, she had two other tricks up her sleeves.

Reaching into the duffle bag she removed a yellow can of pepper spray and flicked the cap open, shook it, nodded. It was full, that shouldn't have surprised her as it had never been used, but it was always good to be prepared: *a bad workman always blames his tools.* She contemplated spraying some, to make sure it worked, but didn't want to give anything away, or the stink to get up inside her mask, self-sabotaging her own plans.

Slipping the can into her coat pocket, she turned her attention to the last of her insurance policies. It was a small plastic box with two metal prongs on the end which when she pressed the button on its side a bluish-white light crackled into life with a terrifying sound of unchained electricity. Letting go of the button, she placed the 70,000-volt, handheld laser into her other coat pocket.

Should her chosen method fail, she was still armed to the teeth, confident that one of these would help her succeed.

Any moment now Doctor Hasan would return with his bitch, and another *bitch* would be waiting for him. Cynthia checked her watch as she made her way back to the driver's side door, opened it wide, and waited.

The Labrador appeared from a cluster of bushes near the carpark's edge, and Cynthia's eyes followed it, observed the bitch as she trotted over to Doctor Hasan's car, stopping on the way to cock a leg near the low fence which separated carpark from park and urinated.

Cynthia didn't waste any time. She leant into the car and hit the play icon on her phone before closing the door. She walked to the back of the car, head bowed, mask hidden by the slight turn of her body and the edges of the hood; each of her movements underscored by the guitar and the steady drum beat of Fleetwood Mac's *'The Chain.'*

Everything seemed perfect.

Doctor Hasan emerged from the bushes and she prayed he hadn't seen the feathered mask as she placed her hand to the side of the car, kinked a leg, and bent over, presenting her rear to him in an almost animalistic way, as if she were some monkey trying to attract a mate.

She waited.

She stepped gently from one foot to the other, causing her bum to rise and fall as she listened to the Mac with their *'wind blowing* and *watching the sun rise,'* trying to lure the doctor in like an angler fish.

Tilting her head slightly as the steady beat and the flowing lyrics drowned everything in the real world out, she observed the hidden spectacle behind her in the wing-mirror, keeping watch for his approach, knowing she couldn't reveal herself too soon. If she did, she would scare him off, regardless of how macho he was.

Then he was there, the bastard of her nightmares, and he raised a hand in front of him. A double flash of amber light lit up the carpark and Cynthia ducked lower to hide herself from any possible onlookers.

Unlocking his car. Soon, soon he'll be mine.

He opened the car door and loaded his dog inside.

Come on, come on…

Slamming the door closed, he walked around the car and began to open the driver's side door.

"No…no, no,no," Cynthia muttered.

Hasan turned to her then, abruptly, and on taking her in, his head cocked to the side, and he eyed her splendid behind. She wanted to rush the leering bastard where he stood, yet she didn't. He was saying something, his breath misting around his head as the words left his mouth. She didn't turn. Couldn't turn. Not whilst wearing the mask. Well, not yet anyway; he'd flee before he got in range of the swinging iron and all her plans and purchases would have been for nothing.

Closing his door, Doctor Hasan took a step closer.

She observed his head as it moved up and down and he took in her long legs and her bottom, which was barely covered by the hem of her skirt. She pulled it higher to reel him in.

"Blast it, stupid damn bloody thing…" she uttered, louder this time, hoping her words reached Doctor Hasan like a fishing lure, bringing him closer, inviting him to take a bite; and when he did, if he did – *Cynthia knew he surely would* – she'd strike.

The Mac were singing about: '*not loving* and *never loving again,*' and the words flooded her mind with images of Daniel. Of how much she wanted to love him again, and realization about how close she was to achieving that aim.

Her hands were shaking, and they were slick with sweat. She rubbed them on the sleeve of her jacket as she glanced down at the ground and observed Doctor Hasan's shadow spreading across it, encroaching slowly on her position as if it were a spilled canister of oil, growing longer and darker as he approached.

She sensed him, behind her, getting closer, the hackles on her neck rising.

Her eyes checked the mirror again, and she could see him, looming behind her, his eyes focused on her posterior, her legs, her suspenders.

She'd *hated* the way he looked at her in the doctor's surgery, and she *hated* the way he looked at her now. It was that same smug look, the look of ownership, the look of ruining something; the wanton desire to have their way with someone, knowing they would then throw them away without a care in the world, and Cynthia despised that about him with every fucking fibre of her being.

Just step a little closer you cocksucker, and I'll show you who owns whom!

Hasan was only a few feet away, his words still misting in clouds of smoke around his head, and she caught a few this time. *Help* and, *you look like you could do with a hand*, and *pretty little thing like you shouldn't be out here at night all alone*, and *I'm going to fuck you now*.

No! You're not even going to get to touch me you piece of shit!

He took a step closer.

I'll be the one doing the fucking!

The stench of his aftershave became a choking smog and Cynthia wondered why a man like this, a man who could afford the finer things in life – *given his occupation* – chose to drench himself in Paco Rabanne: Pour Homme© which made him smell like an old man trying to pick up some young meat in some dive bar.

However bad he smelt, she was glad of that stench now because, even with the owl mask covering her face and restricting her vision, his musk snuck in, giving away his position and proximity to her. But the aftershave wasn't the only thing which announced itself.

As the baseline dropped on *'The Chain,'* something hard press up against her bottom.

DUM, DA DA DUM, DA DA DA DA DA DUMMM.

Is he already hard?

DUM, DA DA DUM, DA DA DA DA DA DUMMM.

It wasn't his member though, it was his hand, its fingers squeezed.

The world, apparently, *was* his bitch, and *he'd* take what he wanted from it regardless.

DUM, DA DA DUM, DA DA DA DA DA DUMMM.

He doesn't own this bitch, though…

With a swift concealed movement, Cynthia's hand disappeared into the shadows of the wheel arch, and her fingers wrapped around the tyre iron. There was no way Cynthia was going to let Hasan take her in any of the perverted ways he could think of. She would be the one *taking* tonight, not of his sex, or of his life – *although he deserved his life to be taken, to pay the ultimate price for his failure and negligence* – no, she would take of his body.

His carcass belonged to her. He just didn't know it yet.

A little piece of her died inside when she gave back, just a little to his touch, in order to keep him on the hook; she pressed her arse back against his hand, and then suddenly there were two hands gripping her hips, his fingers finding purchase as if her body came equipped with handles for his pleasure. He pulled her closer.

Scream if you want to go faster.

And that's when she felt *'it'* as he pressed her harder against his manhood, the wedge of his burgeoning desire hard against her buttocks.

DUM, DA DA DUM, DA DA DA DA DA DUMMM.

She caught a final glimpse of his leering face in the wing mirror; his lips were moving. The world had gone mute around Cynthia, but she imagined him saying things like: *Do you like that you dirty whore*? and *Why don't we get in my car*? and *You were asking for it.*

Men like Doctor Hasan always assumed women were asking for it.

Why are women always asking for it? You vile…vile…sonofabitch.

Five fingers made a fist around the handle of the tyre iron, and Cynthia began to slowly pull it from its concealment, for Daniel, for herself, and for all the women in the world who were told they *'deserved'* what they got for *'dressing like that'*, for *'looking like that'*, for *'why don't you just smile, life can't be that bad'*, and especially for all the women who were told *'they'd been asking for it.'*

As the guitar joined the bass and the screaming lyrics of Fleetwood Mac kicked in, she spun around, tyre iron held high, ready to lay someone low, and in a second it was cutting through the air, swinging down on Hasan as his mouth hung agape and he took her pirouetting form in; eyes springing wide as if they were eating his face as he confronted the owl mask.

The tyre iron connected with the side of his head, and those bulging eyes closed instantly. A hollow thud rang out and the vibration carried up the iron and into Cynthia's wrist.

Dr. Hasan stumbled backwards, his legs buckling and his head bouncing off the boot of the car. However, he stay down on the ground. Instinctively, the doctor bounced back up, hobbling around in front of Cynthia like a punch-drunk boxer before blindly reaching out for her. She shrank back from him as he careened towards her, arms raised, hands blindly snatching at the air, trying desperately to put his filthy hands around her throat.

She swung again, and this time the iron found the meat of his shoulder.

Again.

Cracked against his jaw.

There wasn't an audible crunch when the iron connected with bone, but she felt it reverberate up her arm, into her shoulder, and then her chest, and it was when the numbness filled her chest that Cynthia knew she'd felled the bastard. She watched his legs give out beneath him and he crumbled to the ground as if all the bones in his body had been liquified instant- unconscious.

Bending down, she removed a few sets of cable-ties from her bag, secured them around both of Dr. Hasan's wrists and ankles, then she opened the back door of the car, and she began the mammoth task of manhandling him in.

Prey stowed inside, Cynthia used another couple of cable-ties and connected them to the ones around his wrists and ankles and hogtied him.

From her earbuds, *The Chain* came to an end as she closed the door.

Symmetry.

There was a strange poetic justice in that coincidence, as the chain of events leading up to Doctor Hasan's abduction were also now at an end.

Across the lot, the mutt was barking in Hasan's car, and although it was muted, the dog was clearly furious.

Turning to face the Audi™, Cynthia thought about putting one of the windows in with the tyre iron, to show the dog – *the bitch* – some form of kindness, but she didn't, because Hasan had never shown an ounce of kindness. In the time she'd known him and followed him, he had never showed Daniel the care or attention he deserved, not even at the time when he deserved it the most.

The bitch can freeze or boil. She's made her bed, she can die in it.

Opening her own driver's door, and casting one last glance around the park, Cynthia climbed inside, slammed the door, and placed her hands on the steering wheel.

She'd done it.

Now the hard work starts.

Tears trickled down her face as she sobbed behind the mask.

Removing the earbuds, Cynthia dropped them into the seat well between the passenger and driver's seat, placed a finger to her phone's screen and swiped right, bringing up the album *'Tango in the Night'* – another of Daniel's favourites.

Rolling her finger up, she flicked through the tracks until she found the song she'd planned to drive home to, the ever-upbeat, *Everywhere*, and she pressed the play icon, and the jingly-jangly opening filled the car. The chiming was soon followed by a steady drum beat which sounded like footfalls; running, momentum.

This song signalled the next chapter in her life, of moving onwards – well, backwards – instead of being stuck in the same place, forever on a loop.

She hummed along to the words, about *being with someone everywhere* as she turned the key in the ignition and the car purred to life. She paused when her passenger moaned in the back seat. His head was down in the foot-well, his words lost in the upholstery, it reached her as nothing but a drunken mumble.

Everyone's a critic.

Turning her head slightly as she began to pull away, she spoke over her shoulder to the fallen monster in the rear of her car.

"The best thing about mistakes, Doctor Hasan, Mr. Osman Hasan. Is that sometimes we get the opportunity to correct them."

There wasn't a reply, just a mumble, a mouthful of incoherent words made up of a string of vowels.

"Are you ready for your correction?"

Another grunted reply. His lack of response didn't faze her. She'd said her piece, stated her intentions.

Pulling out of the carpark, with words of *'Everywhere'* ringing true in her head, Cynthia sang at the top of her lungs along with Christine McVie, harmonising like kindred spirits, their voices coalescing majestically as they belted out words about *something strange happening to her* and *friends saying she was acting peculiarly* and *about making a start* and *making it soon, before* he *broke* her *heart.*

PART THREE
PUPA

CHAPTER 12

It had been a few days since Cynthia bludgeoned the interloper in the basement with the pillowcase, banishing him back from whence he came.

The bruises which had blossomed on Daniel's body – *because it was his body now, returned to her once more* – had begun to turn a sickly shade of greenish-yellow. There was no permanent damage that Cynthia could see. No prangs, fractures, or breaks that would need weeks to mend or fix, just swelling and bruising, and Cynthia was more than happy about that.

Apparently, she'd hit him hard in all the right places.

Since his correction, Daniel had been fed and watered, much like a houseplant. Although that analogy was worrying because Cynthia had never been good at keeping houseplants. It seemed they all had a habit of dying on her. But *this* houseplant – *if Daniel could be referred to as such a thing* – she desperately wanted to keep alive, for as long as humanly possible, and only time would tell if she'd be able to break the habit of a lifetime or not.

Knowing plants, and animals, and all living things needed light to thrive – *daylight ideally* – she'd found herself at somewhat of a loss, because down in the basement there was no light at all. The windows were painted black to keep her secret, well, a secret. She wasn't about to take Daniel outside on a leash – *although she had one upstairs for 'special occasions'* – or to let him roam around the garden unshackled. So, Cynthia had settled on synthetic light, because in his current state and her current mood, that was all she could afford him. And so, she left the harsh strip-lights on for two of the six evenings after she pummelled his body with the pillowcase full of soap.

Some evenings – *the ones governed by light, and some of those shrouded in the darkness* – Cynthia didn't even feel like keeping him company in the basement, opting to take her meal in the kitchen where she could think clearly and not be disturbed, or, be forced to speak with the whimpering-wreck restrained in the bed.

It wasn't a big deal to her. She knew the lack of company would help Daniel remember, understand, who was in charge in this situation – *and so she starved him of human interaction, much like she starved his stomach of food.*

The days when she remained absent also allowed her more time to fuss over her risotto, trying out the many varieties of mushrooms which she had delivered by a courier. Each package had been left on the doorstep in a small wooden crate stuffed with straw. Farmer's markets were the way to go, apparently, and she'd spared no expense, because this was the meal of a lifetime, the meal to define her future and rectify her past; it would literally be a meal to die for.

Having given strict instructions for the delivery driver not to knock – *as she did with all her online deliveries* – all Cynthia had to do was wait, and the things she needed came to her. She'd decided long ago that it was better that way. Less human interaction meant fewer chances of *something* happening whilst she signed for her deliveries, and it gave scarcer opportunities of a raised voice reaching out from the darken world below her house, a raised voice with the sole intent of desperately trying to raise an alarm.

One abduction was enough for any house to hold.

People would get suspicious if delivery drivers went missing after deliveries at her house. So, whether it was mushrooms – *not mushroom in here* – or medication, toiletries, bras, knickers, or a vibrator or two or three – *she has her urges* – the tried and tested delivery instructions worked.

Over the past six evenings, it had appeared that Daniel had been adjusting well; he'd slipped back seamlessly into the Daniel which Cynthia cared to care for, and *not* into the Doctor Hasan whom she did not. She'd wanted Daniel to trust her again, and not to fear her as she'd witnessed in their brief interactions after the flogging with soap, where he'd flinched away as she approached, screwing up his face at a suddenly raised hand, or when he'd try and raise his legs to protect himself as she swooped out of the darkness with the owl mask. He'd reluctantly nibbled at the egg in a proffered hand, sniffing it too from time-to-time, fearing – *Cynthia assumed* – that she'd poisoned his food.

There was an innate need, on Cynthia's part, for him to trust her, because a relationship based on fear wasn't a relationship at all. It was a lie; and a lie was not the foundation to build a future on, or a past for that matter, and so she'd presented him her own form of an olive branch, one crafted by electricity and light with the aim to turn fear into trust once more. Light in his otherwise perpetual darkness was that gift.

Unlike her other plants, she hadn't wanted Daniel – her fleshy-houseplant – to wither away in some darkened dungeon from neglect.

Was it even possible, for a person to wither without light?

Online searches had proven worthless in that regard, but the thought of it *possibly* happening forced her hand or, more accurately, her finger.

CLICK.

Let there be light, and there was, for a short time at least.

During those two days of unaccustomed light, Cynthia changed her usual routine too, returning as she would each earthly morning – *which was her early evening* – to check on his progress. It was easier to navigate now that she could see what she was doing, and Daniel was happy to see her, and he seemed more relaxed as he bathed like a pig in shit in the illumination she afforded him. When she'd estimated he'd had enough light – *and enough of a good thing* – she'd removed the chamber pot from under the mattress and turn out the lights.

The chamber pot was stashed on a metallic, rusted shelf below the bed, positioned directly beneath the hole she'd cut in the bed, mattress and sheet – the sheet surrounding this well-shaped hole that funnelled down into the bed and into the obscene cavern beneath it.

The light from the last two days aided Cynthia in noticing how foul the bedsheet had become, and it shamed her something wicked, having neglected Daniel's comfort and cleanliness for so long. It was no wonder he had bedsores.

The sheet was shit-smeared and damp from his personal morning dew, not from arousal – *Cynthia had no idea if the thing in the bed could become aroused any more, having not seen a chubby on him or felt one since the night she almost caved his head in at Norman Park, the night of his abduction* – but from where he'd performed his nightly or, unbeknownst to him, actually his *morning* ablutions.

The light revealed everything that was unwholesome about the grisly process, and on observing it all, she found herself craving the darkness again, to hide the squalor her lover lay in, and to rid herself of the feelings of disgust and neglect she'd put him through.

But you had to do it…you had to bring him back.

It's unsanitary!

He's better now, just remember how it was before.

It had been a messy affair when they'd first started this process. Nothing but a dirty protest each and every night. Over time, however, when Daniel realised Cynthia wasn't going to let him out of his shit-stained sheets to use the toilet, and instead left him to sit and sleep in his shit-stained sheets, he'd gotten really good at using the chamber pot. It was surprising how quickly he'd mastered the act of defecating and pissing lying down, especially given the fact that he couldn't use his hands.

Cynthia remembered the pride she'd felt at her discoveries in the chamber pot over those first few days and weeks, imagining that the joy she found in each new deposit was akin to potty training a toddler, and she'd beamed with pride behind her mask. When she'd discovered a large log in the pot, she'd patted Daniel's head and told him what a good boy he'd been.

It had felt a bit odd at first, a bit sick and twisted if she pondered it for too long, because all Daniel needed was an oversized nappy and she'd have been well on her way to instigating *Paraphilic Infantilism* – and people paid good money for that shit, literally.

Odd fetish aside, Cynthia had taken great pride in how well her lover had adapted to using the chamber pot. They'd gone many months now without incident or accident, never spilled a drop nowadays, or missed depositing a brown nugget when his bowels eventually decided to release their precious, dark treasure from within.

She'd read somewhere that the fastest way to break someone emotionally was to degrade the captive by removing their basic human liberties. Cleanliness had been the first of one they'd suggested. By removing the ability to get clean, it served as one of the best ways to break a captive emotionally, whilst also having a knock-on effect to their spirit and mind; it was truly the easiest way to make them suffer without getting your hands dirty. Many a person – *the online research suggested* – had been broken by letting them sit in their own piss and shit for days on end.

It was unsanitary.
It was inhumane.
It was humiliating.
It was all the *un's* and the *in's* and the *hum's*.

There was a need to persevere, but after a few weeks of the torture, she discovered it was doing more harm than good; not for Daniel, but for Cynthia, because she wasn't able to focus when she went down into the basement. She couldn't seem to find him in the first fortnight of his captivity, because the man she was looking for, the man she was striving to bring back, was hidden behind a stink-screen. If she wanted to discover him again, she had to do something about that god-awful stench. She'd tried to persevere, but in the end, she'd given in to her gag reflex.

Cynthia had decided, shit or no shit, she'd sponge him down and change the sheets every few days.

She rationalized that there were two reasons for this sudden change in her duty of care.

The first reason being the smell, so pungent and foul she couldn't spend longer than ten minutes in the basement without fleeing to the safety of the house above, and if she was going to make a go of breaking him – *Doctor Hasan* – and shepherding in Daniel, she'd need longer than ten-minute slots to do so.

The second reason being that she couldn't afford for him to develop some type of infection from where he'd been laying – *festering, was a better word for it* – in his own shit and piss, as she'd noticed his skin, especially between his legs and arse-crack had become raw and cracked, and from yet more of her online research, it was becoming the perfect breeding ground for an infection to take root.

The ablutions gradually improved over time, as she purged Doctor Hasan's guts of his extravagant, excessive eating habits. Gone was the red meat and Foie gras. The braised beef and the honey glazed chicken. The bottle of red, and the whiskey chasers, and the countless cigars following his meals; the bastard ate like a king, because in his world, he believed he was.

Hail to the king, baby.

There were times when she'd followed him before his abduction, spending many an evening observing him eating alone in all the swanky restaurants in Bromley and the surrounding areas of Sevenoaks and Chislehurst. There was even a time she'd stalked him up to the heart of London, observed him from across the darkened, candlelit catacombs of Gordon's Wine Bar, sinking glass after glass of his favourite – *and of course, expensive* – bottle of red whilst he stuffed his greedy face with various cheeses and slices of thinly cut meat. The man didn't eat, per se. He gorged to excess.

It took a few weeks to fully purge his body of that opulent living, but Cynthia did it. It helped that all she permitted him to drink were a few sips of water a day, and all he had in terms of sustenance were hardboiled eggs – *if* Cynthia felt he deserved them.

The lack of fluids and the constant diet of eggs had bound him up something chronic, although it was better than the alternative, which she was grateful was a long way behind them. The eggs had done a number on him some mornings whilst Cynthia enjoyed her *Mammal-Shit* coffee in the kitchen, pondering what she'd do for her OnlyFan© later that night. Morning. Evening?

She'd sometimes hear him groaning like a cow giving birth as he tried to squeeze something out. Then, when his moaning and groaning eventually subsided, she'd traipse down to the basement, she'd remove the chamber pot – *where she'd find his brownish-black offerings, large pellets of solid excrement, which rolled around the pot like marbles* – and she'd flush the contents before slipping the pot back in place.

It wasn't just his diet which had caused Daniel to become bound up. It also had something to do with his lack of exercise, and his withering body. It seemed his body was sucking every single piece of nutrition from of the scraps he ate, trying to ensure his survival, with the unfortunate downside being that all it left were ruddy great stones of excrement to clog up his bowels.

Cynthia eyed the chamber pot now, all empty and cleaned, resting on the kitchen table, but it was the wooden board sitting next to it which pulled her attention back to the present instead of the past with its shit and soiled sheets.

On the wooden board was an array of food *a tasting menu some would have called it in the swanky restaurants Doctor Hasan had frequented*. She'd been working all morning on their intricate design, complexities and taste, and more importantly, their *mouthfeel*.

Mouthfeel.

It was a funny word, but as someone who enjoyed food – *and no Cynthia was not a* foodie. *She detested that term* – she had come to hear of the term often. It referred to the way an item of food or drink felt in the mouth, distinct from its taste; would the food be dense? Tightly woven? Would it have a complex, chewy texture or would it have a crumbly, velvety tannins appeal?

Over her six days of limited contact with Daniel, it had occurred to her that she hadn't considered what *he* might like to have for their *'date night'* meal. The mushroom risotto was her choice. It was the meal she had picked out as she waited for Daniel to arrive at the restaurant, the meal she'd even ordered and picked at whilst she sat alone, enduring the agonising wait for Daniel to show up. And she *would* have that meal again, even if it killed her.

She'd imagined it so often that it was hard to think of anything else. She'd even thought about it when she got the call from the hospital telling her Daniel was on his way there in an ambulance, wondered / hoped that if she asked nicely the chef could box it up for her to take away. The risotto remained on her mind as she travelled by bus to be by Daniel's bedside –the restaurant wouldn't box it up for her: *'We do not do that in this establishment, my dear. This is a restaurant, not a take-away service.'* She'd even thought about it when she stood beside Daniel's graveside, of how the meal that wasn't a meal – *only a few hurried nibbles* – would taste, should she ever get the opportunity to have it again.

However, through all her preparations for *'date night'* she'd neglected the small question of what Daniel would eat. So, for the past six days she'd researched the meals on the restaurant's website, narrowing the options down to four possible choices, relying heavily on her memories of what Daniel enjoyed.

With the many options available to her, she'd settled for meat-based meals, knowing how much of a carnivore he was, then choosing meals consisting of lamb, chicken, beef and fish. That had been the easy part, though. The hardest part, of which Cynthia pondered endlessly over, were the ingredients; the cooking temperatures, the herbs and the spices used in each meal's creation. All the things that were never listed on the fucking menu.

Sliding the wooden board across the table, she placed the options in front of her, worked her way down the rack of items, memorising the ingredients in case Daniel should ask.

Strips of roasted chicken breast were latticed across a bed of grilled asparagus, with a drizzle of dressing made from white wine vinegar, mustard and a dash of olive oil.

Slow cooked lamb shank was placed on a bed of mint and basil-infused, creamy mashed potato, with a sprinkling of passion fruit seeds and a mango dipping sauce.

Medium steak with a dappling of crumbled blue cheese, served with diced, caramelised shallots and two triple cooked chips.

Lastly, baked Cod in a Cajun garlic butter sauce, tender and juicy, seasoned with garlic cloves, olive oil and Cajun seasoning, served on a bed of fresh spinach and chopped spring onions.

With her nose inches from the four tasting meals, she inhaled the collective aroma.

"Mmmmmm…heavenly," she enthused.

Standing, she pushed her chair back with her calves, and the wooden legs barked across the kitchen floor, and she made her way quickly to the basement door where she readied herself for her own transformation, stripping down to her smalls before unhooking and then dressing in her basement attire.

Not long until you won't need all this gubbins.

Reclaiming the mask from the wall, she stroked a finger over the feathered face before slipping it over her head and securing it in place. After fussing with the shawl, she soon had it covering all the necessary areas and turned back to the table where she picked up the chamber pot and the wooden board, full of all the delicious morsels of food that she intended to feed Daniel, and then she made her way to the basement.

Placing the chamber pot on the chair where she sits to change, she opened the door.

"Hello?"

The frightened voice of Daniel reached her almost instantly, a muted, bewildered utterance from the dark. Reclaiming the pot from the chair, she lets it swing nonchalantly at her side as she balances the board in the other, taking two steps down, and she turns and closes the door behind her.

Darkness reigning supreme once more.

"Hello? Is that you?"

Louder now, panicked.

"Yes, my love it's me..." she purrs into the darkness of the world below.

"What's that smell, honey-bun?"

There's a small pause between *smell* and *honey-bun*, as if he were thinking of what to say, or – Cynthia thought – if he were in fact wrestling with the other him. But therein lays madness, and so Cynthia chooses to ignore it, to give *Daniel* the benefit of the doubt. Nothing could, would, will dampen the joy she feels right now, the utter ecstasy she embodied cooking for her beloved.

He called me honey-bun.

A smile worked itself onto her face behind the mask, although an inner part of her being still dwells on the pause.

Honey-bun *might have been a carefully crafted ruse?*
"Smells divine, sweat-pea, whatever it is?"
No pause this time.
Natural, all Daniel.
How sweet.

The smile broadens. She'd missed his pathetic, sickly-sweet terms of endearment for her.

"Dinner, my dear, is…served." She uttered, continuing her way down the stairs, food in one hand, shitter swinging in the other; knowing full well that by the end of proceedings – *given the rich gastronomical delights she's lovingly prepared for him to sample, and of which he was to make his selection from for their previous* 'date night' *meal* – their future 'date night' meal? Lovers who ate together, more than likely shat together too, and Cynthia just hoped it wouldn't happen at the same time.

There was love, but even love has its limits.

CHAPTER 13

The candlelight reflected off the bulging, prominent whites of Daniel's eyes as Cynthia studied them carefully, looking for any tell-tale signs that would suggest an otherness, as if someone else was sitting opposite her, behind those orbs.

Come out, come out, wherever you are…

Stifling a giggle, she remarked how his eyes resembled two boiled eggs, each one stuffed within large, cavernous sockets.

He's eaten so many he's sprouting them…

So many he's seeing them, no, not seeing *them, seeing the world* through them.

Stop yolking around!

The mask, thankfully, hid her smiling face at her lover's misfortune.

There were an abundance of candles arranged on the table for the evening's meal, Cynthia having raided one of the many cabinets Daniel had purchased to renovate but never had the time, a cabinet he'd procured before he was robbed of all the time in the world to upcycle it. Within, Cynthia had found a box of long, red candles. From where, or why she'd bought them, she had no idea, but they gave their meal a different vibe than usual. More dark-mystical-séance than romantic dinner for two.

She'd arranged the candles on the table in a circle and, looking at them now, it *did* remind her of a séance. No scratch that, a séance an altar for a human sacrifice, where she would have made an offering to appease some ancient and angry god. However, the only person Cynthia wanted to appease tonight, deity or otherwise, was sitting opposite her.

The tasting board was on the table, surrounded by the candles.

She had turned on the lights to Daniel's island, illuminating that scummy piece of driftwood floating in the dark sea of the basement so she could unshackle him and get him out of bed. Still, he flinched away from her touch, fearing she was going to harm him, and it was in that moment she understood why he was so timid, so pathetic, so like the Daniel she knew near his end; and it reassured her, this particular devolvement, because it could only mean one thing:

He's too weak to fight.

Knowing all the fight had left Daniel's body, and with it, that awful, no good, dastardly bastard with it, Cynthia had no problem in escorting Daniel to the table and his awaiting chair, although it did take a lot longer than she'd imagined to get him upright and moving.

Every time she touched Daniel, it felt as if she might break him. And if Cynthia was honest with herself, she'd broken him enough already over his short tenure as her patient. To inflict even more unnecessary damage to his body, in his current state of fragility, was a cruelty not even she thought herself capable of.

Who was she kidding? If he so much as stepped out of line, she wouldn't miss a single beat in his beating. It would pain her, but she would do what needed to be done.

They struggled, arm in arm, across the basement, momentarily stranded in the darkness between the two worlds, light and dark. It was Daniel's shuffling, stuttering, knock-kneed gait which caused so much of the delay. It was as if he'd forgotten how to walk, the muscles in his legs having withered to mere scraps of membrane beneath his sallow flesh.

Cynthia wanted him to enjoy the feast she'd slaved over though, while it was still hot, she settled for tepid, and she didn't rush him. Instead, she slowed her pace and escorted the bag of bones he'd become slowly, but persistently, through the dark plain and into the light.

Daniel stumbled once, and she'd pulled him close to her, his bony hip digging into her side; as her hands had shot out to stop his tumble, her fingers grabbed not an ounce of fat or muscle, instead they seemed to hook under his ribcage, and she'd hauled him back to his feet using his ribs as if they were a handle, then supported him the rest of the way by wrapping an arm around his non-existent waist.

When his bony body pressed against her own, it made her shudder. Not because she was disgusted by it, but she tremored because it felt so real, so him, so like the Daniel who once was, and how he'd felt near the end, rail thin and bony as hell. She didn't relinquish her grip. If anything, she hugged him closer and, in return, as he had done in the months before his life was over, he leaned into her also.

Together again.

They hobbled to within arm's reach of the chair, and Daniel's place at the table, and Cynthia caught a glimpse of Daniel in the mirror as they approached. The same mirror where she'd often watched him whilst she ate, and it caused her to catch her breath; he was resplendent in his metamorphosis, and it took her breath away.

In the last few feet, he pulled free of her grasp, desperation in his faltering steps, an innate desire to get to the table on his own, to feel partway human again. All she could do was observe him in the mirror proudly, like a mother watching their child's first steps.

You're hungry, aren't you?

She could tell that all Daniel wanted to do was to fill his stomach and stuff his face, and she was overjoyed at the prospect, because once he'd tasted, he'd be able to make his choice, and they'd be another step closer to their long-awaited, and overly postponed, *date night*.

It had been a good while since Cynthia had seated Daniel at the table, and as she pushed his chair up to the table, she realised he still hadn't tucked into the meal, which now would have grown cold. She didn't mind though, because in his waiting, Cynthia realised he was himself for the first time in a long time.

He just sat there staring at it, as if it were a mirage which would dissipate as soon as he reached for it, and Cynthia had been frozen in her observations of him, as if she were watching a natural history programme, and she was waiting for the lioness to bring down the gazelle before feeding time would finally start. However, the truth of the matter was Cynthia hadn't moved because she was still in awe of the thing she had created. Daniel, her beloved, was seated at his usual place at the table as if he'd never been away.

His bulbous eyes scanned up and down the wooden board and he swallowed a couple of times. Every now and then there was a wet, sucking sound as he slurped the dribble which had escaped the corner of his mouth, salivating at the prospect of eating, yet he'd still not touched a scrap of food.

He likes it. Good.
I knew he would, the man loves his meat almost as much as he loves me.

Another *smacking* sound as Daniel opened his mouth as if to speak. Cynthia lifted her head, tilted it, in the unmistakable and universal gesture of curiosity and waited patiently for the words, but they never came. Daniel closed his mouth again, licking at the skin of his dry lips.

Is he going to fail this test?
Thoughtful.
If he does, the whole thing's fucking ruined.
Wrathful.
I'll throw it all in the bin and I'll starve him for his misstep.
Vengeful.

As Daniel swallowed again, an audible click emanated from his throat as his Adam's apple bobbed up and down in his thin neck. He opened his mouth once more and she thought that this time he *must* speak, but instead of words, his tongue emerged and just licked his cracked lips before disappearing back into the damp cave it had emerged from. He looked like a lizard in that moment, one of those tiny geckos they'd seen crawling over the sun-baked white walls of their holiday let in Turkey.

The thing about those Lizards, Cynthia mused darkly. *Is that you can squish them under a boot when they disturb you. And if* he *doesn't do what* Daniel *would do, then I'll stamp the life out of him just like a fucking lizard.*

Right here, right now – I'm not playing games anymore. We're running out of fucking time.

Leaning forward, maybe-Daniel sniffed at the fragrant offering before him.

Don't…you…fucking…dare!

The barn owl watched on, ready to strike as Daniel's stooped head swung up and down the wooden board. His filthy hospital gown was tented around either side of his head, held aloft by his bony shoulders protruding up as if there were spikes under his skin.

Shifting in place, he lifted his eyes to the owl lady.

"May I?" He offered weakly; eyes wet with what appeared to be tears of joy.

YES!!! You past the test, thank the lord…and yes, you bloody well may.

All she did was nod her head in approval.

"Thank you, thank you, thank you…" he uttered, sitting straighter in his seat.

There was a great restraint shown in what he did next. Cynthia had assumed that as soon as she'd acquiesced to his request, he'd lower his head and snuffle up all the food like a pig at a trough.

But this is Daniel, Cynthia thought. *Not that pig of a man Hasan… Daniel has manners, we've worked hard on those… beaten them into him.*

A cruel smirk snuck onto Cynthia's face behind the mask as she contemplated her characterisation of *pig* and *Hasan*, and how, if he were here now, she'd have verbalised those thoughts. It would have been an insult which would have riled him like no other, given him being a Muslim and, well, pigs being unclean.

Yet, Hasan *was* a pig of a man.

One, big, fat, stinking boar.

"Where should I start?"

The question pulled her back to him.

"Well, my love. That decision is completely up to you. Start from one end if you like, work your way through, one by one, or pick at them at random. But please, savour them…tell me what you like and what you don't care for. From your selection I'll make a plate of it for our special evening."

"Date night?"

"That's right, *date night*." Her voice cracked with excitement. "It's fast approaching, and I can't wait to spend an evening with you. I believe you have something of a surprise for me?"

"I do?"

"Yes, don't you remember?"

"Remember what?"

A sly smirk worked its way onto Daniel's face. But, no. She couldn't decipher if it was sly or cruel.

They stared at each other, a stalemate.

Was this Hasan making another appearance? Twisting the knife in further, reminding her that he wasn't going anywhere; that he was and would always be in charge.

The wood of Cynthia's chair creaked as she gripped the armrests, knuckles turning white as she crushed the wood beneath her grasp, because she had to do *something* to quell her rising anger, outrage, and wrath. She was moments away from reaching across the table and dealing with Hasan's insubordination. She'd slap his conniving face clean off his head if she had to, and she'd do it too, ruin him again if he spoiled this for her, for *them*.

Finally, he broke the building tension.

"I was just shitting with you," he offered. "Pardon my French."

Cynthia released her grip on the chair. There was a sudden numbness to her fingers as the blood slowly flowed back into them, and she laced her fingers together, placed them demurely in her lap, her thumbs massaging her palms.

"You were always good at that. Playing the joker, I mean."

"I was, wasn't I?"

"You still are."

"I guess you're right. I still am…. what sort of surprise did I have in store?" his eyebrow arched in a comical way, causing Cynthia to laugh, and she cocked her head right back and bellowed with laughter behind the mask. Daniel joined her in her laughter, and they coalesced in the empty basement in a joyous chorus. It gave Cynthia the feeling of ascension, of finally finding their way back, together, from the brink. As their voices rose together – *as they had many times before in this house*

– she suddenly cut the moment short by levelling her predatory mask squarely on Daniel.

"Now eat."

Those two words sounded more of a threat than an invitation. She observed the smile flee Daniel's face, and he gulped once more before lowering his eyes to the four dishes displayed before him.

Were the meals tepid or cold?

Too late to worry about that now, he's passed the test. At least that's something to celebrate. Even if they are cold, they'll still taste fabulous.

Daniel reached for his cutlery and a restraint snapped one of his hands back. The one reaching for the knife. His eyes shot up to Cynthia, bemusement on his face. He'd been so occupied with the opulent tasting board that he'd not noticed her slip a cuff on him at the table after seating him.

"Precautions..." she uttered.

Daniel nodded.

"You know I'd never –"

"Precautions."

The tone she used, deep and brooding, ended any further discussion.

Picking up the fork, Daniel began working his way through the board.

All Cynthia did was observe, leaning in closer, and placing her elbows on the table with her chin cupped in hands under the mask. Each sound Daniel made as he shovelled the food into his gob made her love him all the more.

This...is...bliss.

Daniel made light work of the bite-sized offerings.

"Heavenly...

"Devine...

"Exceptional...

"Delicious...

"You'ff ex'felled yourshelf..." he managed with a mouth stuffed full of Cajun styled Cod, and she allowed him the momentary slip in his table manners, due to the fact that he was famished.

"Please, Daniel, don't speak with your mouthful."

Holding up his hand with the fork, he pointed his index finger at her and nodded in agreement. "Forry…" he slurped.

A tilt of the mask, a *you-can't-be-serious* gesture.

Gulping down the food, her shook his head and levelled his eyes at her.

"Sorry."

"That's okay my love. Just don't let it happen again."

Especially on our special night.

"But…" Daniel's index finger was out again, signalling the importance of his next words. "You've got to try this, it's otherworldly. I know I've not had a varied diet of late, but I've never tasted anything quite like this. You've really excelled yourself."

Flattery will get you everywhere.

"No, I shouldn't…"

"Why?"

"Well, you know, a moment on the lips, a lifetime on the hips… that's what they say, isn't it?"

"Some might…but trust me, it's delicious. Come on, just a little bit."

"No, really. I'm okay. I cooked it for *you*, you eat it… honestly, I don't–"

"Please? You really need to try this."

Forking some of the Cajun styled Cod, he quickly presented it to her across the table, and his arm shook as he held it out to her. She didn't want to eat it, but when she saw the pleading look in Daniel's eye, and the longing flutter of his eyelashes, she couldn't refuse him. Cynthia found herself rising from her chair and moving around the table, pulling out the chair next to him, and sitting down.

"Only a small bite."

"You're gorgeous, my love. You don't have to worry about your figure, just enjoy it."

The gap between her and Daniel had been reduced to mere inches.

Lifting the bottom edge of her mask higher, she exposed her chin and then her mouth. Daniel's eyes drifted from the fork to her lips, where they remained, as he stared longingly at them.

"You're going to love this, it's my favourite…I'll be sure to order this for our date night," he offered as he brought the fork closer. Opening her mouth, she accepted his offering; lips coming together around the fork as Daniel slowly withdrew. Some of the sauce dribbled over her bottom lip, and her tongue snuck out quickly to reclaim it. Closing her eyes to heighten her other senses, she savoured the taste as she'd told Daniel to do whilst she also pondered the mouthfeel of the dish, and the subtle texture of it on her tongue.

Heavenly…he's not wrong about that.

There was a subtle ting of the fork being placed on the table; however, Cynthia continued to keep her eyes closed, cherishing the aftertaste in her mouth, the spices, the subtle heat it left on her tongue and throat.

Something gripped her face.

Not the mask, but her actual fucking face. A finger stroked over her lips. Her eyes sprung open behind the mask, and Daniel's face, or was it Hasan's, was all she could see through the large apertures of her owl eyes.

"What?" Cynthia managed, and Daniel snapped his hand back, holding his finger aloft. There was something wet on its tip. An oily residue. Then, without missing a beat, he placed his finger to his mouth and sucked the deposit off.

"You missed a bit," he uttered.

As he sucked his finger, Daniel's eyes continued to stare longingly at her lips, which were still slightly open from the shock of him touching them, the surprise of *Daniel*, after all this time, touching *her*.

His head dipped closer to hers, eyes closing as he moved forward, cracked lips pressed together, not a pout as such – *his face was too gaunt for that* – but pursed, ready to kiss her; the sight caused her to flinch back.

Cynthia's chair scraped on the floor, and she was standing now. Moving around the table in a rush, desperate to put some much-needed distance between them.

"Did I…" he uttered, not brave enough to finish his sentence.

"No…no…it's not you, it's…it's…me." The words and the saying tumbled from Cynthia's mouth freely, a phrase she'd heard a thousand times before, and which she'd sworn she'd never repeat, yet here she was, spilling out as if it were a cover-all-bases.

"I'm sorry," Daniel said. "I just thought…"

The act was so genuine, so natural, but still, she hadn't planned for it, not like this, not now, and it shocked her. Dipping her head forward, Cynthia quickly blew out the candles.

"Wait, please don't go…I'm sorry…I…I…I…–"

"I'm sorry…I should never have…" a reversal of fortune, and now it was Cynthia who couldn't finish her sentences. With the candles extinguished and Daniel sitting at the table in the dark, she turned and rushed for the stairs, her shawl billowing out around her like giant wings.

"Please don't go…don't leave me here like this…please…"

Work boots crunched on the ground. She was all but running as she stumbled up the stairs, fleeing the basement as if her life depended on it.

"I'll be back. I promise…I just need to…I just need to…"

What was it she needed to do?

All she could focus on was her racing heart and her panicked breathing. Shouldering the door at the top of the stairs, she stumbled into the kitchen, slammed the door behind her, and fell back against it. She slowly slid down to the floor where she peeled the mask from her face and flung it on the chair. Taking several deep gasps of clean and unfiltered air, her panic finally began to subside.

"What are you doing?" she whispered to herself before she struck herself, an open-handed slap across her own cheek.

Again, she hit herself. Not as hard as she wanted to, she didn't want to bruise herself before their *big day*, but it stung more than the first slap had. It felt good. Sobering.

"Pull yourself together you…you…stupid cow."

Once more, she struck her face.

"It isn't supposed to go like this…"

Another crack, an open-handed strike, and numbness spread across her face and her eyes found the calendars on the fridge, alighting on her past, present and future all laid out there in those scratched out boxes.

"You're not supposed to be falling for him...not now...not ever...not again...you can't lose him again...you can't...you won't survive this if you do." Wrapping her arms around her legs, she hugs herself into a tight ball up at the foot of the basement door and weeps.

In her weeping, and in her sorrow, she reflects that in love, true love, the undying kind, the type of adoration she had for Daniel, only casualties are left at its bitter end. Grief, the dark and unfathomable kind she felt at the prospect of losing Daniel again – *regardless of what joy and closure she would gain from that* asked *and* answered *question* – was the heavy price she would pay for having loved someone so completely.

Rocking herself at the foot of the door, she attempts to comfort herself in a world where there is not an ounce of comfort to spare. With each rocking motion, the back of her head slams against the door.

"It wasn't supposed to go like this..."

BANG

"It wasn't supposed to go like..."

BANG

"It wasn't supposed to go..."

BANG

"It wasn't supposed to..."

BANG

"It wasn't supposed..."

BANG

"It wasn't..."

BANG

"It..."

BANG

CHAPTER 14

A sudden movement in her bed awoke Cynthia, and she stretched an arm across the double mattress, her fingers crawling over the sheets in search of the phantom encroacher. But, finding nothing, she laid her flat palm to the mattress in the place where Daniel used to sleep. The mattress still dipped where his body had lain, yet what should have been a cold and vacant space was warm.

Impossible?

Although possible, too.

How drunk did I get last night? And how *alone?*

Did I... did I...did I booty call *Michael?*

Michael was her chemist, although he didn't have a master's degree in pharmacy accredited by the General Pharmaceutical Council, nor did he work out of a clinic. Instead, he operated out of his mother's bungalow in Lewisham. Roberta, his mother, had been a long time dead, but Michael had been left the house in the will, kept up with the bill payments, and paid off what little was left on the mortgage. Michael's mastery of pharmaceuticals came from having a lot of money, white privilege, and a lot of time on his hands.

Given enough time, there wasn't anything Michael couldn't lay his hands on, and over the past year, not to mention the first few months after Daniel's passing, he'd been a lifesaver.

Before Cynthia had gotten with Daniel, she and Michael had been a thing. A small thing, but a thing nevertheless, and when she'd run out of credit or couldn't pay for a bump in those long-ago days, well, Michael would just bump her to even the slate.

She hadn't slept with Michael for years, although he'd tried his luck on numerous occasions after Daniel died, when she'd called him crying, asking for something, anything to take the pain away and help her sleep better.

'*I can tire you out,*' had been a common refrain. So, too, was '*I hear operating heavy machinery can tire a person out. How about it? I got a jackhammer in my pants and nowhere to put it.*'

Exploring the depression in the bed further, Cynthia discovered it wasn't only warm, but the sheets were wet with sweat.

"Did I?" Cynthia said aloud, half-asleep and confused.

If I did, then where did you go?

Rolling away from the empty side of the bed, she pondered the question and pulled the duvet tightly around her naked body; she'd always slept in the nude, whatever the season. She was lying on her front when she sensed movement again, and something clambered across the bed towards her from behind.

Oh, you came back.

Her body rocked gently as the clamouring came closer.

After yesterday, and that kiss, I could go for a fumble beneath the sheets.

The duvet lifted, and she felt someone slide in next to her. If she kept her eyes closed and thought about Daniel, only Daniel, then it wasn't cheating, was it? The mind is a powerful thing, after all, and she could imagine him beneath the duvet with her even if it was someone else.

Suddenly her hair was scooped away from her neck.

Is that you, Michael? She yearned to ask, but if Michael replied, it would ruin the illusion of Daniel that she craved. The closeness of him. And not the Daniel in the basement, but rather the Daniel who lived in her mind, who was with her always. The Daniel she could never touch, hold, or fuck.

The person behind her -*Daniel*- kissed her neck.

Soft and delicate, butterfly kisses. The way Daniel used to do it, when he'd get his face close to her thighs, stomach, and chest. So close that she could feel every flutter of his eyelashes against her skin.

Mmmmmm...butterfly kisses...my favourite...

Stretching her legs out, Cynthia's feet twisted in the sheets with a moan of anticipation.

Pulling her hand from under the pillow, and reaching over her shoulder, she discovered a head nuzzling into her neck. Her fingers crawled their way into the mass of hair where she pulled at it gently, not to stop, but rather to encourage him even more.

They continued kissing her neck, and a tongue licked up and down too from time to time, driving her wild. Her fingers quickly became entwined in their unruly mass of thick hair. A hand stroked down the centre of her back, unseen fingers rising and falling over each of her vertebrate. Once they reached the length of her spine, a warm, open palm pressed flat at the base of her back, resting on the rise of her buttocks.

The anticipation drove her wild.

Freeing her other hand from beneath the pillow, she slipped it down between the sheets and along her body, tracing her smooth naked flesh, enjoying every contour on the way down. In no time at all, she was in a state of ecstasy, her body writhing, bucking back against his. She couldn't delay another moment. Her fingers traced towards her groin, slowly, delicately, teasingly – *just the way she liked*. Her hand, holding his head, squeezed into a tight fist, fingers becoming entwined with a fistful of hair in the process as the hand between her body and the sheets worked in small, concentric circles over the soft flesh of her stomach.

A shudder worked through her body, and she tensed, pulled the head tighter to her neck whilst she pushed herself into the body behind her. It felt good. More than good, in fact; it felt orgasmic.

Daniel, it's Daniel...just think of Dan...iel...Dan...iel...Daniel!

Slowly, the hand on her stomach moved south, tickling its way down.

How long has it been since you've been with a man?

Lips and tongue at her neck, heavy breathing by her ear.

A year? No, it's been longer than that…

A groan of pleasure, him not her.

…stop talking to yourself and enjoy it whilst it lasts.

Cynthia wanted desperately to open her eyes, but instead she squeezed them closed, gave herself over to her other senses, allowed herself to be carried away by her imagination, because she knew that the longer she could keep them closed, the longer she could remain there with him.

"Daniel…" the word slipped from her lips, and she cursed herself inwardly. Yet whoever was between the sheets either didn't hear, didn't care, or was so caught up in the moment that she could have called them anything and they wouldn't have missed a stroke.

Her fingers slipped lower, but she wouldn't go *there*. Not yet. Instead, she gripped her thigh, dug her nails in, and bit her lip at the pleasure and the pain she inflicted on herself. A warmth spread across her stomach, and her body trembled again as the strength of her potential orgasm grew between her legs; the tingle of arousal spreading up and across her breasts in waves. She craved more hands, his or hers, to cup her breasts, to squeeze them as she climaxed.

A subtle inhalation of breath near her ear now, which drove her wild, and she pushed her naked self into him, grinding her arse against her lover between the sheets. The soft panting at her ear soon became heavy as their tongue snaked its way up her neck, their mouth engulfing her earlobe and sucking on it. The panting was louder now, with her need for the physical act of sex growing with each passing second. Seconds which seemed to stretch into hours.

Releasing her grip of her lover's head, Cynthia grabbed at her own breast, forcefully, feeling a hard nipple in the palm of her hand, and she groaned with pleasure at the ecstasy and agony of the moment. She writhed on her bed as if insurmountable pain before pressing herself firmly up to the groin behind her, and she could feel their arousal along with hers. Suddenly what she craved for became a reality, and there seemed to be too many hands on her, all at once.

That can't be right. You're imagining it…

A hand gripped her neck, lightly, delicately; followed by another snaking of the tongue. Another hand squeezed at her buttock before she felt it relinquish its grip, quickly followed by the sting of a cheeky slap. One that didn't hurt, just caused a juddering breath to escape her mouth before she bit her lip to stifle her yearnings. Fingernails clawed down her shoulder, followed by a mouth; soft, wet lips calming the enraged skin with kisses and saliva. Fingers raked down the inside of her leg before grabbing her inner thigh forcefully, dimpling her skin – *oh, how she loved that* – before they ventured higher, crawling around her hips from behind, following the slope of her abdomen to the soft skin of her naval.

She interlocked her fingers with what she assumed to be one of her lovers many hands, and pushed herself against him again, felt his manhood throb against her, matching the same internal throbbing in her chest.

Still, she kept her eyes locked shut. To open them now, when she was so close, would have shattered the illusion, and she wanted nothing more than to enjoy this. For them both to enjoy this most sacred of moments, the becoming of one flesh, again, after so long apart.

A warmth and wetness spread between her legs, a furnace of lust and love threatening to boil over.

"I..." Cynthia moaned.

Hands gripped her hips, followed by the weight of someone mounting her from behind, their hips pressing down on her buttocks.

"I...I...love...you..." she exclaimed in a juddering voice, arching her back, pushing back against the force that was pressing her down. A flurry of kisses followed, not mouth to mouth, but mouth to back, before an arm reached under her, pulling her to him, restricting her writhing, eager hips. The warmth of a naked, sweaty stomach pressed up against her back. Their breath, heavy against her neck.

"I...I...NEED YOU. I WANT YOU," she pleaded; her screaming voice partially muted by the pillow at her face. Suddenly she was spun over, falling on her back to the mattress, arms raised out above her head, seeking the wooden slats of the headboard.

Have me.

Her legs fell open, and a body moved into the vacated gap. A firmness pressed up against her, desire boiling the blood within her body, heat radiating to every inch of her, and she pressed into him.

Still, she kept her eyes shut.

Still, she writhed.

Wanting everything that had been stolen from her.

Him.

Daniel.

That deep and basic connection, flesh upon flesh.

Lowering her head, her mouth found a shoulder, and she bit it.

A sudden moan of pleasure, and pain, as his hardness pressed up against her. It was almost time for them to connect in a way she had longed for. A way which she had resigned herself to never having again. A blissful fog descended over her as her hands relinquished the spindles of the bed and searched for his body.

Their hand was at her throat again, soft and gentle fingers tracing the contours of her neck; there was kissing too, this time, finally, of her mouth, and their tongues wrestled for dominance, each one trying desperately to subdue the other.

"I...want...you..." she moaned with a mouthful of tongue as, lifting her hips slightly, she guided *herself* to *him*. Reaching her arms around his neck and lacing her fingers, she pulled herself to him as he pulled her up from the bed, until she sat straddled his thighs, legs wrapping themselves around his back, clinging to him like a limpet, never wanting to let him go.

Grabbing a handful of his hair again, Cynthia pulled his head back, moving his mouth so that he kissed her chest and neck as she nestled herself onto his crotch, his largeness pressing up against her. Her other hand raked nails down his back. A hiss of pain, or pleasure. It was hard. Still, she squeezed her eyes shut, imaging Daniel beneath her grinding hips.

She wanted him, needed him. She was an addict in desperate need for a hit.

Placing her hand between their rutting bodies, she grabbed him, squeezed him in her hand, and began guiding him to her.

"I need you. I want you...I...I...want...you!" She was panting in increasing desperation and yearning.

Dipping her head forward, her mouth wide, she bit the meat of his shoulder, harder this time. Another groan, this one of pain, she was sure of it, and suddenly Cynthia found herself thrown backwards onto the bed. The duvet was pulled over their writhing bodies, and her lover slipped underneath.

He kissed his way down, and Cynthia let him. Her hands found their way beneath the duvet and relatched onto tufts of his hair.

She didn't pull him up, but instead she guided him lower, pushed him to her ultimate destination.

More kissing; her pelvis, her hips, the tops of her thighs. He was too low now, and so she pulled him higher, guided him to where she wanted as his arms reached around her legs, and he heaved her into position.

She'd missed this. Missed having her needs met. However selfish she was in this moment, it didn't trouble her, because Daniel had always been a generous lover. *Her* needs always placed above *his*. She ground her hips towards him as her body flushed with heat and longing, she was close, really close and he knew it, and so he teased her.

"P...p...please...don't...stop..."

Yet he did, withdrawing slowly, bringing Cynthia back down from the wave of carnal-high she'd been cresting. Squeezing her legs together, she thrusted her hips and her sex at him once more. It was no use though, and she quickly realised she couldn't trap him down there. He was on the rise. She could do nothing to stop him from working his way back up her body, kissing his way north, licking his way up inch-by-painstaking-inch, leaving her in a state of incompleteness, of being only half-finished.

It made her think, fleetingly, of the many bureaus and cabinets which littered the house, abandoned mid-way through their restoration, to spend the rest of their existence in a state of near completion.

She couldn't allow herself to become one of those things.

She opened her eyes.

Maybe if I look at them just once, maybe he'll see how much I need this, how much we need this, Daniel. It won't be cheating, it'll be a moment, a second without you...but you'll return to me when I close my eyes again. You're always there when I do.

METAMORPHOSIS 177

She glanced down at the approaching mass under the sheets.

"I'm not done yet."

Her hands gripped the edge of the duvet.

But the man beneath the sheets ignored her plea, climbed higher and higher, the shape below the cover nearing her breasts.

"Finish me off, please…" she moaned as she felt a tongue flick at a nipple, but still they climbed higher, her pleading words ignored, and she began to lift the duvet as the body continued to rise.

It was dark beneath the cover, and all that Cynthia could be seen was a mass of hair approaching. The crown of a head. They were almost out.

Cynthia reached a hand beneath the duvet whist the other lifted the cover higher. She ran her fingers through their hair, traced her way down the side of their face until she cupped their chin in her hand. Slowly, lovingly, she began to lift their face to hers.

The body between her legs rose higher and higher, but the shadows still hid them. Her hand lost contact with their face and she let it fall to her breast. She didn't know why, but she found herself covering them protectively as the duvet began to slip from the emerging body.

Two hands shot from the shadows, each clamping tightly around her throat.

There was no pleasure in this act. None that Cynthia could find. It was different from the *sexual asphyxiation* her and Daniel had partaken in before, and it felt as though she might lose her life at any moment.

She thrashed and bucked, but couldn't throw them off.

The hands continued to squeeze tightly around her throat, and her windpipe crunched beneath their constricting fingers. Cynthia could feel herself shutting down, oxygen starvation setting in quickly. In her struggles, the hands continued to throttle her, and the duvet slipped further down and suddenly a face loomed over her.

It wasn't Daniel.

Nor Michael.

It was Doctor Hasan.

"I'm going to kill you…you bitch!"

It took all the strength she had left in her body to lift her hands, and she clawed at his face, her fingernails ripping ribbons of his jowly cheeks away. One of her nails lodged itself in the bottom of his eyelid, where it met resistance, and Cynthia braced herself before dragging her hand down, tearing his eye wide open, causing it to suddenly appear even more bulbous than it already was, as if at any moment it would tumble freely from the socket it twitched in.

Blood poured onto Cynthia's naked body like treacle where it spattered onto her face and into her mouth. There was no let-up in Cynthia's assault of him, or his of her, and Cynthia scratched and clawed relentlessly at her attacker's face, the way someone buried alive might claw their fingers to the bone inside their coffin.

Doctor Hasan's face was a mask of raw, shredded flesh, yet even in his agonised state, he continued throttling her; leaning forwards, he bore the entirety of his weight down on her neck, and the fleshy ribbons which hung freely from his face tickled at her exposed, now purplish, face.

With each downwards, forceful thrust, Dr Hasan pushed Cynthia deeper into the pillows, and the streamers of flesh which dangled from his face wobbled with the exertion of his grip and pressure.

"I'll show you who's boss, you stupid whore!"

Blood and saliva dribbled from his open, lipless mouth.

"I'll show you what you get for spurning my advances, you pathetic, weak, woman!"

He roared as his head thrashed wildly from side to side, blood falling on Cynthia's face like dirty rain as she faded beneath him; she only had the strength for one last assault.

Make…it…count!

Cupping Doctor Hasan's face between both of her hands, she latched her fingers to his skull like crampons, her nails biting into the meat of his shredded face. She manoeuvred her thumbs to his eyes as Doctor Hasan shook his head, trying to rid himself of her grip, desperate to get her to stop her assault. Cynthia would not – could not – let him win, and so she pressed her thumbs forcefully into those bulging eyes.

He screamed and wailed, neither of them wanting to give up vital ground, each still believing they could finish the job. It was a battle of attrition now, survival of the fittest. As Cynthia's thumbs pressed in, the liquid of his eyes sluiced warmly down her hands, wrists, and arms. The pressure around her throat began to subside and she found she could breathe again. It was all she needed to finish him, and as she twisted her wrists away from the head, there was an audible *crunch* as she broke apart his orbital sockets.

"D...D...Die..." she stuttered.

Rearing back, with his mouth opened in a silent scream, Dr. Hasan pulled Cynthia with him.

"Why won't you just die?" She screamed.

Flailing hands found her neck again, only this time, once they found purchase, they began to twist, forcing Cynthia to turn in a way that necks were not built to turn.

"GUGAGGGGAAUUUGGGG!" He screamed into her face, and although Cynthia didn't know what he was saying, her mind filled in the blanks.

He's going to break your damned neck.

Although Cynthia fought him with all she had, he was still too powerful. Her head began to turn and twist.

Die, you bastard...just die already.

It was the last conscious thought Cynthia had.

With one final, brutal twist, Doctor Hasan rotated his hands and roared with rage, and Cynthia heard her own neck snap as white, blinding light bleached the entirety of her vision, and finally, she...

...awoke.

Her arms and legs were thrashing within her sheets before quickly rising Cynthia onto her elbows, where she stared down, disbelievingly at her body, the bed, and the duvet which lay draped flat across her naked torso.

Although she could tell there was nothing under it, she lifted it to check. As if Doctor Hasan might have magically become *Flat Stanley* between the moment of her neck breaking and her snapping awake.

But there was nothing there. Just her naked self. And so, lowering the cover, she collapsed back down onto the mattress, her body taking a moment to settle as she stared up at the ceiling; one hand across her stomach whilst the other touched her tender throat, as she pondered what had just happened.

It all seemed so…so, real?

A buzz of fear still roamed through her body, its poison slowly spoiling her stomach.

Why'd you have to kiss me?

She placed an arm over her eyes.

Why'd you have to make me feel…feel something, for you?

Rolling over, she wormed her way to the edge of the bed.

Why'd you have to make me want you…love you…all over again?

"Man, I need a drink."

Clambering out of the bed, she pulled a silk negligée over her nakedness and made her way out of the bedroom in search of something strong and wet to rid herself of her nightmare. Hopefully, if she drank enough, drowned herself too, then, well, she wouldn't have to do what she needed to do.

What she had to do.

Descending the stairs in search of the kitchen and liquid oblivion, she had one final thought which brought tears to her eyes.

There are no such things as happy endings, are there?

CHAPTER 15

Five drinks later, Cynthia's fear of the dream began to plateau, and she finally found herself levelling out.

"Why'd you have to kiss me, why couldn't you have waited?"

The announcement, sudden, in the emptiness of the kitchen, sounded weak and pathetic. Nothing could have prepared Cynthia for how she felt; or could have torn her mind away from the truth and the falsity of how that one kiss had made her feel.

Yes, of course she wanted Daniel to love her again.

She wanted him to crave her once more.

And, above all, she wanted to be his world again.

Although the kiss had been so sudden, so true, so him, that she hadn't been prepared for it, or prepared for that stolen moment to shake her as much as it had – there was a time for everything, and Daniel's chosen moment wasn't it.

Lifting the glass to her lips, she drained the last remnants of her large, fifth double of Redbreast™ – *a twenty-one-year single malt, which she refrained from thinking how much each sip cost her* – whilst she ruminated on her dream, and how good it had felt, and how right it had been, until it wasn't.

All the factors were there for it to be categorised as a nightmare; however, Cynthia couldn't shake the feeling that it had been more of a premonition, an echo from the future, of how things were doomed to spiral out of control.

However much she had tried to erase Doctor Hasan, a part of him was still in there, still living through Daniel like a parasite, and when she'd least expected it, he could, without warning, raise his ugly head to snuff her out. The dream had been a warning. It had to be, yet Cynthia couldn't stop herself from craving the man she loved.

But at what cost?

How do you know he's not trying to dupe you?

Pouring herself another whiskey, a single, no, a triple – she needed to drown her thoughts right now – Cynthia placed the bottle back on the table with a *thunk* before picking up the glass and inhaling its aroma as she pondered what had happened.

He did kiss like Daniel, both in the dream and when he kissed me last night...

But was it him *last night?*

Or was it Doctor Hasan, playing his cruel games?

Hell, you're never going to know. Just have another sip?

Gulping a mouthful of whiskey, she didn't swallow, instead keeping it in her mouth until she could feel it burning her gums and her tongue. There was a warmth rising in her mouth, the notes of the whiskey singing their sweet song over her taste buds and fuelling her temporary delirium and malady until, when she couldn't bare it any longer, she swallowed. The liquid burning her throat on the way down, and in its wake the flavours announced themselves.

Tropical fruit...sweet spice...and dark chocolate.

There was a lingering vanilla-like finish, combined with a velvety-soft mouthfeel.

Holding the glass up to the light, she observed its delicate golden glow.

"Fire water," she muttered. That's what Daniel used to call it. He hated the stuff, and couldn't understand her fascination with it, describing it as *paint thinner* and *fire water*.

Leaning back, she placed her bunny-slippered feet on the edge of the table, her lap suddenly the perfect shelf to store her drink whilst she searched for something to keep her company. With the glass nestled in her crotch, her hands searched her pockets for her phone and, once discovered, she brought up her music app, the deftness of her fingers belying her drunken stupor as she scrolled through her playlist and paused.

Then Play On, by Fleetwood Mac.

She tapped a finger to the album on her screen.

Nothing.

Pressed it again.

Still nothing.

Oh, come on, you stupid little...

Furiously, she tapped at the screen, the nail of her finger clicking on the glass as if she were attempting to send a message via Morse Code.

Still nothing.

"Why the fuck-a-roo aren't you working...damn-blasted-shit."

Manoeuvring the phone closer to her face, the screen swam into focus, and slowly she placed the pad of a finger to the album and the cover lit up her screen, a naked man riding a horse.

"Looks a bit like you, doesn't it?" Turning her head in the direction of the basement door, she paused. When no answer came – *because why would it? Daniel was locked up in the dark, a world away, probably sleeping off his bold statement of a kiss* – Cynthia threw a dismissive hand at the door, and turned her bleary focus back to her phone, unable to tell if it was the sight of the album or the alcohol flooding her system, but suddenly she felt like partying.

Her mood was all over the place, presently, with soaring highs, mediocre middles and abysmal lows and it seemed to go hand in hand with her time slippage. Which was what she'd come to call the moments when she was venturing, existing, and confusing her past present and future – *or were they pasts, presents and futures* — as there were two of them in this folie a deux.

Scrolling down the 2013 remastered and expanded edition, her finger hovered over the track, *Oh Well*. She pressed her finger to the play icon and music erupted from the kitchen speakers. The guitar riff screamed into the house, and Cynthia couldn't help but tap her bunny-eared slippers to its enchanting rhythm.

She sang along at the top of her voice, not caring a single jot if she woke Daniel; she'd transcended giving an actual fuck right about now because nothing made any sense. Nothing seemed capable of remaining in tense. Sex dream nightmares. Kisses she'd wanted and rejected. Two calendars hung on the fridge, taunting her with their contradictions. All that existed in the moment, this, then, that moment, was the music and the drink and the wanton need to express herself. She was so drunk her back teeth were swimming, but Cynthia didn't let that stop her.

The lyrics to *Oh Well*, were so peculiar that she imagined Peter Green being off his tits when he wrote it, an impression which caused her to feel a strange affinity with the song in her current state of delirium; she didn't know all the lyrics and ended up mixing them up with her own rambling thoughts.

"I couldn't help the trouble I'm in, can't sing, sure ain't pretty…"

Instead of singing '*and my legs are thin*' she changed the lyrics.

"And Daniel's legs are thin."

As the words left her mouth, she pointed down at the floor, at the thing beneath the kitchen, strapped into the hospital bed, or was he still in the chair? She shook her head, plucked the glass from her lap, and drank. Lowering her feet to the floor, she thudded them up and down, stamped on the ground like her slipper's namesake, Thumper, from Bambi.

Skinny arsed legs, twiglet legs.

She chuckled at her thought before stumbling over the next line of lyrics.

"You can't ask what I make of you; I won't give answers you want me to…woohoo!"

As Peter Green sung the recurring lyrics '*Oh Well*', Cynthia thought the exact same thing, because in this moment, as the Mac and Peter Green serenaded her and she swayed in place; and the dream, the no-good, awfully bad, disturbing dream which had been so good until it had been hideous, finally slipped from her mind and she took another swig.

She didn't just not give a damn, she didn't give a tinker's damn.

"Oh well," she crooned, again and again.

Draining half of her glass, and suddenly emboldened by the song, she attempted to stand. She stumbled to her feet, held onto the table momentarily to anchor herself and then a beat later she was jiving around the kitchen, swaying wildly as if she were in some hedonistic daze.

"Oh well.. fuck it, it's a party, right?"

Lifting her glass, she doffed it to the closed, basement door, sloshing some of the contents over the floor and her hand.

They're around here somewhere.

Eyes scoured the kitchen, desperately trying to recall where she'd stashed the drugs which would take this party to the next level.

Now where did I put the drugs, Michael?

Where did I...

At the thought of his name, Michael sprung up in her mind, unhindered, causing an echo of her dream to return. There was no diluting it, Michael was who she'd thought she'd been fucking. The person she'd hung Daniel's face on in her mind as they twisted and rutted beneath the sheet.

Until that ghastly thing beneath the sheets tried strangling you.

A shudder wracked her body at the recollection.

The music in the kitchen continued, brought Cynthia back to herself again. The guitar riff was building, the drums kicking in, and all shit broke loose in the song, and in Cynthia too, shattering her temporary paralysis. She was off now, spinning and stumbling around the kitchen like a dervish in search of the drugs, and the possibility of forgetting everything for a few blissful moments.

As she stumbled around the kitchen, she opened cupboards and drawers, searching desperately for her hidden stash of narcotics. She spun to the song's hypnotic melody, and the room spun with her. She thrashed her arms about as if she were in a mosh pit, her head snapping around manically, side to side, up and down. Her spirit was free, she was a *'peace and love'* hippy, a Janice Joplin, Jefferson Airplane, Jimi Hendrix groupie.

Just a little powder, or a little bud. That would work…maybe a tab or two, or three…come on, where you hiding?

With an almost empty glass of whiskey in one hand, she thrashed to the fridge, spilling even more of the precious little she had left as she strutted and postured, giving herself over to the moment, the music, the lyrics, and her slippered feet soaked up the various spillages as she glided across the floor.

In her exuberance, strands of hair flew about her face, sticking to her sweaty forehead, as more of it whipped about her head freely. She was Medusa, her flailing hair a nest of snakes, striking out as she thrashed and danced and spun.

For the length of the song, she'd officially transcended to the realm of *not-giving-a-single-fuck*. Soon however, some external force would bring her crashing back down, to try to force her into *giving-a-fuck* again. But not now. No.

Continuing to thrust and gyrate, kicking her legs, and tapping her feet, and windmilling her arms, she danced as if no one was watching, and she scrambled in search for her party drugs. She crashed into the chair near the basement door, sending it clattering to the ground. She glanced down at the spilled items from the chair. Only one held her attention.

Her mask – the barn owl – stared back at her.

Crouching down, gingerly, with the room swimming around her, Cynthia placed a hand briefly on the floor to steady herself before reclaiming the mask. She held it reverently before her as Peter Green crooned about God, and sticking by God's side, and that God would be his guiding hand.

Well, if some God, or minor prophet, or wise man, could guide my hand right about now, I wouldn't stop them. I'd kinda like to get a little high to match my little tipsy.

Giggling at the thought, she scanned all the possible places she might have stashed the large quantity of drugs Michael had provided her with. He was good, Michael. Never asked questions, even when Cynthia's last request had been for enough to kill a horse ten times over. Scratch that. ~~Kill a horse, ten times over~~. Kill a herd of horses ten times over.

All he did was take her money and ogle her a bit, waited to be invited in to the house and her, and when neither option transpired, well, he just tipped his non-existent hat and excused himself, waving a hand over his shoulder, telling her she knew where he was if she needed anything else.

Dancing again, Cynthia swayed side to side. She'd lost the fast, exuberant tempo from earlier, and now her jive resembled a zombified shuffle, holding the mask out before her, she pressed the glass in her hand to the beak of the mask.

"You look like y' coulddo with adrink."

Her words were slurred as she tipped the glass, spilled whiskey into the barn owl's beak, and watched it drip down the feathers and splashed to the floor. She was pondering something Peter Green had just sung, a line which struck a chord within her.

This... she shook the mask in her hand. *...this is God to Daniel.*

The mask was a sacred thing, a totem, something to be adored, and she slipped it over her face, securing it in place with the strap. The owl woman was Daniel's comforter in a world of discomfort and dislocation. She was his hope in a hopeless, measly existence. He didn't just adore the mask. He worshiped it, and she let him.

Cynthia was also... no, scratch that. ~~Cynthia was~~ The barn owl lady was also Daniel's resurrection from the stranglehold of the grave.

Arise Lazarus.

Sweat trickled down her face from her exuberance, the humidity of her own body within its feathery covering causing the glass in each eye to mist over.

I'm Daniel's god.

No, that's not right, I'm Daniel's goddess.

Dipping her head lower, she stared into the reflective surface of the splash board behind the kitchen hob and observed her feathered face.

Beautiful.

Resplendent.

Peter Green was still crooning about *'not asking what he thought of you'*, and *'that he might not give the answer you wanted'*. As the heavy beat and the silky guitar faded, the room was soon filled with the song's melancholic ending, and the sound of it bummed her out, depressed Cynthia something wicked.

She slid the glass, empty now, onto the counter, knowing she didn't need any more *'paint thinner'* – as Daniel would have called it. There was a history of her being a messy drunk and, in her current state, and with the depressing ending to the energetic song pulling her down, she didn't want to end up doing something she regretted; either to herself, or to the emaciated thing in the basement.

Her eyes went to the knife block.

No. Don't you even think about it.

You haven't gone this far to ruin it all now.

Resisting the temptation, she opened the drawer in front of her and peered inside. Nothing but junk, and not the junk she was craving. She slammed the drawer closed, and moved on to the next one.

Just a little bump. That's all I need. A little pick me up.

There was a chime in the kitchen.

No, that wasn't right.

A sharp guitar chord, ringing like a bell. Turning her masked face to the speaker, she paused, smiled at the recollection. She knew this song.

'Black Magic Woman'

Must have it on random shuffle.

The stretched-out, chiming chord was indeed tolling like a bell. Cynthia half-pictured a cartoon bell ringing above her head as she remembered where she'd stashed the drugs and plodded across the kitchen, opening the cupboard above the ridiculously expensive Bose® speaker.

"VOILÁ."

Removing small plastic baggies, one after the other, the counter was soon covered by an array of drugs. Some were powder, some were tablets, and others were vials of liquid, along with the standard assortment of bags of bud and clingfilmed wrapped resin.

Michael had been right when Cynthia placed her order. There was enough here – *in her personal stash* – to kill a herd of horses, maybe even enough to kill all the horses in England. As she ogled her personal treasure trove, the lyrics to *Black Magic Woman* seemed to match perfectly with her inner mood and dialogue as her fingers pawed through the many items at her disposal.

I need you so bad.

MDMA…

I can't leave you alone.

Methamphetamine…

I need you so bad.

Skunk…

I need you darling.

Chlorpromazine…

I want you to love me.

Valium…

I want you to love me.

Morphine…

Whoah, I want you to love me Daniel, I need your love so bad.

Cocaine…

That's the badger…

Cynthia giggled at her use of the word badger, knowing it was a word Daniel used often and for no apparent reason. 'Rough as a badger's arse' and, 'that's a scary badger' and, 'just one more badger and we'll call it a night'.

From where he'd adopted the word, she had no idea; however it was a small part of him that she loved, and found herself using it from time-to-time, as if she'd absorbed his colloquialisms through her skin, having lived for so long under the same roof together. It was as if she'd assimilated parts of him into her very being through a process of osmosis, or, maybe *Lovemosis.*

Just a little bump, it's a party after all, right?

Opening the baggie, she tapped the white powder onto the marbled surface.

Well, maybe just a little bit more.

Until there was a large mound of powder.

A snow drift.

Reaching over to the fridge, she removed a business card from under a magnet, and chopped the white powder up, dividing her trove into four long lines. Removing a yellow, plastic straw and a pair of scissors from the drawer, she snipped a two-inch piece of tube free and discarded the other piece.

Eeny, meeny, miny, moe.

Her finger pointed at the fourth line.

Lifting the mask, she bared her face and dipped her head over the white line.

Placing the straw in her nostril, Cynthia inhaled, worked her way up the line. The cocaine bubbled in her nose, tickled the back of her throat until, finishing the line, she pinched her septum with her free hand and flipped her head back.

"Woooheee…that there…is the shit!"

After shaking her head, arms, and hands, she returned for the second line.

Eney, meeny, miny, moe'd again.

She selected the first line and, without faltering, snaffled it up the same nostril. She'd missed a bit and instead of sniffing it up, she wet a finger, placed it to the remnant of the chalky powder, and smeared it on her gums before sucking the digit clean, not wanting to waste any of the good stuff.

Another song began to play. A soul, bluesy number.

'Need Your Love So Bad' which was, in her opinion, and Daniel's too, a very underrated Fleetwood Mac anthem. It was more than just a song to them both.

Returning to the lines and her Eney, meeny, miny, moeing the shit out of them, the second line – *of the original four* – disappeared as quickly as the first and fourth up her other nostril. She sniffed deeply of what had originally been the third line, but who was counting? Cynthia certainly wasn't. And once she'd inhaled all of the powder, she gripped the bridge of her nose, squeezed it tight, and there was a click followed by a sharp pain and a sudden warmth, like the onset of a nosebleed. The pressure building in her nose was insane, yet, instead of stopping, calling it a night, she shuddered with delight, her eyes growing wide as she took in the final line.

"Wooooo!" she exclaimed to no one and everyone.

As the Mac sang about *'needing someone's hand to lead them'*, and *'someone's arms to hold them,'* and *'for those arms to squeeze them tight'*,

Cynthia couldn't help being transported back to the nights of slow dancing to the song with Daniel, in that very room. The times when Daniel's prevailing sickness made it hard for him to stand for long periods of time, and when the medication caused his skin to become sensitive, too sensitive for her to even touch him. They'd spent hours dancing to this song on repeat, slowly turning in circles. Some nights her head was on his chest, other nights his was on hers as she held him up, not wanting the moment to end.

"That's when I need your love so bad," she screamed at the top of her lungs.

Only one line remained and there was no need to *eney, meeny miny, moe*. Cynthia inhaled the last of it and turned her back on the drugs. Resting her rump against the lip of counter, she lowered the mask back over her face and swayed on the spot, arms wrapped around her midriff. She hugged herself tightly, and imagined she was hugging Daniel, or he was hugging her, as something sharp scratched against her arm. Glancing down, she discovered the card she'd used to cut the cocaine was still clutched in her hand, and as she reached over and placed it back on the fridge, her eyes fell on the calendar. Taking the pen from its bit of string, she put a huge red X in the square for today – *as she'd neglected to cross it off* – and counted the remaining squares.

One, two, three…three fucking days… wow.

Three days until their *'date night'* — since their date night? —where nothing would ever be the same again.

"Shit, shit, shitty-shit-shit."

Cynthia turned abruptly from the calendar. There were places she needed to be; things that needed to be done. She'd gotten so carried away with drowning and sniffing her sorrows away that she'd forgotten the very thing that afforded her these expensive luxuries in the first place; her OnlyFans© were waiting for her.

The note on the calendar, on today's date, which she'd just crossed off, detailed that tonight, right now in fact, was her grand farewell show. There'd be no use for the platform after today, what with all the things she had to do.

Plans had already been made on how she would spend the next three vital days, and there were a great many things to be prepared and organised. Then of course, at the end of it all, there would be a *'date night'* to be had, a past to be forgotten, and a future, together, forever, with Daniel to reclaim.

Although this was an end of an era, a severing of the purse strings which had kept her afloat – *both of them afloat* – and comfortable over the past few years, tonight's session especially had been one that Cynthia was looking forward to, because at the end of it she would know what underwear she'd be wearing for their special occasion. Something to drive a man wild. Her OnlyFans© would help her decide.

The words on the calendar were '**Ask Me Anything**', and so Cynthia would frolic around in an assortment of skimpy outfits and underwear, whilst she answered their many banal questions, whilst also asking several of her own in the hopes of narrowing down her choices.

She wasn't deluding herself, though. The *Ask Me Anything* event usually turned into an '**Ask Me *'To Do'* Anything**' event, but for her farewell show, she might just accept a few of those requests – *within reason of course* – because she might as well go out with a bang.

Gripping the banister, she began to climb the stairs, her body swaying not to the music playing in the kitchen – though the Mac was still audible as she made her way upstairs – but rather she swayed with the effects of the cocaine and the whiskey.

Gritting her teeth, she anchored her hand to the banister and began pulling herself up the wooden staircase, smiling the whole way, knowing that after tonight there would be no more appeasing strangers for money, there would be no more OnlyFans©, there would be no more sorrow: Only joy.

After tonight, she would begin the descent into her new – *old* – life; where she would – *if things went her way* – be betrothed for all of time, in sickness and in health, until death do them part – *once more* – to the love of her life.

Whatever the cost…she would pay it and pay it gladly.

Together…forever…as it should have always been.

PART FOUR
BUTTERFLY

CHAPTER 16

ate again, like a whore's period.
 With everything moving steadily along to its culmination, and the additional time she'd put into his transformation and rehabilitation, she couldn't seem to stay on top of her Only Fans© obligations.

How many times can you keep showing up late before they start leaving in droves?

It was a pointless question because after tonight it would be over. Forever.

Staggering into her bedroom, out of breath from the brisk ascent, she powered up her computer. Whilst it loaded, she clicked her playlist and pressed the play icon. Music trickled through her speakers as she picked out a selection of her finest underwear for the stream. As the landing page loaded, Cynthia quickly, albeit rather drunkenly, raided her drawers and cupboards, flinging all kinds of crazy, skimpy underwear onto her bed. This was gearing up to be the farewell party to end all farewell parties.

Arrivederci suckers!

Standing with her hands on her hips at the foot of the bed, she ogled the random selection.

Where…when…why did I buy all these things?

Cynthia had enough bras scattered about her bed to dress a field of cows and their innumerable tits.

Udders. They're called udders, not tits.

Sure… sure…

How about we meet in the middle and call them Udd-its?

No, they're udders…

Or how about, Tit-ers?

The effects of the alcohol and the cocaine were making their effects known and Cynthia was finding herself somewhat hilarious as her eyes roved over the assortment of underwear. Some of the garments were lace, some satin, silk, rubber, or lacquered leather. Others had additional padding, whilst some looked as if they'd been savaged with scissors – *more string vest than bra*. Further items were bejewelled with silver and rhinestones, while a couple more had chains and zips. There were even some that made Cynthia look like a 50's starlet; lots of fabric, and padding, and when she'd wear those ones, they made her breasts look like cones. But not Madonna-esq cones. More Marilyn Monroe in *'Some Like It Hot'* cones.

She didn't need the padding, per se, but if the padding did anything, it helped to accentuate her already curvy body into that hourglass figure that drove men wild. She'd also been known, on occasion, if it was a Fan's birthday; to dress up as Norma Jeane and to sing happy birthday to them. Warbling out the song in that sultry, *come-to-bed* voice that – *apparently* – JFK loved so much.

Her OnlyFans© always ate that shit up, and the money would fly in.

Turning back to the computer, Cynthia pulled the monitor down slightly, adjusting the built-in camera so her punters would get the full view of her skimpies. The view which mattered the most: breasts, legs, and arse. She could be decapitated for all they cared, just as long as they got the *'BLA trinity,'* they'd be happy. And so, Cynthia would oblige.

She quickly typed in her password – TheNoonDayDemon64 – and her username – <HoneyCynth> – and waited patiently for the website to log her in.

Why, when you're in a rush, does it always bloody lag?

When her computer failed to log her in immediately – *the spinning wheel of doom in all its rainbow glory reining on her screen* – she turned back to the bed to make sure she had all she needed for when things kicked off.

Rummaging through the assorted items, she uncovered the naughtier, top shelf items, which had been hidden beneath the first layer of more *acceptable run of the mill* – lingerie that she'd thrown on the bed.

Knickers, thongs, G-strings, stockings, garters, suspenders, and corsets; there was even a pack of edible knickers which she'd bought a few years ago to use with Daniel, but sadly they'd never got around to using them. Wondering if edible underwear had an expiry date, she picked the pack up and turned it over, eyes scanning for a date. It didn't really matter, though. She knew if she was wearing them, regardless of them being out of date or not, Daniel would have chowed down either way. She dropped the packet back onto the bed and took in the mattress' full glory.

The bed looked as if an Anne Summers / Victoria Secrets party had thrown up on it. The only things missing were a few vibrators and a bucket-load of lube.

Now that's what you'd call a party.

There were several matching brassieres and panties which left little to the imagination, like the lacy, black, plunge number, and the Tallulah Open-Chested Bra. There were others, though, which yearned for a little more imagination on behalf of the viewer, the lover, her fans, *her* Daniel; ones that covered over all her modesty, her favourites, in a way that kept the goods hidden from view, reserving her sex for that special someone who she chose to tumble beneath the sheets with, and not just anyone who stole a glance and flung some change.

Some of the bras were strapless, and therefore easy to slip on or off, whilst others had too many straps; some others were corset-like, big straight-jacket type things, and Cynthia had a love / hate relationship with those ones. She hated the way they took an age to get on or off, and she especially disliked how constricting they were, feeling as if something or someone were squeezing the air from her lungs, milking her of oxygen, but she did love – *adored, even* – how the corset gave her cleavage a sculpted-by-the-gods look. One that Dolly Parton would have been proud of.

'A place to park my bike,' was a common refrain she'd hear from her punters on the rare occasions when she'd worn one for their benefit, and every time they said that phrase, the poor, pathetic losers pretended to own it, acting as if they were the person who'd coined it.

Cynthia had heard it plenty of times, though. Daniel even said it once. Jokingly, of course, but when Cynthia squeezed his balls in her hand and told him never to use it again, he took the request as seriously as he took his cancer diagnosis.

Appearances – like customer services – were everything though, and Cynthia would titter and laugh at her customers' *'oh, so brilliant wit.'* She'd tilt her head back and flick her hair as if it was the funniest, sexiest thing she'd ever heard. A compliment to beat all compliments. She'd also ensure to keep eye contact with them throughout the whole flirty business, leaning in closer to the camera, creating an even deeper cavern for them to *'park their bike'* into as she pressed her breasts together by crossing her arms, treating her fans – *all over the world* – as if they were the most important person in the room, scratch that. The most important person in the ~~room~~ chatroom.

Taking in the large assortment, Cynthia swayed from foot to foot. She was drunk, and under the influence of some pretty sweet powder; however, she wasn't swaying from the drink or the drugs. Instead, she'd transcended the tricky moment when the night could go one of two ways, down the shitter, or into the stars. The music which filled her room from the speaker on her phone: Fleetwood Mac's, Rhiannon (*live at the Fabulous Forum, Inglewood, CA, 08/29/77*), had her ascending into an orbit all her own.

Turning slightly, she glanced back at the computer.

It had finally logged her in.

Even while traversing some other astral plane, Cynthia could clearly see the display. Eighty-seven people were waiting in the queue to join her stream.

Pirouetting back to the bed, Cynthia's head swam for a moment, and she pinched the bridge of her nose until her discombobulation subsided. Then, she stared down at all the possibilities on her bed, her eyes lingering upon a lacy, mint-green number.

It was one of Daniel's favourites.

Slipping her negligee from her shoulders, Cynthia let it fall to the groundlike a snake shedding its skin. Stepping gingerly out of the discarded layer, she stepped instead into the mint-green, French knickers and slid them up her long, tanned legs; though partway up she noted that she'd need to shave before date night. She still had time for pruning herself before then. And she would. Because she didn't want Daniel seeing her legs like that, rubbing his hands up against them and wondering when he'd started dating a hairy lumberjack. She matched the knickers with an open-chested bra. There wasn't much fabric, and it looked a lot smaller – *a lot more revealing* – than she remembered as she fingered the lacy frill on its lower edge, marvelling at its silky-softness as she held against herself and admired her reflection in the mirror.

That'll do nicely.

The prude in her was satisfied, while the exhibitionist in her was ecstatic.

This was never about porn; this was about art – regardless of what her friends and family had said to her before she cut them out of her life. She reached her hands behind her back, secured the strap in place, and turned to check her look in the computer.

She rearranged her breasts, pulling them here, lifting them there, squishing them in place, ensuring they – *the nipples especially, because apparently on some social media platforms a slipped-nip was still classified as porn and not art* – were housed successfully. She could only see herself from her neck down, but that was fine. That's what she'd be showing off when the time came anyway.

Nobody cares about the face when the body's so smoking hot.

It was Cynthia's voice, yet it also wasn't hers.

The phrasing was off, and the voice sounded deeper in her own head. That's when she realised, she was recalling a past memory, the voice of one of her classroom bullies, Jamie

'*Put a bag on her head and I still would, though*' Howard. She recalled his vile words as if he were in the room with her. '*She's a munter, fugly as hell, but that body, those tits, and don't forget that smoking arse. I'd tap that in a heartbeat.'*

On that day, so long ago, Cynthia had sworn she'd never be spoken to – *or of* – again like that, and she had made it her personal mission to ruin the objectifying sonofabitch's life. He would get his.

And get it he did, on a rainy Tuesday afternoon when they were queuing up for Drama Class. She hadn't *planned* for it to be that day. It was a day that had started like any other, but when Jamie held out a brown paper bag two eyeholes cut in it, and offered it to her? Well, Cynthia had no other choice but to act.

'Hey, Cynth, you wanna stick this on your head? That way I might just let you sit on my dick.'

She didn't give him and his goons (*Michael, Bradley or Billy*) a chance to snigger at the remark. Instead, she marched directly over to him and produced a mightily, well-placed, knee into Jamie's groin. The impact lifted him off the ground and caused the ugly, acne-riddled, weasel-faced-prick to crumble to the ground at the feet of his impish tribe of reprobates. She had stood above his quivering, eye-watering body as he struggled for breath and her classmates cheered behind her.

The knee solved all her problems. After that day, Jamie had never taunted her again. It wasn't enough to stop his bullying ways for good, though. After he'd been discharged from the Urology Department of Bromley Hospital, where he'd been admitted with a severe case of acute testicular trauma, he proceeded to move on to other, weaker, prey.

Someone – *Cynthia* – in his four week-long absence had spread a rumour that he'd lost a testicle because of their little altercation, even though she'd found out through her mother – *who knew someone who had their hair cut by Jamie's mother* – that all that had happened was her knee had split the membranous bag around one of his testicles, it didn't matter. Two balls or one, his new moniker stuck: *One-Ball-Jamie*.

That's what the girls at school called him every time he tried to act as if he were THE BIG I AM. And within no time at all, the bully became the bullied, and although she was an empath, she didn't feel an ounce of pity for him, or shame about what she'd put into motion.

She'd taught him a valuable lesson on that day with her swift knee to his groin: **Whatever you do in life, don't be a dick.**

She'd only ever felt a power like that one other time in her life, in Norman Park, when she abducted Doctor Hasan. Another beast laid low.

Checking out her curves once more, she absently wished she'd brought another drink, because she could have gone for another treble around about now. Bending over slightly, she checked her arse in the mirror, to see what her fans would be seeing.

"Nice ass," she uttered, and she did look great, even if she did say so herself.

There was a ding from the computer, and she turned to face it. The waiting room had reached its maximum number of viewers and there was a flashing message on the screen.

That's odd?

And it was, because Cynthia could have sworn she'd disabled waiting room messages. But it appeared one of the horde couldn't wait patiently like the others. She couldn't blame them, though. She'd left them waiting for around forty-five minutes.

"Dogs in heat, ready to hump everything in sight," she mumbled as she leaned in and clicked on the comment, expanding it on her screen.

JackInYrBox <*When does this show get on the road? Limp dick immigrant.*>

What? her face screwed up in confusion.

The bell chimed again, another message.

JackInYrBox <**Limp dick imminent* >

Cynthia chuckled at <JackInYrBox>'s faux pas as she swayed to the ethereal *'Rhiannon'* with its killer beat and haunting lyrics and she tried to focus on the screen, her head still swimming with the booze and drugs. It took a considerable amount of concentration to move the mouse over to the admit all button, the tiny little square in the upper-right corner; it was as if the tiny arrow weighed a thousand pounds, but eventually the arrow hovered over the green icon.

"And wouldn't you love to love her." She crooned, the song mirrored her life – *then* and *now* – perfectly, knowing that, yes indeed, her fans would *love to love her,* and a special someone in the basement would *love to love her* too.

Double checking the view on the camera, a tight, mid-shot revealed the bra and her French-knickers. Her head remained out of shot, and that was good. She didn't want to put them off their stride once they saw the deadness, the coldness, the *this-is-just-a-job* in her eyes for her last performance – she wanted to go out on top.

She wanted to be remembered as a legend.

She wondered, fleetingly, if Jamie was tuned in to her stream, hiding behind a cartoon avatar and some smart-arse name that a spotty, horny, teenager could have come up with.

The mouse still hovered as she gave considerable thought to just shutting it down, regardless of the consequences; turning the stream off and leaving her *would be* audience blue-balled, and blue lipped.

How'd you like those apples?

Head nodding, she could do it if she wanted.

They'd get over it soon enough.

A shake of the head as she questioned her possible actions and repercussions.

No. That's not right. They too, deserve a happy ending, don't they?

And, if *they* deserved one, then so did Cynthia.

They've kept you fed and watered and clothed and housed, Cynthia reasoned. *They've been there for you in your darkest moments. Not that they knew it, but they were there for you when you felt alone; that's more than can be said for your so-called friends and family. When was the last time they checked in? When was the last time they thought of you, do you think?*

She shrugged like a petulant child and struggled to think of an answer to the questions her mind fired at her. She assumed that the last time she spoke to her family and friends was around the time she went bat-shit crazy and told them not to bother her, that she was grieving, and didn't need them haranguing her; that they should stop calling because each time she picked up the phone to their wittering all it did was tear the scab right off her healing wounds.

It's the least you should do.

One last hurrah.

You don't even have to tell them it's the end. Leave them wanting, go out on top, become infamous!

Just as she was about to click *admit all*, the music changed and Fleetwood Mac's, *'Second Hand News'* sprung to life through her speaker.

Although it was an upbeat track, there was a slice of dread attached to it too. It made her wonder that if she did cancel the stream, deleted her account, left them all with their paid perks unfulfilled, there'd be an awful lot of second-hand news flying about, and the sudden devolvement of her platform would surely draw attention. Attention wasn't something she craved right now, which was rather ironic given that was how she'd made her ivory tower.

Stop being stupid, they don't know anything about you?

They've no idea where you live, or what you're up to, why would they even care?

What if someone on here does know me?

If they decided to pay me a visit, to check up on me?

And what if they told the police I'd swindled them out of their money?

If they raised concerns about my mental wellbeing?

Surely the police would act on that, just to perform a wellness check or something?

Second-hand news is how rumours are started.

A chuckle escaped her lips at the word *Rumours*.

"What a song, Mac at their finest."

The last thing she needed, was for some busybody, keyboard warrior, drawing attention to her, or finding her location through her IP address, handing it off to the police or some online-true-crime-nut who'd come looking for her because she'd swindled all these pathetic perverts out of their money. It was more than possible, hell, even *Netflix*™ had a show about someone killing a cat which caused the whole keyboard-wielding, true-crime-loving, loner-brigade-world to come looking for the perpetrator.

That was a good documentary to be fair.

They'd watched it to pass the time during Daniel's recovery from his chemo appointments:*'Don't Fuck with Cats'*

Cynthia didn't want a starring role in the follow-up series:*'Don't Fuck With <HoneyCynth>'* and so, with a heavy heart she relented.

Tonight's session would be a quick one; and she'd keep the details of it being the last show hidden from her ardent, loyal followers, they'd only ask questions, and when people asked questions that's when things went tits up. She'll give her fans what they wanted, what they'd paid for, and what she'd advertised: *'Ask Me Anything'*.

After that, she'd be gone, she'd clock out and they'd be none-the-wiser.

Later tonight, she'd be free to get on with what needed to be done, and even in her drunken, drugged-up state, she knew there was a shit-tonne of things that still needing to be done to make *'Date Night'* a success.

Thinking about all the chores that needed doing caused her to huff dejectedly because there were so many things that still needed finalising and she couldn't grow apathetic at this stage, she was coming in to land, the runway of their future stretching out before them.

Finally, she'd convinced herself that no one would come looking for her – *and even if they did, which she highly doubted* – it would be too late for them...too late for her...and definitely too late for Daniel. The metamorphosis, *hers* and *his*, would finally be complete.

Cynthia clicked admit and the chat box on her screen filled up instantly and the shit-talking tumbled relentlessly down her screen.

.

Randy4U < *Well at least I have somewhere to park my bike ;)* >

Never heard that before, you dim-witted, prick.

JoytotheWorld < Jesus loves you – John 3:16 >
RampantRover69 < Now that's a sight for saw eyes…and hands (aubergine and squirting water emoji) >
FlirtyBerty < Nice jugs… (emoji of two beer glasses) >
LiverpoolLambert < JUGG-osaurus… (dinosaur emoji and two beer glasses clinking) >
BlackBeauty < Got milk?!? >
SevenInchKing < Christmas must've cum early, could hang my balls on those nips. >
HussyforLusty < You look beautiful. >
Gspotter7656 < Stunning… worth the wait >
RoastedBob < When does this show get going? >
KillTheRich < Skank. >
KillTheRich < Whore. >
KillTheRich < WHY DON'T YOU KILL YOURSELF YOU DUMB, UGLY, BITCH. >

GROUP NOTIFICATION: USER <KillTheRich> WAS EJECTED FROM THE CHAT

SomethingBlue < What a jerk. >
FlirtyBerty < I could do with a jerk. *(winking emoji face)* >
OnlyTheCumStainsRemain < Why can't we see you? Where's that beautiful face hiding? >
OggOnTheBog < There's a pair of tits and you want to see her face? >
OnlyTheCumStainsRemain < Need something to aim at…lol… >
OggOnTheBog < Those titties aren't target enough for you? >
OnlyTheCumStainsRemain < Nope, need a challenge. >
SomethingBlue < Limp dick. >

RazorBackRhyno < So, when does the ask me anything start? >

After she scrolled her way to the bottom of the messages, she began typing her own message to the group.

HoneyCynth < ASK AWAY… but first, what do you think? >

She'd intentionally turned off her microphone, wanting to immerse herself fully in a world of Fleetwood Mac, it was a party after all. As she watched the screen, emoji's began to rain in the chat room; thumbs up, hearts, faces with tears, smiling faces, there was even an aubergine or two, a peach three or four, a fist followed by a squirting water emoji seemed to be a fan favourite. It all appeared to Cynthia as if it were a modern-day equivalent to hieroglyphics, as her baying crowed told her what they thought of her outfit without using words.

But do they love them?

Would Daniel love them?

Or is it too much, too slutty? Not enough girl next door, he did love that about me…

KillerInBed < What other's you got? >
HoneyCynth < Is that a question? >
KillerInBed < What do you think? Do you have any crotchless ones? >

Whilst wagging a finger at the camera, she typed a response with the other hand.

HoneyCynth < @KillerInBed I do, but they're not for you, (cheeky wink emoji) would you like to see some others? >

KillerInBed < Some guys get all the luck. Well, if you ain't going crotchless, what else you got? Anything slutty? >

HoneyCynth < I believe I've got a little something that fits the bill. Would you like me to wear it for you? >

SomethingBlue < We'd ALL like to see it. >
RazorBackRhyno < Suck up. >
FlirtyBerty < I could do with a suck up. >
HoneyCynth < Well, whilst I get changed, why don't you all think about what you want to ask me? >

Turning away, she sashayed her way towards the bed, peered over her shoulder at the camera, smiled to herself as the angle was flattering, the camera tight on her arse and the French knickers accentuating her curves.

Still got it, never lost it.

She gave her bottom a little wiggle, knowing her fans would appreciate, it before bending over the bed in search of her slutty gear. The pings and dings of new deposits into her bank account trilled from the speakers and there was no doubt in her mind that most of those deposits had filthy requests attached to them, of thing *they* wanted *her* to do.

The garments she sifted through on the bed were mainly pastel shades, oranges, greens, blues, purples, and yellows. Daniel had loved those colours on her. He'd mentioned often how they complimented her English-Rose complexion, and how they turned him on something chronic. And so, Cynthia had obliged his craving, bought every shade in the shop; they'd cost a pretty penny, but the expense had been well worth the outlay, given the look of desire and joy on Daniel's face when she stripped down to her underwear each evening.

They'd quickly become her uniform for sexual relations with

Daniel, but if she had to pick *her* favourite pair? The underwear that made her feel sexy and slutty in equal measure? It would be the deep red (*blood-red*), open-chested, number with the matching lacy thong. They were the only pair of underwear which survived the migration from her single life into her steady relationship with Daniel. They were a rare artefact from her previous life, before she'd found true love and she'd reserved this particular pair for special occasions – *usually a birthday or an anniversary* – when they'd roleplay Cynthia being a hooker and Daniel being a naïve, cuckolded punter.

They did, indeed, make her look like a slut. And she'd been okay with that, because sometimes she wanted to be a slut. A slut for Daniel, but a slut nevertheless. She picked up the bra, her fingers playing with the lacy, delicate fringe as she kept her back to the camera and unclipped the bra she was currently wearing. As she did, there was a steady chiming from the computer's speaker, a litany of cash donations and – she assumed – comments tumbling onto the screen which annoyed her slightly, because their chorus was drowning out Fleetwood Mac's, 'Over My Head'.

I'm in over my head, she thought as she replaced the first bra with its slutty sister before bending over the bed – *a movement which brought another round of chiming* – as she reached for the red thong.

"Just you wait, the best is yet to come…" she whispered, not to the morons on her screen, but to the body waiting patiently in the basement.

Peeling off her existing underwear, still with her back to the camera, Cynthia peered over her shoulder demurely. It didn't matter that her head was out of shot. The subtle twist of her waist and spine detailed to those watching that she was watching too. Watching them, watching her.

More deposits rang out, followed quickly by a flurry of messages *ding, ding, dinging* on her screen. She knew it was because she'd never flashed as much flesh on her stream as she was tonight, and it appeared her fans had become ravenous for it over the months and years of their pent up unfulfillment finally being answered and unleashed.

Stepping into the thong, she slid it up her long, athletic legs, once more remarking to herself that she'd need to shave before their special night, just in case things went *that* way, and secretly Cynthia hoped they might. She didn't just want the lust of the man in the hospital bed in her basement, she wanted the love of the man she'd brought back from the deepest and furthest echelons of the grave – lust was a moment, love was, and forever would be, eternal.

'I can't help but feel I'm wasting all my time.'

The Mac continued to serenade as Cynthia swivelled to face her waiting, online congregation, sauntering over to the monitor she bent forwards and began typing.

HoneyCynth < *What do you make of this one?* >

She stood back from the screen, danced to the song, writhed her hips to its guitar, and stroked hands over her curves as her whole body thrummed to the melody and hearts exploded all over their screens at her performance. But she wanted more. Craved more. Desired more. Wanted exploding aubergines, and fists, and squirting emoji's, because she knew if she could seduce these hardened porn veterans, then Daniel would be a breeze.

He's only human after all. And, of course, the weaker of the two species.

She wanted Daniel to want her more than he'd ever wanted her in his first life, before everything had changed. She wanted him to feel that he couldn't exist without her, so he would know what it had been like for her when he left her all alone; she needed to be the glass of water a man dying of thirst craved, and in doing so, she would be his salvation.

Having given her fans so much over the years, the least they could do, during their final moments together, was to give her the damned answer she craved: what lingerie should she wear.

HoneyCynth < *I've got some that look good with suspenders and stockings. Would you like to see those, too?* >

No sooner had she asked the question than she was swamped with replies.

Emoji's of aubergines and fists and squirting water rained, and reigned, over her screen. Tottering like an excited child from foot to foot, excited by the buzz, she made her way swiftly to the bed, and as she scampered across the room, her foot became entangled in her discarded negligee, and she stumbled and could do nothing to stop the back of her head cracking on the floorboards.

The lights went out for a moment.

Not the lights in the room, but the ones in Cynthia's head.

It felt like she'd been out for ages by the time she eventually came to.

Her neck ached and, after massaging it, she rolled over onto all fours and crawled the short distance to her bed, where she pulled herself up like an octogenarian who'd taken a tumble getting out of the shower. She eventually collapsed onto the edge of the mattress, letting out a little huff at the stiffness she felt in her back and neck as what felt like a migraine took root behind her eyes.

When will you learn that mixing your drinks and your drugs never ends well.

Her head hung low, chin to chest as she rubbed the base of her neck before her hand ventured higher and she discovered the rather large egg which had formed from where she'd connected with the floor. She pulled her hand back and winced in pain before looking at her fingers, relieved there was no blood she let out a sigh.

Well, that's a positive.

It was at that moment, as she sat on the edge of her bed, with a raging headache, in her underwear, in the silence of her room – *her playlist having come to an end* – that she remembered what she was doing before she fell.

The computer.

The stream.
The camera.
All of them were still on.
And she heard *it*.
A ding, followed by another ding.
Soon it was all she could hear.
DING...DING...DING...DING...DING...DING...DING...DING...DING...DING...DING...DING...DING...

Lifting her head, Cynthia turned her aching neck towards the monitor.

Furry4Life < *Well, I wasn't expecting that...this is some kinky shit.* >
KillerInBed < *Damn straight, this is Eyes Wide Shut stuff.* >
FlirtyBerty < *Why are you wearing a mask?* >

Her focus shifted from the messages to the largest box on the screen which held the image of her, collapsed on her bed.
SHIT...SHIT...SHIT...SHIT...SHIT...SHIT...SHIT...SHIT...SHITTYSHITSHIT...
The first thought in Cynthia's head was:
How could they still be watching?
Quickly followed by:
Surely, they must have been worried for my welfare?
She rose from her bed and hurriedly scoured through the messages in the chat, discovering, thankfully, that she hadn't passed out for the hours that she'd assumed. It had only been mere minutes. Seconds, probably.
So, if I was only out for a moment, then why do I feel so rough?
She didn't bother trying to decipher that mystery because her next thought had her running towards the computer.
I'M WEARING THE FUCKING MASK!
As she launched herself at the keyboard, and her migraine surged

with the sudden movement, flushing her body with a debilitating power, causing her to almost stumble again. She made it though, clung to the table with all the strength she had left in her body. Her fingers fumbled for the mouse to end the stream, her barn owl face large on the screen as she hovered over it, as if it were a nature documentary and someone had snuck a camera into its nest to observe animals in their natural habitat – an ethologist.

How could you have been so stupid?

FlirtyBerty < *I still would though...Bird woman of the Internet...* >

How could you not know you've been wearing the mask all this time?

RazorBackRhyno < *Mask, bag, it doesn't matter, any hole's a goal... am I right?* >

You've screwed it all up. They know now, everyone will know, you really screwed the pooch on this one you bloody idiot!

KillerInBed < *U ain't wrong.* >

Why? How could you be so dumb?

SomethingBlue < *I kinda like it, its naughty... you branching out into uncharted territory?* >

What the hell's got into you?

       FlirtyBerty < *SluttyOwlWhores for the win!* >

The mouse hovered over the *disconnect live stream* button as Cynthia glanced once more at the screen. Her vision grew cloudy, and tears welled in her eyes before bursting their banks. She stayed that way for some time, just staring at the screen, her huge owl eyes reflecting the monitor and the never-ending comments back from her viewers – in a wormhole of a reflection that went on and on into infinity.

 None of her sinful congregation could see her tears. They were a private penance.

 As she wept behind her mask, Cynthia realised two things, above all others.

 She was alone; surrounded by an online community, but utterly alone.

 And secondly, she realised as she finally clicked the button to end the stream – *for now and all time* – that she was still none the wiser about what she'd wear for Daniel.

 After closing the laptop screen, Cynthia stood on shaking, trembling legs and shuffled over to her bed. She didn't pull the covers back, instead crawling onto her sheets and, collapsing onto the various pieces of underwear, she began to tend her nest. Cynthia opted to keep the mask on, to hide her shame, her stupidity, and her disgrace, she told herself. But the real reason, which she wouldn't, no, couldn't admit to herself, was that it had become a part of her now.

 Always and forever.

 "Once something is on the internet, it's on there forever," her family had told her, right before she cut them out of her life.

 How could you let them see you like that?
 You're stupid, do you know that?

You might have just ruined everything you've worked so hard to accomplish.

Are you happy with yourself?

You're a stupid whore.

A dumb bitch.

Finally, she closed her eyes behind the mask, hoping to stop her tears from flowing. But, if anything, the darkness made everything that much worse.

Cynthia dragged the sheets closer, pulled her legs into her chest, hugged them as tight as she would a lover whilst she rocked and cried the ache out of her heart in the middle of the nest she'd made for herself.

As sleep began to claim her addled mind, a smile creased her face as her tears continued to trickle, because however bad she felt now, she hoped that in the coming days she'd have everything she ever wanted.

Joy will come in the morning.

She was sure of it.

CHAPTER 17

Dead man walking…dead man walking…DEAD MAN WALKING!

Over and over, the words tumbled into her mind as scratched into a record, the needle of her thoughts jumping and skipping back in a never-ending refrain.

Dead man walking…dead man walking…DEAD MAN WALKING!

The lungs of her mind continued to scream each word as Daniel shuffled out from behind the dressing screen she'd erected in the basement, mainly to protect Daniel's modesty; he'd become increasingly shy over the last few days, ever since his beating with the soap for the stolen kiss.

However, the real reason Cynthia had put the screen up was that she wanted to be surprised when he finally emerged, all dressed to the nines. She wanted her heart to leap at the sight of her beloved, as it would have done when he'd walked into the restaurant all those many moons ago. She wanted that buzz, the quickening of the heart, butterflies in her stomach, surprise, shock and lust all at once.

However, her heart didn't leap as she imagined. It only fluttered – *like a dying bird's wings* – before it succumbed, surrendered, and collapsed in on itself like a dying star.

It'll be different on the actual night.
There will be butterflies in your tummy too, I imagine.
This is just a dress rehearsal. Who gets excited about those?

Daniel hobbled further out from behind the screen, stepping fully into the harsh glare of the strip lights and the warm orange glow from the ever-present candles on the table. He wobbled, like a toddler learning to walk, before placing a hand on the foot of the hospital bed, desperately attempting to keep himself upright, momentarily stopping gravity's pull on his wasted body; although for how long he could keep this up, and remain erect, had yet to be determined in his weakened state.

His body seemed to thrum from the exertion, but he soldiered on regardless, standing before her as if he were a rare specimen waiting to be discovered, picked up, harvested; Cynthia with a silver pin to be thrust through his chest, where it would trap him to a fabric cushion for all time, imprisoned not in the basement, but rather under a pane of glass for people's entertainment, for them to stare at what he had become.

To witness his metamorphosis.

Lifting his head, Daniel's doe eyes searched her out, and she observed a weak smile creasing the parchment-like skin around his mouth. Cynthia returned the smile, but there was no way Daniel could tell. The owl-woman's mask, as always, remained emotionless, stoic in her appraisal of him.

Although he was the weakest he'd ever been, Daniel was stronger in so many other ways. He was a survivor, and that gave him the strength to bare her avian stare, to rise above the humiliation, the beatings, the uncertainty of his future, all of it.

Instead of crumbling before her, Daniel fanned a hand towards the ground, bowing ever so slightly, as if he were a court jester, here for Cynthia's amusement, and her amusement alone.

'*What do you think?*' The action seemed to request.

Tilting her head, Cynthia silently observed the specimen before her. She took in his scrawny, withered, malnourished body. Although she could see his neck and head – *gaunt and hollowed out, skin thin and pulled tight against the internal scaffolding of his face* – the rest of his withered form was thankfully hidden within the baggy fabric of his clothes.

The blazer jutted out in all the wrong places, his bony shoulders appearing beneath it as if someone had left a coat hanger in there. The trousers swamped his stick legs too, and around his non-existent waist, he'd rolled the band down several times, which caused the length of the trousers to shorten, exposing the socks he was wearing.

Hey, Daniel, Michael Jackson called, he wants his trousers back!

A muted giggle escaped her mouth.

I'll see if I can fashion a belt out of something; it'll bring all of this together nicely.

Daniel was drowning in all that loose fabric, but he'd been drowning in it all those moons ago too, as the weight fell off him with each passing day, so it didn't cause too much offense or spoil the look which Cynthia was desperately trying to hone.

Lifting a hand in the air, she circled her finger, and Daniel turned around slowly, giving her the opportunity to view him from all angles. And angles there were. The way he shuffled, staggered, and corrected himself, she could tell that he desperately wanted to please her. However, whichever angle he offered to Cynthia only revealed the truly, sickly, specimen he had become, and which she had created. She smiled at the fabulous job she'd done in crafting Daniel's likeness out of that mound of flesh she'd abducted all those months ago.

The twirl was an achingly slow spectacle, and as Daniel continued his spinning before her, she couldn't help but hum the funeral march, softly to herself, her rouged lips behind the mask muttering each low, bass-like note.

"DUM…DUM…DUM…DUM…DA…DA…DA…DA…DA…DUM"

The feathered mask acted as somewhat of a filter, softening her hum to an almost inaudible level, of which Cynthia was grateful. She didn't want Daniel to think her cruel. Not now. Not when things were so close to completion. She could see he was really trying, and the last thing she wanted to do was to embarrass him, and so Cynthia let him spin at his own pace, to show all of what he'd become to her.

There really wasn't anything for him – *the man who once was* – to be embarrassed about because, if Cynthia was being honest with herself, he was proving to be somewhat of a natural at transforming. He was mimicking Daniel's personality perfectly, as this act, this show of character – *his acting the clown* – was exactly the type of thing Daniel would have done, finding the funny side of things in a terminal situation.

Uncanny, it's as if he's Daniel.

Because he is Daniel, her mind replied instantly.

Dead man walking…Dead man walking…I got a dead man walking over here…

Shut up, he'll hear you.

Cynthia shut the voice in her head down. She needed to focus, which was proving increasingly harder to do with *'dead man walking'* and the funeral march going around and around in her head. After a few more pivots, and as a bout of dizziness rocked him, Daniel finally perched his frail body on the end of the bed, to wait for what came next: his appraisal.

Her head twitched to the side, a floorboard creaking upstairs pulling her attention away from the moment.

Was that? Is that? Are they coming for me?

Cynthia paused, waited for the sound again but nothing came, and so she beckoned the skeletal waif over to her with a curled finger, and Daniel followed, slowly getting to his feet again, then shuffling towards her with all the speed of an lobotomised inmate of a mental institute, his feet *shuck-shucking* across the floor as he was too tired to lift the worn leather shoes; shoes which had once housed Daniel's dead feet, and the sound grew as he drew closer. It sounded like a shovel being forced into the ground, of someone digging a fresh grave.

Dead man walk–

-SHUT UP!

As he approached the table and the candlelight – *a creature from a Boris Karloff film* – Cynthia noticed how the flickering flames gave his skin a vibrancy, a vitality which had been sorely missing over the intervening months since his captivity, as the many months had stacked up into one hell of a long year.

This will work…it's going to work…it has worked…

Is that? No. It can't be...but it might be...was someone knocking at the door?

The police? A nosey neighbour?

"May I?"

The suddenness of his request pulled Cynthia back to the present, shunting her out of her day dreaming/night dreaming/troubling/whatever-the-hell-time-it-was-in-the-real-world-dreaming of how their *date night* would transpire.

Instead of uttering a reply, she placed a foot to the seat of the chair opposite her and pushed it away from the table in an invitation for Daniel to sit, a broad smile spread across her features behind her mask. She was overjoyed. The bag of bones before her didn't just sit down at the table with her; *he'd asked if he may*. And that was what counted; what proved to Cynthia that it was indeed Daniel standing there and not that interloper and permanent pest, Hasan.

Daniel's parents had religiously instilled in him the need for good manners, and in doing so – he explained their reasoning – it meant that no one would ever have to tell him to mind them.

It had been his politeness that had won Cynthia over, even before she knew she needed winning. He'd approached her table in the pub, after he'd been knocked down by some drunken fool – *a good six years ago now, but the memory was as fresh today as it was then* – and said: 'Would you mind awfully if I borrowed the end of your table? I won't be a bother, and I promise I'll give it back when I'm done. Just need somewhere to lick my wounds.'

Cynthia had consented to that polite little request and spent what felt like most of the evening chatting to this roguish man with a freshly broken nose; and she'd ended up consenting to a lot more by the time he'd left her house in the early hours of the following morning.

'May I?'

It was such a minute detail, yet it was a detail which galvanised Cynthia's hope, made it swell and bubble over within her like water over a brook. Things – *even things out of her control, like Daniel's mannerisms, the small tics that made him,* him – were progressing wonderfully well.

Pat yourself on the back, you've only gone and done it.

As she continued to observe Daniel in the silence of the basement, he collapsed into the proffered chair opposite her. The strain and exertion from the short walk – *dressing screen, to bed, and now chair* – clearly showing on his face as Daniel ground his teeth and wiped sweat from his brow before hooking a finger into his shirt and pulling at the starched shirt collar which was plainly rough against his skin.

Using his trembling hands, he lifted his leg into position, crossing it over his other leg at the knee. It was something Daniel would have done, and again, Cynthia swelled with pride at the creation which sat before her as a quivering hand reached out towards the glass of water on the table.

When Daniel eventually picked up the glass, the water inside rippled with the tremor, as if it were the scene out of *Jurassic Park*, where the boy and girl were stranded in the car with the T-Rex approaching.

Teeth clacked against glass as Daniel brought the water to his mouth, his hands quivering with the strength it took to hold the drink to his lips. It was as if the glass were a dumbbell, too heavy for him to manoeuvre in his wasted state. Conscious of the noise he was making, he quickly brought his other hand up to steady it, to help lessen the burden that hydration had become, until soon the palsy in his hands and the sound of his teeth clinking on the glass subsided.

The silence was filled with four greedy swallows. Cynthia counted each one, noting his Adams Apple bulging in Daniel's non-existent neck with each swallow as if it were a flesh-covered shuttle zipping up and down a loom.

"Thirsty?"

"Pardon me?" Daniel uttered back, lowering the glass to the safety of his lap.

"Thirsty?" She repeated, an octave louder, wondering if the feathered mask had softened her initial words, as it had her humming of the funeral march.

"Oh, yes. It's thirsty work looking this…this…"

He paused.

"Ravishing."

He chuckled at his remark.

Cynthia stifled her own amusement, not wanting him to feel that she was on his side just yet. There was still one final test for him to pass, and Cynthia still needed to be a bitch if, and when, the moment suited her. It was probably the biggest test to date, not due to its size, or the taxing nature of it, or for that matter the severity of her wrath should he get it wrong. But it would be the biggest test to date due to the time constraints imposed with their *date night* lurking just around the corner.

If Daniel failed, then tomorrow – *date night* – would have to be postponed. And if it was, then Cynthia wasn't sure she'd have the strength or the courage to keep him around for another year.

That's how you got caught. And how she'd ended her OnlyFans last night, she could feel that net tightening around her by every moment she'd be forced to keep him any longer than she needed.

No. She wouldn't wait another year to do the right thing, and Daniel, in his weakened state, probably wouldn't last another month of captivity, let alone another year of it. So, if it came to that, it would be better off, for all intended parties, if she just put him out of his miserable existence, sooner rather than later. Although it would pain her to do so, she couldn't allow him to suffer through another year of recreation.I It'd be downright cruel. She would instead choose the high road, show Hasan a kindness he'd not afforded her or Daniel. She wasn't a monster. Although, when her deeds saw the light of day – *as they would, there was no doubting that* – she assumed *monster* would be the first word on many a lip.

No. If he failed this test, then Hasan would be like a racehorse that had broken its leg. She'd shoot it. show it mercy.

They shoot horses, don't they?

Euthanasia was a kindness Cynthia *could* offer because what else did she have, if she didn't have Daniel?

"Sorry. I overstepped again. How uncouth of me to compliment myself. It's so crass, so vulgar, I'm so very, very, sor–"

Cynthia raised her open palm and Daniel stopped talking instantly.

Cynthia noted the slightest of flinches in his face from the swift action, and his eyes narrowed in fear of a reprimand.

"Please," Cynthia enthused into the room. "You've nothing to be sorry for. It was funny. It was your sense of humour that first attracted me to you."

"I believe you've said that a few times over the years."

Good save, Daniel. Because I never told you that. Well, at least, not to the you who's sitting before me I haven't. I never got around to implanting that particular memory, but, your response was perfection, a covering-all-bases reply.

By jove, I think we've cracked it!

Cracked him, more like.

"I have."

She played along with the deception.

"Let me just say, you look wonderful this evening, very dapper…"

"In these old things?" Daniel released one hand from the glass and waved away his comment as if his words hung in a fog around his face. Her eyes went back to the glass, worried he'd drop it, but he quickly replaced his hand and secured the precarious breakable.

Her gaze roved back up his body, unable to stop her mind from recalling where his clothes had come from. Not the shop, or the brand, but rather the fact that they'd come from the hospital, all wrapped up in a little plastic ziplocked bag. His name written in capitals on its side in Sharpie. They were Daniel's *Death Clothes*, the final things to have touched his skin before he died.

Why couldn't it have been me?

Cynthia's eyes climbed higher.

Trousers…

Shirt…

Blazer…

Tie…

Shirt collar…

Dull penny eyes stared back at her from Daniel's pallid face, waiting for a response. All she could see in that moment was how the light shone off the sharpness of his cheekbones, his hollowed-out eye sockets, the largeness of his teeth in his shrunken, puckered mouth; the downy hair which had spread across his thin cheeks as if he were anorexic and the dips in his skull near his temples revealed the intricate shape of his skull.

DEAD MAN WALKING…DEAD MAN WALKING…DEAD MAN WALKING…

"SHUT UP!"

Cynthia screamed the words out loud this time, and at them, Daniel flinched, spilt some of the water in his lap, and the spillage spread near his crotch and ran down his trouser leg. If she hadn't seen it happen, Cynthia would have assumed he'd pissed himself at her outburst, which wasn't uncommon. He'd done it before.

"Sorry, I…" Daniel offered in a frightened voice.

"I wasn't talking to you."

A dismissive wave of her hand.

Daniel strained his neck and looked around the room, and Cynthia presumed he was wondering if it wasn't him who she was speaking to, but maybe instead, someone who lurked in the shadows. Leaning forward, she placed her elbow on the table, cupped a hand against her masked chin, and leaned into it. Her owl face stared ahead at Daniel, and she imagines she looks somewhat like Auguste Rodin's 'The Thinker'.

"Looks like you've spilled your water, you…mucky pup."

Reaching out his quivering arms, the glass held in both hands, Daniel placed the mostly empty drinkware on the table before glancing down at his wet trousers.

"Yes, I seem to have spoiled myself…"

He said it with a smile which didn't reach his eyes.

He's worried you're going to hurt him again.

Nonsense.

"It's okay. Accidents happen, and it'll dry by tomorrow. -*Yesterday? The red circles from the calendar upstairs can't decide*- It's not like it was red wine or oil, not that you'd be drinking oil, I'm not that cruel, but you catch my meaning, I suppose?"

"Yep, caught."

He mimed catching something in his hand.

Cynthia continued to observe him, and watched on as his eyes darted from her to the table, then to the shoe box at the table's centre. She wondered why his eyes looked so sad, so scared, so on edge?

He's wondering what you've got in the box?

WHAT'S IN THE BOX?
Seven. Great film.

As Cynthia sat straighter in her chair, the legs screeched on the floor as it slid back slightly.

Daniel's gaze immediately returned to her, and he placed his hands on his crossed knee, his body tensing as he prepared himself for another beating. When the expected beating failed to materialise, he relaxed slightly, shoulders slumping back down from their tensed position near his chin. He began to breathe slowly again as his hands busied themselves with an attempt to wipe the water from his trousers, a fruitless exercise, but Cynthia assumed his needless fussing with his trousers was to take his mind off what was soon to emerge from the box.

"We've got one last thing to do before tomorrow. A little game, as it were…" she said as she pulled the box to her. She'd wanted to say *test*, but she'd tested him so much over his captivity and his metamorphosis that it felt cruel to say the words again, knowing he still might fall at the final hurdle.

"Oooo…I do like games, don't I…"

Cynthia paused, turned her owl face back at him.

Is he unsure? Does he not know?

The words hung in the air between them, metastasising. Cynthia couldn't tell if it was a question or a statement. A hand formed a fist and just before she was called into action, Daniel continued.

"…always beat you. You say I've got the luck of the devil."

Her hand relaxed.

Ahhh, good, he does remember.

Cynthia took a deep breath of relief.

"That's right, you've always had a strange knack for winning every game we've played. Even games of chance, it's like the universe is always on your side."

"I'm just lucky I guess, especially if you think how I landed you. Right place, right time, and of course, being devilishly attractive helped me land the woman of my dreams…"

A small chortle escaped her lips, muted once more by the mask, and from the way Daniel reacted, her laugh must have sounded more huff than amusement because it was certainly interpreted as such.

"Sorry, there I go again, complimenting myself. I just don't know what's gotten into me of late, it's very unbecoming of me."

"It's okay," she said, pulling the box closer and lifting the lid. "You do look rather…spiffing, very handsome!" Even in the dim light of the basement and the flickering candlelight, she could see colour flush in Daniel's wan cheeks. He was blushing.

"Well, thank you. I just hope I'm enough."

"You're everything I want you to be and more."

She placed the lid of the shoebox on the table, turned her masked face back to Daniel.

"Right. Are you paying attention?"

He nodded.

"Then we shall begin."

Daniel's slumped form shifted in the seat as he shuffled himself higher, sitting as straight as his bony, hunched body would allow, peering intently at the box as Cynthia parted the pink, crepe paper within. Her hands disappeared into the box, and she rummaged through its contents.

"In here are three boxes. Each one is different. Each one has something hidden within it. You're not allowed to peek or know what those things are until our date night. I'm going to place each one on the table, and from those three, you're to make a choice. You're not allowed to touch the boxes; you can't pick them up and shake them. You can't even remove them from the table until you've made your choice. You're only permitted to look at them. Do you understand the rules of the game?"

"Yes." The word seemed lodged in his throat like a fishbone, and once it was out, he devolved into a fit of coughing, Cynthia waited until he was finished before she continued with the spectacle. She removed the first item, holding it in her hands reverently. A ploy, a deception to influence Daniel's decision making, to see if he chose this one because she lingered on it, touched it so fondly. A small deception to see if he chose what she'd implanted in his mind or if he would, in fact, choose with his own heart.

Placing the box on the table, Cynthia ran a manicured nail over the brown leather, tapping the top of it twice before returning to the shoebox again to remove two more boxes. One, another ring box, covered in a red, velvet trim; the other, a long box, with the words Tiffany & Co.® embossed on the green felt. The type of box that would contain a bracelet.

Of the three boxes, only one of them would move them on to the next phase. The others, well, Cynthia didn't have the heart to contemplate that right now, although she would — *and ruthlessly* — if she needed to.

Cynthia into the box again. She withdrew the final pieces which she'd refused to mention before, placing each on the table before Daniel as she studied his face.

A worn, brown leather wallet, a keychain, a signet ring, and a chunky silver ring followed the forespoken three boxes. She kept reaching in, and laid a St. Christopher necklace on the table, the silver pendent winking in the candlelight before she scattered a bunch of loose change to clatter noisily onto the table. Lastly, she placed a pack of chewing gum – *Cherry Delicious* – which was half-used next to the assortment of personal items.

"These you can take now; however the boxes remain on the table."

Cynthia made a shooing gesture with her hand.

"Thank you," Daniel replied before reaching forward to pick up the St. Christopher.

He placed it over his head, the chain and pendant hanging outside of his clothes, it wasn't how Daniel would have worn it, but Cynthia let him off, rationalizing that his shirt and tie were in the way. But if he didn't correct it by tomorrow, then she would.

He pocketed the keys into his left blazer pocket and, once they'd jangled inside, he turned his attention to the rings. Cynthia watched in fascination as Daniel placed each of them on the exact same fingers Daniel would have. Whether this was luck or a happy coincidence, Cynthia had no idea. She was just glad it had happened the way it had. Picking up the change, he placed it into his trouser pocket, and then returned to pick up the chewing gum.

He held it to his nose.

Inhaled.

"Mmmmm... our favourite," he said before sliding the chewing gum into the right pocket of his blazer.

"I'm glad you remember."

"How could I not? I remember when you gave me one after we first met, on the way back to yours, when you said it would help with my beer breath."

This was true, and it made Cynthia smile. Daniel appeared to remember their first meeting fondly.

"Well, let's cut short the trip down memory lane and focus on the task at hand."

Daniel gulped, and she watched on as he turned his eyes to the three boxes.

"You need to pick one of them. Only one, mind you. Take your time and pick the box that only you would have picked."

"This is all sounding a bit like Indiana Jones and the Last Crusade," he uttered before shifting his weight forward slightly, a hand creeping out from the safety of his lap.

Cynthia was about to shout at him, her hands balling instinctively into corrective fists, but Daniel remembered her warning before it was too late and pulled his eager hand back.

"Just one, and remember, no touching."

She wagged a finger at him.

He nodded; however, his gaze never left the three boxes as concentration carved up his face and a deep crease appeared between his brow. He licked his lips before chewing the inside of his cheek.

The same thing Daniel did when he was nervous.

Come on, pick the right one.

Not the right one, but the right *one.*

You can do it!

He rubbed his stubbly chin with one hand as he leant back from the table.

Come on Daniel, I believe in you.

He pondered the choice deeply, *umming* and *ahhing*.

This was the biggest game – *test* – of his life, a game of winners and losers, where the winners won big, but the losers lost *everything*.

Extending his hand, the one with his rings on, he pointed at the Tiffany & Co® box.

"You've made your choice?"

Her heart sank in her chest.

"Yes."

Fingernails bit into the palm of Cynthia's hand as she clenched her hands into fists again in the seat of her lap.

It wasn't supposed to go like this…it wasn't supposed to end this way…

"That one…"

Damnit!

"I wouldn't have picked that one."

His eyes shot up to the owl mask.

"I know you don't *do* bracelets; you hate the way they jangle and get in the way."

Halle-flipping-luiah!

"Correct. Now there were two." Cynthia placed the rejected item back in the shoebox, leaving two ring boxes on the table. Both were pretty much identical, except for their coverings; one lacquered leather, the other smooth velvet. Daniel's eyes flitted back and forth between the remaining two items before he clapped his bony hands together, and the sound made Cynthia flinch.

"Oh, I'm sorry. I didn't mean to scare you. It's just that I've made my choice."

"Which is?" Eager, desperate to get this game of Russian roulette over with.

"That one."

He pointed a quivering finger at the velvet box.

"You're sure?"

"Positive."

"There's no changing your mind now. You're sure you want to pick that one?"

"Nope. I'm positive. That's the box you'd have wanted. It's more… more romantic, less S&M…" he giggled.

Cynthia remained silent in her appraisal of him.

Picking up the rejected item, she threw it into the shoebox and covered it with the lid, leaving the chosen box on the table between them.

Cynthia stood, and walked over to the foot of the stairs, to the awaiting drinks trolley. It was a sixties monstrosity of polished brass made to look like gold and wood, but it did the job she needed. She began wheeling it over to the table, the bottles and glasses chiming together as she traversed the uneven floor.

"Did I pick the right one?"

"Only you know that, Daniel." Cynthia uttered as she parked the trolley next to the table. "What do *you* think?" There was a coldness to her voice, and she was surprised her breath didn't fog out from under her mask.

"I…I…I think it's what you would have wanted, and so yes, I believe I made the right choice."

Clapping her hands together, mimicking Daniel from moments before, she watched him flinch in his seat as if someone had just fired a gun.

"Congratulations!" She roared.

"So, I did well?"

"Very well indeed. You may now collect your prize, but no peeking, for tomorrow all will be revealed. But don't you worry, I'll act surprised."

"As surprised as someone *can* be when they picked it out months in advance."

That's true, we did pick it out, when you were still with me.

Twirling a glass from the drinks trolly like a baton, she began wetting the rim of it before placing it into a bowl of white powder which looked like cocaine, but which had the powdery-granulated appearance of sugar. Once dusted, she placed the glass on the trolley, next to her undusted glass.

"My surprise will be in the moment, I can assure you. I can't wait to see how you'll do it, ask the question I mean."

"Well, I'm sure you'll enjoy the surprise."

"I will, but first, we drink today to celebrate tomorrow!"

"Drink? Honey, I haven't had a drink in, what, months? I'll be plastered and I want to be able to enjoy our special day."

"One won't hurt…trust me, I'm a professional."

He nodded, and Cynthia watched as he picked up the box and placed it in his inner jacket pocket. The same jacket pocket where it had been until it was removed by the emergency team that had announced him as deceased. Would announce him as deceased. Will announce him as deceased. Red circles on warring calendars.

"Thank you." Daniel uttered as Cynthia began mixing cocktails.

"For what?"

"You'll think I'm stupid."

"No, I won't. Go on, please…" she said, finishing the shaking of the cocktail.

"No. It's silly."

"You know I hate it when you do that. Just tell me. You know I won't be able to let it go, so why bother keeping it a secret when we both know I'll badger you until you tell me."

"Badger?"

"Well, you've quite clearly rubbed off on me haven't you."

She placed the frosted glass in front of Daniel, who immediately reached for it, claimed it, and held it within his two hands like a sacred artefact.

"Go on," Cynthia offered. "Tell me, and drink up, we've got a busy day tomorrow."

Daniel took a sip.

"What is that?" Daniel said, pointing to the dusting around the glass as he licked his lips. "Is that sugar or something?"

"Yes," Cynthia said, but the face behind the mask took on a deceitful glare. "Just sugar."

Liar. Why don't you actually tell him what it is?

He doesn't need to know. A dose that small won't kill him, it's just to see what I can get away with. How much he's still able to function before…well before he becomes incoherent… and well, you know…

"Odd, it's got some…well…it's making my lips tingle."

"Oh, that'll be the lime and lemon I soaked the sugar in."

"Tastes divine."

"Well, there will be a lot more on the menu tomorrow, you can be assured of that. Come on, what was it you were about to say?"

"I'd thought you might have forgotten." He took another large swig of the drink, and worked to puff out his cheeks, which didn't really puff given they were almost moulded to his skull. "This is going straight to my head; I feel all kinds of woozy right now."

"Lightweight."

"Lightweight, indeed."

"So?" Cynthia asked again, demurely, as she lifted the mask, exposed her mouth and took a sip of her drink, free of the frosted glass.

"Oh, right. Well, I just wanted to thank you is all."

"For what?"

Daniel necked the rest of his drink and Cynthia assumed it was for Dutch courage.

"For loving me," he said before licking the dusting from the rim of the glass. "I know it's not been easy, what with the diagnosis and being my carer all this time, but I really do appreciate what you've done for me. How you've been there at my worst. You're an angel and I'll be… I'd be…well, dead if it wasn't for you."

Oh, how little you know.

Tears tickled their way down her face, and Cynthia sniffed behind the mask. Daniel instinctively turned his face to hers.

"Are you okay my love? I didn't mean to upset you. Hey, are you okay?"

"I'm fine," she waved a dismissive hand at him. "It's just, well, that was beautiful. Really beautiful. And you don't have to thank me for loving you. You make loving fun."

"Fleetwood Mac?" Daniel raised an eyebrow at her.

She nodded, came forward and collected his glass, and placed it back on the trolley. Returning, she knelt in front of him, placed a hand on his crossed knee, the owl mask tilted to the side as she gazed lovingly upon him.

Daniel placed one of his bony hands on hers and squeezed it tight.

"Tomorrow, darling," Cynthia said. "We feast."

Removing one of her hands, she lifted the mask slightly, exposed her mouth and kissed the top of Daniel's hand. She lifted her face to his before continuing.

"Now how about we get you back into bed, you've got a... *we've* got a busy, exciting day tomorrow and you'll need your beauty sleep."

"That sounds about right. Actually, that sounds perfect. My head is really spinning."

Cynthia smiled behind the mask as relief washed over her, her skin prickled with pins and needles. They'd done it, Daniel had done it, is doing it, will do it.

Tomorrow, we'll put everything right, as it should have been, and in its proper place.

CHAPTER 18

Today, tonight, this morning; whatever time it was in the real world, outside this place, didn't matter, because in here, as Cynthia descended the stairs gingerly, for them, it was *Date Night*.

Darkness reigned, as always, as she crept down the stairs. Her hand curved to the left as the banister continued to lead her around the bend and down, down, down. Pausing at the bottom step, she turned her masked face towards the hospital bed.

The green glow from the heartrate monitor picked out a ghoulish vision in the dark.

A face, hollowed-out, yet still a face, sleeping like the dead.

Each blip which rose from the tiny screen flashed a modicum of green further into the room, bathing Daniel's angular face in green light.

A goblin face, a *Wicked Witch of the West* face.

Breathing deeply, she waited, silently, and enjoyed the moment.

"It's time..." she mumbled behind the mask before stepping from the wooden staircase to the roughhewn floor of the basement. As she navigated the dark, her heels clacked softly, as if in the dark some supersized insect's mandibles clicked, scissored over and over into whatever prey had wandered too close and had become dinner.

She walked with purpose, the heavy boom box swinging in her right hand, piloting the darkness with a deft ability. Like her mask's namesake, she sidestepped the chairs with ease, because there was a place for everything and everything was in its place.

Depositing her cargo on the table, lightly, as not to awaken sleeping beauty, she sets about positioning the boom box – *a leftover relic from Daniel's past* – next to the light switch on the table. She'll get to that soon – *the light* – but first, some musical accompaniment.

If music be the food of love, play on!

There was a tattoo of that on her left ankle, in a swooping script. She loved that line, although she'd never heard it until Daniel read *Twelfth Night* to her. They both loved to read; Daniel with his classics and fantasy, Cynthia with her horror and science fiction. However, when they read communally, it was a sacred time enjoyed by both parties, a moment where nothing existed except the words on the page.

It didn't happen often. Not often enough to become something you'd classify as a routine or a habit, and they only really started it once Daniel got his diagnosis and struggled with reading, as the tiredness that wracked his body caused even his eyes to tire quickly. He hadn't wanted to waste the time he had left with the mind-numbing entertainment called television, though. Not when there were so many books in the world he'd never get to read.

He'd wanted to do what he loved, with the person he loved most, for as long as they could. And so in the evenings, and more so on the weekends, each would pick a book and, instead of putting the television on, and plugging themselves in for an hour or two or three watching some utter gash from across the globe; a spoilt, rich family and their inept children prostituting themselves any way they could for fame or a buck; a teenage mom; or some other reality show about America's next talentless buffoon who'd been told they had talent when they quite clearly had none.

Leaving those thoughts of television behind, Cynthia reached into the clutch bag which hung from her shoulder. Her fingers searched blindly in the dark for what she needed and, after passing over her honey flavoured lip gloss and lavender scented hand moisturiser – *which made her think of Daniel's mother and her obsession with the smell* – she bypassed a pack of tissues and a compact mirror and eventually found what she was looking for: the plastic case.

If music be the food of love, play on!

Daniel had mentioned that music played an important part in Shakespeare's plays, and that it was often used to carry the plot. And rumination wasn't that different from the plot playing out before them now, *music being the food of love*, because it had never been far away from either of them. Then or now. Their house was a chamber where melodies rang out constantly; it serenaded them when they ate, cleaned, showered, worked, argued and made love, their lives were surrounded by the soundtrack that their entwined lives had constructed, and Fleetwood Mac was the mixtape to their lives – every season of it, the good, the bad, the fallow spells, and the bountiful harvests.

Give me excess of it, that, surfeiting, the appetite may sicken, and so die.

Closing her clutch, Cynthia fingered the plastic box, turned it over in her hands, and searched blindly for the opening. Sliding a manicured nail inside, she popped it open.

The sound it made caused her to pause.

Her head snapped back to the hospital bed, and she expected to see two green, goblin eyes staring back at her in the dark. However, Daniel remained blissfully unaware of her presence, and that, for now, was a blessing.

She needed light for what came next, yet the flick of a lighter, or the striking of a match would, she assumed, be too loud. Instead, her fingers trickled over the plastic buttons and knobs on the boom box. She found the volume button and turned it, there was resistance followed by a dull CLICK, like the sound of a knuckle cracking.

A soft, yellow-green glow emanated from the small display screen, and she leaned closer until she could hear the subtle electrical hum emanating from the two speakers. She held the tape out in front of her, tilting it to the display, searching for the right side.

Side two.

Lowering her head to the cassette tape, side one. She flipped it over.

With a finger to the eject button, she depressed it slowly, and the front of the boom box opened, the door squeaking weakly as it yawned wide, waiting to be fed.

'Feed me'

Cynthia imagines the boom box speaking to her in the deep baritone voice of James Earl Jones, because why wouldn't it?

Slipping the cassette inside, she presses a finger to the small, hinged door to close. Another *CLICK*. Not as loud as the first, the sound of biting a sliver of a fingernail in your mouth, but still loud enough. Head snapping towards the bed, she stares at the withered green goblin through the large eyes of the mask.

Sleeping like the dead…but, not for much longer, with any luck.

Observing the bed like a hawk, no, scratch that. Observing the bed like a ~~hawk~~ barn owl, she slides her hand to the top of the boom box. Her fingers search blindly for the play button and trickle over the copious others: fast-forward, rewind, record, pause, eject.

Aaha…that's the badger.

The embossed letters announced themselves on the pad of her finger as if it were braille – P L A Y. She also feels, or senses – *a more accurate description* – a small triangle shape, tilted on its side. *PLAY*.

With her head swivelled back to the bed, she breathes, waits, weighs up her decision of when to start, although her decision has already been made.

She starts now.

Wakey-wakey, rise and shine beautiful!

Cynthia presses the button.

There's a small squeak, and some mouse-like chatter, as the wheels begin to spin, followed by a low hum as the speakers prepare to blast Fleetwood Mac into the basement.

If there was a light down here – *more than the little oblong display screen, or the green blipping flare of the heart-rate monitor in the far corner of the room* – Cynthia would be watching, totally absorbed and equally obsessed, as the brown tape unspooled from one spoke and magically deposited itself onto another. Even as a kid, she had loved the way physical media worked and looked; the artwork, all hand-painted and psychedelic, although her love for these things went deeper than her physical attraction to them. She loved how they felt in her hands, as if she owned a little slice of history, rather than just leasing it or streaming it like people do now in *'The Digital Age'*.

Also, young Cynthia had enjoyed learning the intricate ways things worked, and her childish, then adolescent, mind continued to be astounded at how sound could be captured in various ways: on a vinyl record or a tape, and later a CD, and now, music seemed to just hang around in the air – *digitally, that is* – in clouds that no one could see, but could share and download and listen.

As a young whippersnapper, she also marvelled at how moving images and sound could be captured, stored, and trapped on a VHS and through the magic of the VCR be brought to life.

Resurrected.

Daniel had loved physical media too, and because of their mutual love for the various formats, they fell further in love with each other, discussing the look and sound and feel of each album and film they loved, long into a many night. They had – *still have – will soon have again* – shelves of the stuff, a formidable collection of two lives/two collections, melding, growing, entwining together like tree roots, to live as one.

VHS tapes, and Laserdiscs and DVD's.

Vinyl records, and cassette tapes, and CD's and mini-discs.

'All of this is a dying artform. No one collects this shit anymore, but you wait and see, it'll all come back. Everything cool always does. Nothing this beautiful stays dead for long.'

They both knew Daniel's predictions were true about physical media coming back; they'd both witnessed it over the intervening years after he'd said it. Yet, what came to her now, afresh, as she remembered those words from Daniel so many moons ago, was that the same could also be said about him too.

Nothing this beautiful stays dead for long.

And Cynthia was on the cusp of a revival, not in the biblical sense, but in the bodily sense. She'd reached into the grave and brought him back from the brink – *arise Lazarus* – and she'd ensure Daniel would have a resurrected soundtrack to go along with his bodily resurrection.

The slow hum continued, and as Cynthia twisted the volume knob to the right, it grew steadily louder, reverberating off the walls. It sounded like the many voices of the wind, no scratch that. It sounded like ~~the many voices of the wind~~ a busy train station platform.

It reminded her of Victoria Station, in London, and when they'd travel through it on their many excursions to attend Daniel's various oncology appointments. The memory of those journeys will bring goosebumps to Cynthia's arms in the basement, more than the cold ever had.

The bed creaked and Cynthia looked up, frozen in place, reduced for a moment to a naughty child caught dipping their fingers into the biscuit barrel before dinner.

Daniel was stirring.

He yawned, attempted to stretch his arms out, his restraints quickly snapped his wrists back down before he searched the darkness for the sound and from where it was coming from.

He looked scared as he stared directly at her, although she was sure he couldn't see her. He must have just been drawn by the sound, and so she waited patiently for her moment. Soon…soon she would make her move.

The haunting sound which accompanied the disturbing memory of that echoing train station lasts for only sixteen more seconds, sixteen *long* seconds. It is a torture, but one she had to bear, if she wanted the good stuff that is, and boy did she crave the good stuff.

The echoing train station and its hubbub of chatter died and became replaced by the tribal beat which was immediately identifiable as '*Tusk*'. She reached across the table and fingered the light switch.

Not yet, soon…soon…

Daniel continued searching the inky black for the origin of the sound, and the woman who'd brought it into his dank dwelling. It was a treat for him, music. A slice of the real world in a world that had been, up until this very moment – *as the sound of drums throbbed through the speakers* – known only as *other*.

A purgatorial existence.

The air was pregnant with anticipation, electrified, like the coming of a huge thunderstorm. The drumbeat worked them both into a frenzy of anticipation before the whispered words from the speakers penetrated the dark, and the voice of Lindsey Buckingham began to croon.

Cynthia whisper-sang along with Lindsey: *ask him if he's going to stay.*

Daniel?

Lindsey and Cynthia continued their impromptu duet, their voices coalescing: *asking if he's going away.*

Doctor Hasan?

Cynthia had waited, yearned, and craved for this exact moment to transpire. Well, not this exact moment. She'd had no idea when she abducted Doctor Hasan, that things would end up this way. She had her assumptions – *of course* – however, she never once assumed she'd be able to reach the levels of barbarity she'd resorted to in order to achieve her aims and desires, but she was glad she *had,* and she *could,* and now she wouldn't change a thing.

Well, maybe she'd change cleaning the shitty sheets, and that stolen kiss from the other night which she'd not foreseen happening, and which had thrown her for a loop. It was only now, as she listened to Buckingham singing the lyrics to *Tusk,* with her finger to the light switch, that she realised how frequent a theme of Fleetwood Mac's songs were of the singer suspecting his partner of being unfaithful.

Never…Daniel would never be unfaithful to me.

HOOGA HAAGA HOOGA.

The Mac sung on, and Cynthia knew what came next, and she prayed Daniel would heed the words. That he wouldn't go against their wishes; she wasn't strong enough to face that now. Of course, she wanted to hear it, had always yearned to hear those words again, with meaning, since the time he spoke to them for the last time.

Don't you dare say those words to me now Daniel…please don't you say them.

DON'T SAY THAT YOU LOVE ME.

That was her que.

She flicked the switch and the harsh strip lights exploded into life above the bed. Daniel flinched at its suddenness as his eyelids narrowed, fighting the glare of the tube lighting as he stared into the darkness past the foot of his bed. He appeared almost hopeful with the prospect of catching a glimpse of his beloved owl-woman, his keeper, the object of his Stockholm Syndrome'd affections lurking somewhere in the dark.

JUST TELL ME THAT YOU WANT ME.

"Hello, are you there?"

Good enough.

At least he didn't say that he loved me.

The brass band kicked in, and Cynthia sashayed towards the light.

TUSK!

Even though the drums and guitar and brass band and singing were loud, she could still hear her heels *clicking* and *clacking* away in the dark as she made her final approach. The heels gave away any advantage she had, and Daniel zeroed in closer on her position. Yet still, she remained hidden from view as she crept closer.

CLICK…CLACK…CLICK…CLACK…CLICK…CLACK.

With the sound of her heels building up pace, she swooped out of the dark at him, and Daniel appeared visibly taken aback at her emergence; she observed him observing her and noticed his mouth hung open in surprise as his head, led by his eyes, traversed her body, from the tip of the mask to her ankles, and then back up again.

"You…you…you…look beautiful," he stuttered.

Tilting her head down.

Yes, yes, I do. So, kind for you to notice.

She stood before him in her little red dress; a figure-hugging number which was sinfully expensive – *but he was worth it* – and which clung to her all her curves in all the right places. The dress finished just above the knee, and her tanned – *fake tanned because she was such an English Rose* – muscular legs ran down to her black, strappy high heels.

She was resplendent.

A vision.

A keeper.

And Cynthia knew that Daniel – *back then*, and absolutely *now* –

had and continued to punch above his weight, as his friends and family had a habit of reminding him.

"You're not wearing your overalls?"

"Oh, I hadn't realised," a demurely placed hand on her hip. "Did you want me to go and change back into them?"

"No...NO! I much prefer this look on you...not that I didn't enjoy the other look. Listen, I don't really know what I'm supposed to say here. The last thing I want to do is offend you.

"It's just that, wow. I never realised how truly stunning you were under all that garb. Forgive me, please. I'm just a little taken aback...like I knew you were *you*, love of my life. B...b...but this is the *real* you, the you that you've been hiding under a bushel.

"The you I'd forgotten about...does that make sense? I'm sorry, I'm jabbering on, I'll shut up..."

Rounding the foot of the bed, she hopped up onto the mattress, perching herself at the end of the bed, near Daniel's matchstick legs, crossing her own at the knee. She observed as his eyes travel down to her bare knee, where they slowly worked the rest of their way down the entirety of her muscular calf to her delicate ankle. Cynthia glanced down too at that point, and observed the light shimmer on her smooth, moisturised shin, glad that she'd remembered to shave and, in doing so, her look was complete... well, almost complete.

The grand reveal, her de-masking would happen later, over dinner; whether that was before or after Daniel said what needed to be said had yet to be decided. The details were still a little hazy, and so she turned her focus back to Daniel, who was still ogling her legs, and she didn't blame him.

Why wouldn't he be ogling me? I'm a catch.

Cynthia bounced her foot up and down, flexing her ankle, teasing him with it, as a conductor's baton would an eager, debutant soloist, and she allowed him this moment of observation.

He was still wearing his clothes from last night – '*Death Clothes*' – because it seemed cruel to get him to change only to put everything back on again for this evening's fare, given the amount of time, effort, and discomfort it had taken to get him into them in the first place.

The clothes were a little creased, but he was as dapper as he was ever going to get and it took her breath away, how much he looked like he did on *that day*, when the nurse escorted her into the hospital room. When she was shown to his bedside to firstly identify him and, secondly, to say her final goodbyes. He'd been full of death by then, but now? Well, now he was full of life. Returned to her as he once was.

Tusk finished which meant there was only one song left on this side of the cassette.

After a brief pause, *Never Forget*, sung by the wonderful Christine McVie, filtered through the speakers. It was an upbeat number, full of warmth and love, which perfectly matched the feeling of the room and the butterflies which fluttered around in Cynthia's stomach.

We'll never forget this night; everything will be all right…

It'll be all right…we'll never forget tonight.

Cynthia placed a hand to Daniel's trouser and felt the fabric crumble beneath her hand, folding in on itself until it stopped, her fingers finally alighted on the stick-thin leg, hidden beneath the many folds of fabric. She squeezed it gently.

"Are you ready?"

Daniel lifted his gaze to the mask.

"Ready?"

"For our date? You didn't forget, did you?"

"No…no…of course not. I'm just feeling a little groggy from last night. It's been a long time since I had any alcohol."

Long time? It's been a lifetime, because Hasan, the you *you were before was a Muslim. But you're not* Him *anymore. You're Daniel. And I'd say you handled your drink pretty well, considering the little surprise I put in it.*

She patted his leg.

If only you knew.

"Don't you worry. I'm going to take good care of you," she said as she hopped off the bed, heels clacking on the ground as she landed before sashaying her way up to his restraints and unbuckling his right hand.

Once released, she leaned over Daniel's body to work on the other restraint, and her breasts rubbed against his chest as she worked. She peered out of the corner of her eye, noticing that Daniel's focus wasn't on his freed wrist, which she assumed it would be, but rather his focus was on her heaving bosom.

Park your bike in there if you like?

She smiled behind the mask as she unfastened the other restraint before standing straight and brushing a hand down rumpled dress, smoothing out where it had rucked up; and with a final look down, she was ready.

Daniel rubbed at each wrist as she let down the guardrail on the side of his bed.

"Shall we?" she offered and held out a hand which hung in the air for a moment, waiting to be taken.

Come, take my hand.

"Yes. I'd very much like that." Daniel offered back as he placed his hand in hers, and she helped him out of bed.

Once Daniel was on his feet, Cynthia placed an arm around his waist and helped him walk away from his island of isolation for the last time. He probably could have managed on his own, however it was important they made good time, and that he wouldn't be exhausted by the time they got to their table.

"Not that I'm prying, but do you still have the thing?"

Daniel pulled up slightly, forcing them both to stop at the edge of the light. It felt to Cynthia as if he wanted to say one last goodbye to the hovel which had been his home.

"Thing?"

There was a pause. A long, excruciating pause.

He's forgotten.

Spiralling thoughts assailed her.

Fucking messed this whole thing up...is it you, Daniel, that stands before me? Or is it that snake, Doctor Hasan I'm carrying?

"Thing?" Daniel said again, the corner of his mouth raising in a sly smirk.

It's you, isn't it?

You bastard...why can't you just leave us alone...give me back my–

"Of course, dear. It's in my pocket." The sly smirk stretched into a broad smile as he tapped his pocket to emphasise he had the box. "I wouldn't misplace that, trust me. Cost me an arm and a leg if you remember?"

"I do…silly me, I just wanted to make sure."

"No problem. You're a real keeper, do you know that?"

There was no need to respond. She knew she was, and so she got them moving, hobbling through the dark, and past the table where the boom box sat. Daniel pulled away from her as they passed the chairs. *Never Forget* came to its melodious conclusion, yet Cynthia didn't head to the table with Daniel, instead pulled him back to her.

"W…w…where are you…taking…me?" His words came in short gasps, with him visibly out of breath from the exertion.

"To dinner, silly."

"But…" Daniel offered as he gripped the back of a chair.

Cynthia pulled him forcefully away, and the chair scrapped along the ground before he relinquished his grip and let her lead him.

"Not here. Not tonight. It's a special evening, and a special evening deserves a change of scenery… wouldn't you agree?"

"Yes, of course, but where are you taking me?"

There was an edge of fear to his words, or was it…anticipation?

"Well, you're too sick for us to go out anywhere."

"Of course," Daniel went along with the lie, which was a truth of the man he was before. "I don't want to pick up an infection or a cold or something…that would…finish me off…of that I'm quite sure." he chuckled awkwardly but there was no mirth in it, only the unmistakable sound of fear threading his voice.

"That's right, your immune systems very poor at the moment. So, I hope you don't mind, but I brought the restaurant to us, for one night only. We're going upstairs to the kitchen. I've prepared everything for us already. Everything is as it was and should have been."

"Was?" Daniel asked questioningly.

"Should have been?" He shook his head, confused as they stumbled their way to the bottom of the staircase.

"Never mind." Cynthia exuded in a calm voice as she bustled him across the basement.

"Smells divine," he said as he reached out to grip the banister.

Cynthia paused, inhaled; the subtle aromas made her mouth water as she recalled the delicacies which awaited them.

"So, we're going upstairs? To the house?" There was a sense of wonder to his voice.

"Of course, silly. The basement's no place to have a meal of this magnitude. You said so yourself. You wanted this to be special, a meal we would look back on in years to come and remember that it was the night we…well, you know. I'm not going to ruin the surprise."

"Roger…" he tapped the side of his nose, the nose which was kinked in the middle from where Cynthia had broken it all those months before.

"Are you ready?" She intently eyed the man she'd pulled apart and stuck back together again.

"Yes…" he said, as he placed his foot on the first step to the staircase which led to their new future.

They climbed higher and higher, and Cynthia supported him every step of the way as they left the basement far behind, a place where neither of them would venture again.

It was finally finished.

For better, for worse, for richer, for poorer, in sickness and in health…

They continued to climb; the door ahead ringed with the glow from the world beyond its barrier. It appeared almost mythical, a Narnia-esque door, a gateway to their past, present and future.

Cynthia reached for the handle, turned it to the left, and pushed.

Until death do us part.

CHAPTER 19

"You've got a little something," she said, pointing at her teeth. "Here."

He paused, placed his knife and fork on his plate, where they rested next to the half-finished, Cajun style cod and covered his mouth with his bejewelled hand.

"Th'orry," he uttered, as he used his tongue to dislodge whatever *'little something'* it was.

"Just a bit of basil, from the bruschetta I think." Cynthia proffered.

After a moment, Daniel removed his hand, smiled.

"Did I get it?"

She shook her head, no.

"If by *'get it'* you mean that you've somehow moved it to another tooth, you're doing a great job."

She giggled.

Daniel tilted his head down, hand covering his mouth again, and aggressively tongues his teeth. There's a smacking, sucking sound before he lifts his head once more.

"How about now?" He beams.

"No, it's still there."

Quick as a flash he grabs his drink, his fourth from a relatively young evening, and takes a large gulp.

Slow down, slugger. I still need you coherent.

He covers his mouth again, remembering his manners.

Good boy.

Swilling the drink around his mouth like mouthwash, he swallows.

"How about now?"

It's still there, stuck between his front teeth, and she shakes her head.

"Look, come here." With a wave of a hand, she beacons him to lean across the table, he does. "Let me just get it for you."

"What did you do for your date night?" Daniel says in a voice that's not his. "Oh, nothing much, just spent the evening having my girlfriend pick food out of my teeth." There's a chuckle as he leans in, the drink making him louder, bolder, and more fun.

Girlfriend?

Not for much longer, with any luck.

Soon, I'll be your fiancée.

"Come here, you silly badger."

"There you go again…" the piece of basil slides over his teeth as he speaks, yet somehow it still clings on. "Sounding like me… who'd have thought it, huh?"

She leans forward, reaches her hand out, and uses the tip of a nail to scrape the green from his teeth, finally getting it on the third attempt.

"There we go, all better," she says, discreetly picking up the napkin from her lap and she deposits the green fleck inside before placing the scrunched-up napkin on the table by her plate as Daniel takes another large gulp of his drink. Cynthia keenly watches him lick the granulated dust from his lips as he places the glass back on the table, with just a small splash of liquid left in the bottom of it.

"Let me get you a top up," Cynthia says eagerly, already reaching over to reclaim his glass before standing.

"It's okay. Please, just sit and enjoy your…what is it you're eating?"

"Wild rabbit risotto with Chanterelle mushrooms."

"Oh, that would be why there's not *mush-room* in here then." A giggle, and Daniel shakes his head; not in regret at how bad the joke was, or when they're caught laughing at their own joke, but in the way someone does when they feel discombobulated.

I'm not surprised you feel like that, it's powerful stuff and you've had a skin-full already.

As she reaches the kitchen counter, she leans into it, juts her bum out, and catches Daniel ogle her behind from her peripheral vision. Whilst he's occupied with her rump she deftly wets the rim of the glass, dips it in the powdery substance, ensuring she covers the entirety of the rim in a thick glaze.

"Don't worry," she says, peering over her shoulder. He's still checking out her arse "It's still piping hot."

"Like the view." Lifting a hand to his mouth, Daniel immediately tries to apologise. "Sorry, that was crass, I don't know what's gotten into me..."

I do.

"Must be the drink talking…"

Definitely.

Waving a dismissive hand, she pours the cocktail from the pitcher into his glass.

"You never have to apologise for complimenting me…just for your silly dad jokes."

"I can't help it," and without missing a beat. "I'm just such a *fun-gi* to be with."

Cynthia returns to the table, drink in hand.

"Really? One mushroom joke not enough for you?"

She places his drink on the coaster near his meal.

"I could do this all day."

"Well, here's to hoping you don't."

She replies with a chortle of her own, glass raised in a toast, forcing Daniel to lift his own to cheers her and to drink; Daniel, he'd always mentioned it was the height of rudeness not to drink once you've toasted someone. Although tonight she didn't have to worry about him not drinking, as he currently didn't need any encouragement in that regard.

A few more of these and he'll be putty in my hands.

We better pace things though, don't want him not living up to the task at hand.

He still needs to ask you, don't forget.

After he does, hell, he can drink like the proverbial fish.

They'd been listening to Fleetwood Mac's 'Rumours' album over dinner. It was, in both their opinions, one of the best albums ever created, but in truth they hadn't really been paying much attention to it; Cynthia too busy ensuring the evening went according to plan; Daniel, well, he was too absorbed in the gastronomical creations presented before his very eyes. That, and coming up with bad mushroom jokes.

Her eyes flicked down to her phone, which was on the table by her plate.

They'd already listened to half the album.

Where does the time go?

Scanning the track listing, she observed all the songs that had come and gone and not a word had been remembered.

Second Hand News.

Dreams.

Never Going Back Again.

Don't Stop.

Go Your Own Way.

Absolute masterpieces, each and every one.

Cocking her head, she swivelled it ever so slightly, a barn owl zeroing in on its prey, as she attempted to hear the next song working its way into existence. There was a lull, and the only noise filling that silence was Daniel's cutlery as it scrapes on his plate before the soft tinkling of a piano faded in. She recognised the tune immediately, she didn't need her phone to remind her of the title, she'd recognise that tune anywhere, and she smiles behind her mask; 'Songbird' began to play.

It was a very special song indeed. It was playing the first time Daniel told her that he loved her. The old Daniel, that was. Not the new one who sat scoffing his face before her.

They're one and the same now though, aren't they?

You're right, they are.

As Daniel forked another creamy piece of cod into his mouth, his glance returned to her as he chewed, his equine-teeth going at the delicate fish in his tiny, pinched mouth as if his life depended on it. And maybe it did.

Do you know the relevance of this song, little piggy?

A scowl quickly replaced the smile as the lyrics, sung so *hauntingly*, so *perfectly* by Christine McVie, slipped freely from the speakers.

There'll be no more crying.

The lyrics could be speaking to Daniel and Cynthia both, and she knew it.

She forced the tears away, not wanting to contradict the lyrics or the moment. It was more than that, though. She didn't want Daniel to see her crying, hear her sobbing, witness her uncontrolled bawling, because if he did, it would only put a dampener on their evening, and this evening deserved to be devoid of any such sadness. Hell, this evening was supposed to be a celebration. And it would be when they finally got to the task at hand.

Cynthia willed the tears away.

Only joy…only joy…only joy…

Pulling the bottom of her mask away from her face, she forked in another mouthful of risotto as Daniel placed his cutlery on his plate. She glanced over at him, there was still food on the prongs.

He can't be finished, he can't be…how rude.

As the thoughts bubbled to her consciousness, and as she pondered his rudeness, he opened his mouth to speak. No, scratch that. He opened his mouth to ~~speaks~~ sing to her.

"When I'm with you, it's alright." He lifted his glass, tilted it in her direction, a mock *'cheers'* and took a sip before continuing. "And I know it's right."

Pulling the mask back down, she covered her mouth before she spoke.

"Thank you." She offered with a nod of her head.

Placing the glass down, he tilted his head to the side a little.

The way he stared at her, in that moment, Cynthia couldn't help but feel naked, exposed, seen; as if she were sitting here de-masked already, as if this was the first time he'd truly seen her since his captivity, and dare she even think it, say it?

He's falling in love with me...all over again.

She wasn't brave enough to word her thoughts, but she thought them nevertheless, and that's got to count for something, hasn't it? Falling in love. Fallen in love. Fell in love. It's all a matter of semantics really.

Must be the drink and the, well, the other stuff that's loosening him up.

His gaze is blazed at her, and if Cynthia were a houseplant she had no doubts she'd be wilting from the solar glare of his stare. She proposed asking him: *What are you staring at?* However, he beat her to the punch and her proposed question was instantly made redundant.

"You're so beautiful, do you know that?"

Wilting, just a little, her stiff shoulders from moments before soften and, instead of leaning away in outrage, she leans in, placed her elbows on the table, tenting her fingers in front of the mask.

"Go on," she encouraged.

Colour returned to Daniel's cheeks, not from the candlelight, although she had to admit the flickering flame had bought some colour to his usually pallid, bleached face.

He's blushing...he's literally blushing over me.

"No, it's silly really."

"Daniel?" There's was a sharpness to her voice, and she's worried she'd spoiled the moment.

Was that the moment he was going to ask you?

Did you just ruin it?

She's back in the restaurant. The night is ruined. Forever.

Forever?

"You know how I," Cynthia wants to say **HATE**, but chose a better word; a safer, softer word. "You know how I *dislike* it when you go to say something and then don't. It gets me all in a tizz. So, please, just tell me...unless it's another mushroom joke, that is?"

She noticed a smile crest Daniel's face, which reached all the way to his eyes, and she knew she'd won him back to her.

"You got me," Daniel says, holding his hands out, palms up briefly, where he waited for some imaginary cuffs. They hung there for a beat before he reached for his drink again. Whatever it was he wanted to say, it was apparently thirsty work, given the three large gulps he consumed.

"Please, go on," Cynthia encouraged, and that was all the encouragement he needed.

"Well, I was going to say that…well. I'm falling even more in love with you, more than I thought humanly possible." He screwed his face up. "Is that weird?"

"No! Of course it's not weird."

"Oh, okay, cool."

"Why would it be weird?"

At the question, Cynthia observed Daniel place a hand to his breast pocket, gently investigating it, his fingers tapping the box within, checking he hadn't misplaced it, before returning his hand to his fork and absentmindedly shifting the food around his plate.

Cynthia discourages herself from telling him not to play with is food.

Don't ruin it, softly, softly…build him up, don't cut him down.

It's almost as if Daniel hears her inner voice because he stops, places his fork down and looks back up at her. His face suddenly a mask of confusion and fright.

What's going on inside that head of yours, how heavy are your thoughts?

"Well, and don't take this the wrong way…" he pauses, testing the temperature of the room. "And I don't mean any offence by it…"

This is getting better and better.

"But…I was wondering, if it's okay with you…but it's perfectly fine if it's not. I'd completely understand. And if you don't want to, that's fine too. Because who am I to ask anything of you after you've looked after me for so long, but I was thinking if it's not too much of a problem…"

"Just say whatever it is you need to say, we haven't got all day. I'm not going to bite. Well, not unless you want me to?"

"Kinky!" Daniel says before making a growling noise, miming two paws with his hands; Cynthia doesn't reply, just sits there before him, stoic. A nervous laugh tumbles from his lips before he lowers his clawed, lion-miming hands and, shaking his head, he shifts uncomfortably in his chair before clearing his throat and pressing on.

"Well...forgive me, I just wanted. Well, thought I'd ask, if...if..." He pauses, places a hand to his forehead, and fingers and thumb begin to massage his temples.

"Sorry..."

A shake of the head, trying to rid himself of his apparent befuddlement before finally struggling on. "I appear to be all sixes and sevens at the moment. What's in this?" Daniel points at his drink.

"Nothing you haven't had before, my love."

A reflex reply.

LIAR...*he's never had a sip of alcohol in his life.*
He's a damned Muslim for goodness sake.
No...he's...NOT.
He stopped being Doctor Hasan months ago...
He's Daniel now, and this was, and still is, his drink of choice.

"My mouth's all tingly. What's in it, though? the ingredients? Maybe I'm allergic?"

"I doubt it, honey. I think I'd know if you were allergic to something?"

"Humour me, please."

The way his jaw twitched, and how his eyes narrowed, she thinks she noticed a flicker of the man she'd banished creeping back into his face.

"Well, it's got vodka and Southern Comfort in it. Freshly squeezed orange juice, Hayman's Sloe Gin and some Galliano L'Autentico... plus a slice of orange and the sugar dust around the glass."

"Oh, right. Well, there's nothing in it I'm allergic too, right?"

"Right."

He takes another large gulp.

"Whatever's wrong with me, I'm sure another one of these will fix it."

Said like a true alcoholic.

"I'm sure it will, honey."

She eyes the empty glass as he places it back on the coaster. Quick as a whip, she reaches across the table, plucks his glass from the coaster, and stands. "Another?" she offers in her best hostess voice, all throaty and flirty.

"Shh…ure ff..ing," his words are slurred. "As Dean Martin used to sww…ay: 'You're not drunk if you can lie on the floor without holding on.' So why the hell not, right?"

"I shall bring you liquid refreshment, post-haste." She CLICKs and CLACKs her way over to the kitchen counter, tottering on her heels as she prepares a fresh drink.

"What do you call a drink like that?"

"You don't remember? It's your favourite…" turning back to observe him, she realises in his forlorn form that her extra special ingredients are beginning to take effect.

You should pace him; maybe lay off the glaze for a while, there's enough drugs in his food to kill a horse…well, as long as he eats it all, enough to get the job done, just trust in the plan. You don't want him passing out before he asks you, do you? Or slipping away with no way of bringing him back before you are his and he is yours?

DON'T MESS THIS UP.

You've only got one chance…don't screw the pooch on this Cynthia, don't you do it.

I WON'T!

I'LL TRUST IN THE PLAN!

"I honestly think I'm too drunk to recall it…like I know it's in there somewhere, probably hiding out in the place where all the phone numbers and birthdays and special dates go to hide, although where that stuff's stored? I've no frigging clue."

Cynthia returns to the table, drink in hand, no frosting this time – *she'll trust in the plan* – and hands the glass to Daniel, who takes a wee nip even before Cynthia's taken her seat opposite him.

"A slow comfortable screw against the wall."

He almost spits his drink out, but in his desire to save face he ends up choking it down and spluttering a little. Placing a hand over his mouth – *to stem some of the spray that escapes his mouth* – he buys himself enough time to swallow.

"A what now?"

"A slow comfortable screw against the wall," she nods at the glass. "That's its name, I'm surprised you don't remember."

"Oh, I do, now you mention it, because if my memory serves me well, we did that once or twice, following a few of these if I'm not mistaken?"

Heat rushes to her cheeks, and she's instantly thankful the mask is there to hide her arousal.

"Oh, you naughty boy!"

"The naughtiest," followed by a cheeky wink and a devilish grin before he returns to his meal, shovelling in a large piece of cod and sauce. His lips smack together when he removes the fork, *ooh*'ing and *aah*'ing loudly, drunkenly, drugged-up-to-his-eyeballs-ly, savouring the tasty morsel and exquisitely rich flavours in his mouth.

'Special Sauce'…he doesn't have a clue.

Cynthia smiles, watches him tongue a splash of sauce which had dribbled out of the corner of his mouth.

That's it, take your medicine.

"So," Cynthia intones. "You've successfully talked us around the houses. If I was a betting woman, I'd say you were hoping I might forget. But as you well know, I've a memory like an elephant, and I'm not going to let you get away with it that easily…." She leans her elbows on the table, places the chin of her mask in her cupped hands. "What was it you wanted to say to me? And don't you try getting out of it…again."

"That's a fair cop guv'nor!" Uttered in an awful cockney accent as he moves the remainder of the food around his plate with the fork.

STOP PLAYING WITH YOUR GOD-DAMNED FOOD!

She wants to yell, but doesn't. Her silence is shout enough, it would seem, and placing his cutlery down once more, Daniel commences his awkward ants in the pants routine, squirming before her on his seat, as if he'd rather be someplace else.

Whatever it is, he sure doesn't want to say it.

"Okay. Okay," he says and she realises he's not talking to her, he's talking to himself, convincing himself to continue.

"Whenever you're ready."

"Look, I love you, you know that, right?"

A nod of agreement.

"Well, I was wondering, and it's completely up to you, if it makes you uncomfortable, honestly it's no skin off my nose…but…but…but…" Daniel's head nods forward as if it's suddenly too heavy for him to keep up, swinging to and fro on his stick thin neck a few times.

Cynthia's about to get up. She's even pushed her chair back in anticipation of his nose dive into the table. Suddenly though, he shakes himself awake again, his head snapping up, his eyes swimming in their sockets.

"S-s-s-sorry, I seem to be…a…bit…woozy."

"Well, I'll get you some water."

"That would be marvellous, thank you." He pinches the bridge of his broken nose, then yawns without placing a hand over his mouth. It irks Cynthia, although she doesn't say anything. It's clear he's struggling, and she'll lets it slide this time.

"Now, go on. Once you tell me, I'll get you some water."

"Sounds like a fair trade." He rubs his tired eyes. "So, you know I love you–"

"You've already said that." The reply short; curt.

"Sorry, I don't know my arse from my elbow at the moment." He opens his eyes wide, blinks a few times. "So, I was wondering, would you take it off?"

"Take it off?"

Lifting his arm, he points a shaking finger at her face.

"The mask?"

This impasse was bound to come sooner or later, yet she wasn't ready to reveal herself just yet. She glanced down at his plate, notices a few more mouthfuls remaining.

"Well, I was kind of waiting for a little something from you before I did that."

"Oh right, shit…I forgot. No. Shit. Sorry. I didn't forget, per se, I just lost track of the time."

All she hears is that he forgot.

"*Forgot?*" She spits the word at him incredulously.

"No, no. Please, I haven't forgotten, I just haven't found the right time…but it's coming, I promise."

She wants to slam her fist on the table. No, scratch that. She wants to slam ~~her fist on the table~~ Daniel's forgetful face *into* the fucking table, to split his face wide open on his china plate.

"What's wrong with right this very second?"

"You're an eager beaver…what's got into you?"

"Into me? What's got into you? You forgot? It's the most important thing in the world to me, and you just *forgot*? What are we even doing here, Daniel?"

The restaurant swims into and out of focus. It looks all wrong.

He shrugs his shoulders like a petulant child.

"Don't you shrug your shoulders at me?"

Rolls his eyes.

"Did you just roll your eyes at me? Did you? You did, didn't you?"

Opening his mouth to speak, Cynthia cuts him off.

"Do you know how long I've had to wait for this moment? What I've had to do to earn this time with you? How long it's taken me to craft this entire night, this meal, to make everything perfect the way it *should* have been? Well, do you?"

There's a moment of silence before Daniel speaks.

"Should have been?"

He's got you there, Cynthia.

"I mean should be…SHOULD BE."

"I knew I shouldn't have said anything." The utterance sulky, childish. "I knew you were going to act like this, and I should've just kept my mouth shut."

"Like this? How am I acting, Daniel? Do tell me how I'm acting?"

"Well, you're acting a little crazy right now."

"*Crazy?* You haven't seen crazy, but you will, trust me."

Her eyes widen as Daniel picks up his fork and begins clearing the rest of his plate like they weren't in the middle of a blazing row. One mouthful, two mouthfuls and the meal – *his meal* – is done.

They sit in an awkward, broiling silence, neither willing to give ground to the other. There are no olive branches here. The meal, the night, their long-heralded *date night* has taken a dramatic turn, and Cynthia's worried she won't be able to claw it back.

The damned drugs have messed it all up.

You should have just gone with a syringe full of heroin or Ketamine.
That would have been less messy.
You've only gone and fucked it.

The sound of Daniel's cutlery clattering on his plate brings her back to the moment, and he looks up at her, sheepishly, a scolded child waving a white flag.

"C…c….c…" he stammers as Cynthia's head snaps up and the owl faces him, his words falling away immediately. She stands, walks over to the sink, and begins pouring a glass of water.

"Couples that stay together…fight together…am I right?"

"I guess," a sighed reply.

Cynthia's head hangs low as she turns off the tap, unable to bring herself to look at Daniel, because she knows that if she did, in the rage that causes the glass in her hand to tremble, she might do something she'd regret. She already has more regrets than she can handle. She places the glass on the marble work surface, grips the edge of the counter with both her hands, and squeezes. Her knuckles turn white with the rage she's expelling. She's a volcano about to blow its stack.

"I'm sorry, I'm such an idiot."

Her head inclines to the weak sound.

"Yes, you are. Of that we *can* both agree…"

There were more mumbled words, but Cynthia couldn't make them out as she was far too busy pondering the argument – *small as it was, petty as it was* – because there was something about it she couldn't shake, something that didn't sit well with her.

Daniel spoke again, but she chose to ignore him.

And then she had the small something that didn't sit well with her; she'd thought she'd heard her name, but that couldn't be, as she'd never given it to him.

Just your mind playing tricks on you, or the drugs?
Could be the drugs?

"…use me?" A mutterance from over her shoulder.

How much have you had?
As much as him?

"…ook at me?" His weak voice persists.

Possibly, hard to tell when its mixed up in the food…

Cynthia squeezed the edge of the counter, harder, heard her knuckles crack – *the sound of dice being shaken in a loosely closed fist* – with the pressure as she continued to ruminate over their spat.

That's it isn't it? It's not the drugs or the drink. You saw it, didn't you?
Yes, I did…and I don't like it.

Unnerved, Cynthia knew, without a shadow of a doubt, that something of *the thing*, the person Daniel was before – *Doctor Hasan* – had snuck back into his face, voice and words during their squabbled argument. No, scratch that. During their ~~squabbled argument~~ minor disagreement.

"Would you please look at me?"

His voice, Daniel's, urgent and beseeching.

Swiping the glass from the counter with one hand, the water spilling over its edge and wetting her hand, Cynthia turned.

Shit.

"Shit!" Her hand rose to cover the mouth of the mask as the glass in the other fell to the floor and shattered at her feet.

He's doing it.

On one knee, crouched by the table, Daniel stared up at her. In his hand, his skinny, skeletal hand, he held the ring box, open, and smiled at her.

"Oh, it's happening, *it's happening*." Her hand fanned at her masked face.

"I'm…. I'm…. mmmm…" Daniel muttered, shook his head, and Cynthia noticed his eyes swimming deep within their sockets, and it was at that very moment, when everything was about to come to pass, that she realised she might have just fucked everything up beyond all recognition.

FUBAR.

Stepping towards him, her feet crunched on the broken glass. She didn't falter at the sound, instead she rushed towards him, because she knew he couldn't – *in his drugged-up state* – come to her.

"Yes?" She questioned, and she glanced down at the ring. Even knowing what to expect —*they'd bought the ring together*— the sight of it now, and the thought of it soon being in place, was everything she'd ever wanted. It took her breath away. It was an early 19th Century

Victorian, 5ct Sri Lankan Sapphire and Diamond Ring, made of 18ct yellow gold; with a price tag of £10,500.

In this moment, as she glanced upon the ring as if it were the first time – *and in a way, it was* – the price of it fell away, because right now, in this occasion, the ring within it was priceless.

"Would you please…" he paused. There was no befuddlement in his face now, just a look of someone desperately trying to remember something.

"Go on…" Cynthia enthused, her hands clutched together in front of her, her shoulders curving in, her head tilting to the side.

"Sorry, I… this is going to sound silly, but I can't remember your name?"

That's because I haven't told you it.

"That's okay sweetheart, it must be the drink… Cynthia. It's Cynthia, silly, remember?"

"Cynthia…right, right…sorry."

"No bother."

"May I please start over?"

There was the subtlest of nods, an acquiescence to his request.

Closing the box with a snap, he gazed up at her again before opening it.

Take two.

"My dearest Cynthia, we've had good times and bad, but the one constant, the one thing that has made this life, even in its worst moments, worth living, is you. You complete me in ways I never knew needed completing; you make me a better man and a better person and a better lover…" he winked at her, and she smiled back, although he was none the wiser given the mask.

"I can't give you much, as I don't have much to give, but I give you my heart. All of it. And so, would you, dearest…Cynthia, do me the tremendous honour…of being my wife?"

Cynthia swooned, her legs not feeling her own, as the butterflies in her stomach pounded at her insides and a numbness spread down her extremities and rocked her. She almost stumbled – *swooned would be a more accurate word* – but managed to correct herself by placing a hand to the table.

He said it.

We did it.

I did it…I got back something that was lost, something that was taken from me.

The restaurant from before fell away, and in its place, only the kitchen remained.

Placing a hand on her stomach, she nodded her head.

The barn-owl nodded its head.

"Y-Y-Yes," she managed. "Nothing would give me greater pleasure than to be called your wife." She soothed before presenting her left hand, and letting it hang between them as if it were the final bridge to cross in their life, and in a star-crossed lover's way, it was.

Daniel fumbled with the ring box until he eventually removed the glistening ring. He took Cynthia's proffered hand in his cold and bony one, then slid the ring on.

A perfect fit.

Withdrawing her hand from his grasp, she held it out in front of her, eyeing her prize as Daniel struggled back to his feet. He leant on the table, knocking over a glass and displacing some cutlery and crockery as he struggled to remain vertical. The tablecloth rucked up under his splayed hand.

"It's…it's so beautiful," Cynthia said absentmindedly, her focus squarely on the ring she'd waited so long to finally have. And it wasn't just the ring, it was the commitment, what the ring stood for, that mattered most.

Communion, for all time. Two people, finally cleaved together as one.

"For all time," a soft mutter escaped the mask.

"Cynthia, my love, I'm feeling a little…woozy…do you think I can…if it's okay with you…see your beautiful face, because I would love to kiss you right now, if that's okay?"

"You'll see more than that by the end of the night…"

"Good, good. I've ached to look on your beautiful face for longer than I can remember."

His head hung low, and Daniel rubbed at his temples.

Cynthia placed one hand to his downturned chin and lifted his face to the mask. He was blinking heavily, and Cynthia knew she had to act fast. If she wanted to seal this union with a kiss, then there wasn't a moment to lose.

"I'm going to kiss you now, Daniel," she purred as her finger stroked his cheek.

"I...I'd...like...that."

Slurred words which appeared extremely hard to come by.

Lifting her hands, Cynthia placed both to either side of the mask.

Another glass crashed on the table as Daniel swayed.

Cynthia began lifting the mask free of her face.

Revealing her chin...mouth...nose...her eyes...her whole face, before discarding the mask onto the table like one would throw away rubbish.

There was no need for it anymore.

Here I am, my love. Your future wife…

She smiled at him, but he didn't smile back.

Instead, Daniel's brow knitted together. His mouth drew back in a vicious sneer, to bare his oversized teeth in his undersized mouth; the picture of a rabid dog, his face suddenly allected by, riddled with, a cruelness Cynthia had not expected.

"I REMEMBER...YOU!"

Cynthia took a step back.

Within a heartbeat, her beloved had morphed into the thing it had been before, as if the person she'd buried under the layers of Daniel had torn its way free from the prison she'd locked it in. His mind and body pushed its repulsive self back into her new creation. Dr. Osman Hasan appeared to her, in that moment, as if he were a double-negative, a picture within a picture, a body within a body. Although Cynthia could still see Daniel – *the sculpted and new Daniel* – it was Doctor Hasan who made his presence known.

"YOU!" He roared, as saliva dribbled from his snarling mouth.

"It's me, Daniel. Cynthia..."

"DON'T CALL ME...DON'T CALL ME THAT. THAT...ISN'T WHO I AM–"

"But you are! You're my Daniel."

Cynthia held her hand up, showed him the ring. "Now and forever, for all time…you were gone, but I brought you back."

They – *because clearly there were two of them now* – took a faltering step towards Cynthia, and she instinctively took another step back.

"YOU BITCH…I'M GOING TO KILL YOU FOR WHAT YOU DID TO ME…YOU FUCKING. FUCK…FUC…FU…" he shook his head as if a swarm of bees buzzed around it.

"I LOVE YOU!" She cried over his yelling, ignoring his cruel words and his screaming and his threats. "WE'RE TOGETHER AT LAST."

"NO…WE'LL NEVER BE…YOU'RE HER… THAT <HONEY-CYNTH>, YOU UTTER BITCH…WHAT DID I EVER DO TO YOU… WHY DID YOU…I'M GOING TO…KILL YOU!" Daniel screamed. Or had he become fully Hasan now?

He raised a hand, swiping the clawed appendage through the air between them, aiming for her throat, as he'd done in her dream between the sheets.

This time, he missed, his hand glancing off her shoulder as he stumbled forwards, his equilibrium finally giving out on him. Dr. Daniel Hasan collapsed onto his knees in the broken glass on the kitchen's floor.

He didn't yelp, or moan as the glass cracked and popped beneath his knees. He just remained there, kneeling in the glass.

"Please, Daniel," she begged as she circled his prone body. "You're ruining the moment…you're ruining everything…"

"There's still time for us to make this right. Do you want to make it right? Please, Daniel, tell me that you do, because I couldn't handle it if you said no…so do you? Do you want to make it right?"

She stood in front of him once more, glancing down at his bowed head where he wavered in place. "DO YOU?" She was desperate to get through to him, and waited patiently for his head to rise, for his eyes to meet hers.

Finally, slowly, they did.

"I…I…don't feel…so…good."

Crouching lower, she dusted down her skirt before levelling her eyes at his.

"That's because you're dying, Daniel."

"D…D…Dying?" He managed to slur.

"Yes, you've always been dying. However, tonight we'll make it right…we *have* made it right, in a way. We're engaged. Together at long last…forever."

"F-o-r-e-v-e-r…" Daniel uttered, taking his time to say the whole word as his head rolled about, and his hands pawed at the glass on the ground, oblivious to the cuts and blood he was causing himself. His face lost its viciousness and spitefulness, as if his own mask had been unceremoniously torn away, leaving a vacant, peaceful thing in its place.

"Yes, that's right." Cynthia clapped her hands together before turning her head.

A cow bell rang out from the speakers.

Perfect timing.

'Gold Dust Woman', a bluesy-folky number brought the glorious 'Rumours' album to its beautifully melancholic conclusion, trickled from the speakers in the kitchen. Stevie Nicks spoke a prophesy over them, and into the chaos which surrounded them.

Dig your grave.

Cynthia needn't follow Stevie's advice this time – *thanks anyway Stevie* – because her grave, their grave, was waiting for them upstairs with fresh, lavender scented sheets and topped off with hospital corners.

A gasp escaped Daniel's throat before he fell to the ground like a dead tree. His face smashed into the broken shards of glass on the floor with a sickening wet-thuddy-crunch.

Bending further forwards, Cynthia gripped a fistful of Daniel's lank and greasy hair and proceeded to lift his head from its grisly resting place. She turned his un-masked face towards her un-masked own and observed his bloodied face twinkle at her from the glow of the candlelight, his skin bejewelled from the many shards of glass sticking in his flesh.

"Shall we pick up the pieces and go home?"

A subtle whisper from her lips.

Daniel didn't speak – *words, it would seem, were something he used to know* – and only grunted.

"Good. Would you like to come to bed with me?"

Another grunt which she took as consent to her proposition.

"Perfect. We'll be together, Daniel. Forever. As it always should have been. *You* and *me.*"

She yanked his head back further and planted a kiss on his gaping mouth.

"I love you, Daniel. I've never stopped loving you. Never stopped believing we'd got this time back...and now look at us, we're engaged."

She lowered his head gently back into the glass and moved around his prostrate body to his feet. Picking up each ankle, she hauled the bag of bones which her lover had become from the kitchen as Stevie Nicks continued to croon her prophesy over them.

Cynthia dragged her fiancé to the foot of the stairs and glanced up into the gloom above.

Death woman...

...pale shadow....

...of a woman...

...black widow.

CHAPTER 20

"Have you ever wanted something so much that you'd do literally anything to have it?"

Silence.

Lifting her hand into the bedroom air above them, Cynthia observed the ring, her obsession, her end. Cynthia's head rested on Daniel's chest, her other hand holding his cold, bony, and now dead hand tightly, as lovers do, their fingers entwined together like tree roots.

"Beautiful, isn't it?"

Silence.

Lowering her hand, she rested it on Daniel's chest. A chest vacant of the rise and fall of breath and the soft *thud thud* of a beating heart.

It had taken her longer than she'd anticipated to get Daniel up the stairs and into bed, having overlooked how heavy an unconscious body – *even one as withered as Daniel's had become* – would be. No, scratch that. She'd overlooked how heavy a ~~an unconscious~~ dead body would be, and she almost – *almost* – didn't make it.

Her own drug cocktail had begun to take its toll when they were halfway up the stairs.

A fit of dizzy spells, and a great sickness, had rocked her. But she was in better shape than Daniel; had more meat on her bones, and it was a good thing too, because after expelling her stomach on the stairs – *her sacred meal of wild rabbit risotto and Chanterelle mushroom* – she'd pushed on through. That her sickness which would eventually become her death was a trivial thing in that moment, a small inconvenience compared to her unquenchable desire to get everything she'd lost, and wished to have again, even for just a short while.

Collapsing and dying on the stairs was not an option.

That's what old people did, and we're not old. We're in the primes of our lives, she'd thought darkly. *We're going to go out the way I've always imagined it, hand in hand, body to body, together forever.*

With her head pressed to Daniel's chest, Cynthia couldn't help but imagine their future, as couples often did in such moments of intimacy.

"So, how many children do you think we'll have?"

Silence.

"I'm thinking we'll have three. Two boys and a girl." Her hand slipped around Daniel's side, and squeezed his bones to her body.

"The first two will be boys, then we'll have our beautiful baby girl, Daphne. Named after Du Maurier of course. You know I love that woman's books, and you'd always said you loved the name."

There was a tiredness swooping over Cynthia, and she blinked, felt the heaviness in her eyelids no longer as a brief flutter, but more of a moment, an act, a pause; an encroaching blackness which she could do nothing about.

"I think Ben and Jonathan would protect their little sister, don't you? Older brother's…tend to do that…and we'd instil it in them, that they need to protect their little sister."

She began rooting in the place between their bodies.

"Children can be cruel, especially when they start going to school… and she'll need protecting…she'll need someone she can count on, if we're not there…"

Pulling her hand out from between them, she clutched her phone.

"I think we'll have to move though, don't you?"

Silence.

"Because this house wouldn't be big enough, would it? We'd need at least a couple more bedrooms…and a big garden. Maybe we should move to a place in the country…with a smallholding…the children would love that, wouldn't they? All that fresh air and green space and animals. Can you imagine how happy we'd be there? All of us, together?"

Resting the phone on Daniel's chest, she swiped a finger and brought up her playlist, *THE SWEETEST GOODBYE*.

It was only one track long. 'Landslide' by Fleetwood Mac.

She pressed, play, then quickly clicked the repeat icon as there was no way of telling how long they had left together, or how long she could still remain in control of her bodily functions.

But she prayed their song would play forever, in this place where no one would come to turn the music off.

She closed her eyes as the music started.

"I can see them, our children, our babies. They're so happy, so contented."

Cynthia squeezed her body against the bony bag that Daniel had become, until a rattle of breath left his lips.

"What was that?"

Silence.

"Yes, my love, they're all here."

And they were.

But in Cynthia's mind, now, they weren't babies any longer. They were in their adolescence. "They're growing up so fast…you were a wonderful father to them; do you know that? The best father any wife could have asked for. And my goodness, Johnathan is maturing so much. He looks just like you did as a teenager."

She opened her eyes and her breath caught in her throat.

'Can a child in my heart rise above?'

"Yes," Cynthia uttered. "A child can rise above. The heart…can only keep them in for so long." Her eyes passed over their children, standing at the foot of their bed, watching over them, and she couldn't contain her joy at what they had become, and Cynthia smiled.

"Wow, look at you all."

They were adults now.

Oh, where does the time go?

First, she glanced at the tall and strapping Ben, their first born. Next to him stood the quiet and rakish Jonathan, who now resembled his dad, as if Daniel was standing right there before her. And lastly Daphne, dear Daphne. She appeared sombre and motherly.

"Always a thinker that one, wasn't she Daniel? Our little Daphne?"

Can the child in my heart rise above?

"She always felt things harder than the others. She'll make a wonderful–"

The word she aimed for failed to materialise, stuck in her throat like a fishbone.

She could see that Daphne's hand, the one not holding her brother's hand, was wrapped around the shoulder of a child. A small, impish girl, with mousy blonde hair who looked the spitting image of Daphne.

Tears streamed down the child's strawberry-shaped, freckled, and ruddy face.

"We're grandparents. Can you believe that, Daniel?" She shook his chest with her hand. "Daniel, did you hear me?"

Silence.

"We're a Nanna and a Papa…everyone is here. Everyone came."

Fleetwood Mac continued to sing about seasons of a life, and as Cynthia stared at her gathered brood, and the ever-expanding generations, it was as if all the seasons of their lives were passing before her very eyes with each laboured blink.

"They're all here, honey. You don't have to be…we don't have to be afraid. They came to be with us…They're here to see us off…together… forever…"

Lifting her head slightly, Cynthia gazed at the face of her fiancé, her beloved, her world. Reaching her hand up, she cupped his bloodied, glass-speckled cheek.

"We did it, my love. We got it back. All those years that were stolen from us. All the plans we had for a family, all the memories we could have, *should have,* made together. All the love we would have shared, not only between us, but between all of us...we got it... all...back...in the end."

There was a dampness to Daniel's shirt, and Cynthia raised her head slightly, the small action taking all the reserves of strength she had left. The wetness pooling on his chest wasn't blood. Not this time. But instead, her own tears, had pooled there. Tears which Cynthia hadn't known she was shedding, because they were tears of joy, and tears of joy never stung as much as those of hurt, and pain, and suffering.

Sighing heavily, Cynthia collapsed back into her lover, damp cheek to damp chest, eyes still fixed on his angular, bloodied, twinkling face.

"I don't know...what...I was...what I would have become without you Daniel, I missed you so much. I've built my life around you." Her hand traced its way down from his cheek to his neck, then over his chest and rested on his heart. "What am I without you?"

Silence.

This time, though, she didn't mind the silence. Didn't feel the need to fill it.

It gave her time to think.

"Lost. That's what I was...that's what I would have been if you'd not come back to me...unable to function...you were...my...scaffolding. My foundations, my rock...and I only noticed how much I needed that scaffolding, that sturdy rock to build my foundations on once you were taken from me. I fell apart without you...but I found you again, Daniel. And I brought you back...made it right...and good...didn't... we... we... made... it... right... and... goooood..."

For how long her eyes remained closed, Cynthia had no idea. But when she opened them again, the children, their children, and their children's children, were crowded around the side of the bed.

She peered up at them.

"We're proud of you..." she uttered. "Mummy and Daddy are proud of what you all became...we love you...we've never stopped loving you..."

Our children get older and we're getting older too.

"It's almost...time..."

A breathy croak.

Cynthia climbed higher in the bed, every movement possibly being her last as a dullness, a lightness, a numbness flushed through her body. She'd continue to climb until climbing became an impossibility and death finally claimed her.

She was face-to-twinkling-face with Daniel now.

"My…love…I'm coming…wait for me…please wait for me…I don't want to…be…alone…"

For one last time, she turned her eyes to her children.

"I've…always…loved…you…and…I'm…sorry…we…couldn't…all…be…together…"

"Go and be with Daddy, he's waiting for you…" her children said in unison.

If her body would have allowed her too, she would have hugged and kissed them all, but her body was too busy dying for that. She turned her face back to Daniel.

"I…got…you…back…"

Her lips pressed up against his, and she kissed his cold, dead lips.

She pulled, gently, away from their embrace, to lay her head on his shoulder.

She was fading, although she'd not go yet.

Reaching over Daniel's body, she grabbed his arm. Hauled it from the mattress by the sleeve of his jacket and draped it across her waist.

Better…

Placing her hand over his chest, she nuzzled into him, and her eyes focused on her hand over his heart. On the engagement ring on her finger. A smile, contented and broad, crept onto her face, and she sighed deeply.

"Have you ever wanted something so much you'd do literally…anything to have…it?"

Her eyes closed.

"I'm…coming my love…wait for me…find me…please…I don't…want to be alone…anymore…"

With one final, juddering breath; surrounded by the children she'd not birthed, but which she had longed for and mothered in her aching, desperate heart all her life, Cynthia gave herself over to death, wrapped in the arms of the one she'd loved, the one she'd lost, and the one she'd found again.

Betrothed for all of time.

Love was…

…and is…

… and forever will be…

… the purest and cruellest of all afflictions.

THE END

ABOUT THE AUTHOR

Ross Jeffery is the Bram Stoker Award-nominated and 3x Splatterpunk Award-nominated author of *I Died Too, But They Haven't Buried Me Yet*, *The Devil's Pocketbook*, *Tome*, *Juniper*, *Scorched*, *Only The Stains Remain*, *Milk Kisses & Other stories*, *Beautiful Atrocities* & *Tethered*.

He has been published in print with a number of anthologies and his short fiction has also appeared in various online journals and some of his work has been translated into other languages.

Ross lives in Bristol with his wife (Anna) and two children (Eva and Sophie). You can follow him on X here @RossJeffery_

He is represented for Film and TV rights by Alec Frankel of IAG (Independent Artist Group) – please email afrankel@independentartistgroup.com for any film/tv rights queries.

ALSO BY ROSS JEFFERY

Harvesting The Nightmare Fields

I Died Too, But They Haven't Buried Me Yet

The Devil's Pocketbook

Only The Stains Remain

Beautiful Atrocities

Tethered

Milk Kisses and Other Stories

The Juniper Trilogy

Juniper

Tome

Scorched

CONTENT WARNINGS

- Sexual Content
- Violence
- Self-Harm
- Drug and Alcohol Use
- Abduction and Imprisonment
- Death and Illness
- Explicit Language

Printed in Great Britain
by Amazon